## "I'm not going to have sex with you, Martinez."

"I didn't ask you to have sex with me," he said slowly, but the naturally seductive quality of his voice only tempted her all the more, despite his rather flat denial.

The flame that kindled to life in his eyes further belied his words and made her ache in places too long neglected. "Yes, you did."

He moved a step nearer to her. "I didn't ask. I won't ask." There was no mistaking the added layer of huskiness in his voice.

"Don't come any closer," she warned, though her words were meaningless, since she couldn't possibly bring herself to move, much less run away.

"Don't worry, *querida,* I have no intention of starting anything neither of us wishes to pursue."

Oh, but she did wish to pursue—that was the whole problem.

Dear Harlequin Intrigue Reader,

We've got another explosive lineup of four thrilling titles for you this month. Like you'd expect anything less of Harlequin Intrigue—*the* line for breathtaking romantic suspense.

Sylvie Kurtz returns to east Texas in *Red Thunder Reckoning* to conclude her emotional story of the Makepeace brothers in her two-book FLESH AND BLOOD series. Dani Sinclair takes *Scarlet Vows* in the third title of our modern Gothic continuity, MORIAH'S LANDING. Next month you can catch Joanna Wayne's exciting series resolution in *Behind the Veil*.

The agents at Debra Webb's COLBY AGENCY are taking appointments this month—fortunately for one woman who's in serious jeopardy. But with a heartthrob Latino bodyguard for protection, it's uncertain who poses the most danger—the killer *or* her *Personal Protector*.

Finally, in a truly innovative story, Rita Herron brings us to NIGHTHAWK ISLAND. When one woman's hearing is restored by an experimental surgery, she's awakened to the sound of murder in *Silent Surrender*. But only one hardened detective believes her. And only he can guard her from certain death.

So don't forget to pick up all four for a complete reading experience. Enjoy!

Sincerely,

Denise O'Sullivan
Associate Senior Editor
Harlequin Intrigue

# PERSONAL PROTECTOR
## DEBRA WEBB

HARLEQUIN®

TORONTO • NEW YORK • LONDON
AMSTERDAM • PARIS • SYDNEY • HAMBURG
STOCKHOLM • ATHENS • TOKYO • MILAN • MADRID
PRAGUE • WARSAW • BUDAPEST • AUCKLAND

ISBN 0-373-22659-4

PERSONAL PROTECTOR

Copyright © 2002 by Debra Webb

Visit us at www.eHarlequin.com

**Printed in U.S.A.**

## ABOUT THE AUTHOR

Debra Webb was born in Scottsboro, Alabama, to parents who taught her that anything is possible if you want it badly enough. She began writing at age nine. Eventually she met and married the man of her dreams and tried some other occupations, including selling vacuum cleaners, working in a factory, a day-care center, a hospital and a department store. When her husband joined the military, they moved to Berlin, Germany, and Debra became a secretary in the commanding general's office. By 1985 they were back in the States, and finally moved to Tennessee, to a small town where everyone knows everyone else. With the support of her husband and two beautiful daughters, Debra took up writing again, looking to mystery and movies for inspiration. In 1998 her dream of writing for Harlequin came true. You can write to Debra with your comments at P.O. Box 64, Huntland, Tennessee 37345.

## Books by Debra Webb

HARLEQUIN INTRIGUE
583—SAFE BY HIS SIDE*
597—THE BODYGUARD'S BABY*
610—PROTECTIVE CUSTODY*
634—SPECIAL ASSIGNMENT: BABY
646—SOLITARY SOLDIER*
659—PERSONAL PROTECTOR*

*Colby Agency

HARLEQUIN AMERICAN ROMANCE
864—LONGWALKER'S CHILD

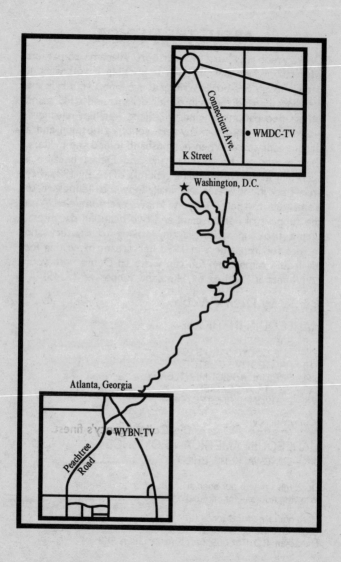

# CAST OF CHARACTERS

*Piper Ryan*—The hottest news reporter in Atlanta. A terrorist organization wants her dead. The word is that they have special plans for her.

*Ric Martinez*—This is his first big Colby Agency assignment. He has to stay focused, but the beautiful and intriguing Piper makes it difficult.

*Victoria Colby*—The head of the Colby Agency.

*Lucas Camp*—The deputy director of a highly covert government organization. Piper is his one and only niece.

*Jack Raine*—A trusted confidant to Victoria and Lucas.

*Townsend and Green*—FBI agents assigned to Piper Ryan's security detail.

*Dave Sullenger*—The news director at WYBN-TV.

*Keith*—The news desk assistant at WYBN-TV.

*Senator Rominski*—The president has named him head of the United States' new antiterrorist organization. He has plans for Piper, as well.

*Jacob Watts*—Personal assistant to the senator. He wants to make a name for himself.

*Alex Preston*—One of the Colby Agency's finest.

Life is what we make it, some say. But in my opinion, life is also about who we are and who we meet along the way. I have been extremely fortunate in my journey, and this book is dedicated to someone who has helped to make my dream of writing come true. She has encouraged me to stretch my imagination and to go where I wasn't sure I could. This one is for you, Denise O'Sullivan. Thank you so much for your faith and encouragement. You are the very best editor an author could wish for, and a truly wonderful person. It is both my professional and personal privilege to know you.

# *Prologue*

"I hope you're not leaving out anything relevant, Lucas."
Victoria leveled her gaze on her oldest and dearest friend.
That sprinkling of gray at his temples and the sparkle in
those devilish gray eyes wreaked havoc with her usual
strict control.

Lucas's smile widened at the implication. "Don't you
trust me, Victoria?" He propped his cane against the arm
of his chair and tilted his head, emphasizing his question.
A hint of amusement flickered in his eyes.

In blatant skepticism, Victoria arched one eyebrow a
fraction higher than the other. "I don't trust anyone who
has worked for the Company and Special Ops as long as
you have."

"Well," he offered in that smoky voice that did strange
things to her ability to think rationally, "I suppose I can't
blame you there. But you know I would never deceive you,
Victoria."

The sound of her name on his lips sent a rush of warmth
through her. Yes, she knew he was telling the truth. Lucas
would never do anything to hurt her. He had always been
there for her, and now she would have one of those rare
opportunities to repay him just a little of what she owed.

"All right, then, I believe I have the perfect man for the

job." Victoria pressed the intercom button. "Mildred, please ask Ric Martinez to join this meeting."

"Martinez?" Lucas frowned. "I don't think I know him."

"He's fairly new," Victoria agreed. "But he's good. And he has the right background for the job."

"Mind if I perform a little screening test of my own?" All signs of amusement had vanished from his expression. "After all, this is my one-and-only niece we're talking about."

Victoria shrugged lightly. "Be my guest."

The door opened and Ric Martinez stepped into the room. Tall, dark and handsome, the man's Latin good looks combined with his fountain of charm proved valuable assets in this business. Ric Martinez could charm or con anything out of anyone.

Ric's gaze darted from Victoria to Lucas and back. "You wanted to see me," he said as he closed the door behind him.

"Yes. Please have a seat." She gestured to the vacant chair in front of her desk. Before Ric could sit, Lucas made his move.

"Close your eyes, Martinez." Lucas stood next to Ric now, the barrel of his weapon pressed to the younger man's temple. Despite his physical handicap, Lucas could still move with more stealth than most when it served his purpose.

Ric's gaze, still locked on Victoria, widened, then narrowed with suspicion. "What's going on, man?" he demanded uncertainly.

"Close your eyes," Lucas snapped.

Victoria gave Ric a nod and he immediately complied. She had no idea what Lucas had in mind, but whatever it was, it would be harmless yet prove immensely telling.

"Okay, man," Ric said stiffly. "Just stay cool."

"Oh, I'm cool, Martinez." The tip of the weapon bored a little deeper into Ric's skull. "The question is, are you?"

"I'm anything you need me to be."

"What did you see when you walked into this room?"

His eyes still closed tight, Ric frowned. "What?"

"Give your boss a profile on the man who might just blow your brains out in the next thirty seconds."

"Black hair, with a bit of gray," Ric began, his posture considerably more relaxed now that he had an idea what was expected of him. "Fairly tall, lean build. Fifty years old, maybe." His brow creased in thought. "You have a small scar on your cheek just beneath your right eye. And you obviously use a cane."

"Anything else?" Lucas barked impatiently.

"Oh, yeah," Ric continued, in that cocky tone that set him apart from Victoria's other investigators. "You're wearing a knockoff watch, a cheap navy blue suit and loafers just like my *abuelo* used to wear."

Victoria watched the smile inch its way across Lucas's grim mouth. She smiled, as well. Lucas was definitely one of a kind. And so was Ric Martinez, the grandfather remark not withstanding.

"All right, Martinez." Lucas lowered his weapon. "You can have a seat now." Lucas's smile widened to a grin when Ric's annoyed gaze connected with his. "Unless, of course, you need to go change your shorts."

"I'm cool," Ric said, grinding the words out as he took the seat she had offered earlier.

"You're right, Victoria." Lucas settled back into his own chair. "He *is* good."

"Does anyone mind letting me in on the joke?" Ric demanded, irritation clear in his tone. "I knew there was a certain level of risk involved when I signed on," he said pointedly as he pinned Victoria with that dark gaze. "I just didn't expect to find it in your office."

Victoria reined in her smile and adopted a more businesslike expression. "Ric, this is Lucas Camp. He's with a highly covert special ops organization of which I'm not at liberty to discuss. And he's a very dear friend of mine." Disbelief clouded the younger man's eyes briefly. He probably wondered how she knew a man like Lucas. She knew a great many things that Ric was entirely too new in this business to even fathom.

Ric felt certain he wouldn't soon forget this meeting. Just who the hell was this guy anyway? Ric shifted his gaze to the man who had held a gun to his head only moments before. Despite his lingering uneasiness, Ric leaned forward and extended his hand. "I would say that it's a pleasure, Mr. Camp, but I wouldn't want to lie."

Lucas shook Ric's hand firmly. "If you'd said it was, I'd have to change my opinion of you."

"Ric, I have an assignment that I feel you are particularly suited for," Victoria said, drawing his attention back to her and away from the man who had seriously annoyed him.

Ric straightened in his chair. Maybe he was finally going to get a real assignment. "That's great," he said with a new sense of anticipation. It was well past time that Victoria recognized his potential.

She passed a manila folder to him. "This is Piper Ryan," Victoria explained. "She's a news correspondent for WYBN-TV in Atlanta."

Ric opened the folder as he listened. His gaze instantly riveted to the glossy head shot of a young and extraordinarily beautiful woman. "Whoa! This is one hot number."

"Piper is Lucas's niece," Victoria added pointedly.

Ric's gut clenched. *Damn.* He lifted his gaze to meet

the death ray Lucas aimed in his direction. "I meant beautiful in a sisterly kind of way."

Lucas's intense gaze cut to Victoria. "And you're certain he's the best man for the job?"

Ric tensed. *Damn.* His first big chance and he screws up by sticking his big foot in his mouth.

"Quite certain," Victoria affirmed.

Relief rushed through him. Maybe he hadn't stepped too far out of line. "What's the deal with Pi—Miss Ryan?" he inquired, doing his level best to ignore the daggers still emanating from Lucas's deadly glare.

"One month ago Piper and five other reporters were invited to a secret press conference for a terrorist group called the Soldiers of the Sovereign Union, or SSU."

Ric nodded. Though he hadn't seen Piper on the news, he had watched some of the highly publicized results of the secret press conference. He remembered that the reporters had been blindfolded and taken to some remote location. The leader of the group had hoped to garner sympathy in the press. But what the media had reported was anything but sympathetic to the terrorists' cause.

"I saw a couple of the news reports," he told Victoria.

"Then you know that to date three of the reporters have died violent deaths at the hands of these people. The FBI is investigating and is providing protection for the remaining reporters, including Piper."

"What role will I be playing?"

"Lucas is going to coordinate that part of the setup," Victoria told him. "With your videographer expertise, I'm certain you will fit right in as Piper's new cameraman. Your assignment will be to shadow her every step."

"What about after work hours?"

"I've taken care of that, too," Lucas answered this time. "I arranged for Piper's next-door neighbor to win a two-week vacation in Hawaii. He left today. You'll be apart-ment-sitting, so to speak, while he's vacationing.''

Ric cocked an eyebrow. ''And your niece won't be suspicious of my sudden appearance in both her professional as well as her personal life?''

Lucas met Ric's questioning gaze. ''My niece is a very busy young woman. She won't waste time wondering anything about you.''

Ignoring the blatant attempt to take him down a couple of notches, Ric smiled politely. ''Good.'' He rubbed at his chin a moment, his gaze lingering on the older man's. ''It does seem rather strange to me though that you don't trust the FBI to take care of your niece. Any particular reason?''

Victoria cleared her throat in warning. He was pushing it here.

''I didn't survive so long in this business without taking extra precautions, Martinez. I never leave anything to chance.''

''Does the FBI have anyone inside?'' Ric asked, effectively moving past the nerve he had obviously just hit.

''They have a man in the SSU.'' Lucas propped his hand on his cane. ''And I have someone special waiting to provide you with any backup you may require.''

''Jack Raine has come out of retirement,'' Victoria added for clarification. ''He's the best there is. You can count on him.'' She glanced at Lucas. ''Though I am surprised you talked him into taking time away from his wife and new son.''

Ric remembered Jack Raine well. His case was legendary around here.

''The bottom line, Martinez,'' Lucas interjected, ''is that I want someone watching my niece who has no political stake in any of this.'' He shifted in his chair, looking directly at Ric now. "I want you to eat, sleep and breathe Piper Ryan until I can stop these bastards."

"I can do that," Ric assured him.

"I hope so, Martinez." Lucas leveled a warning gaze on him. "Because I'm counting on you *personally* to keep my niece safe. Don't let me down."

Ric met his lethal glare. "Trust me, Mr. Camp. Keeping Piper Ryan safe will be a walk in the park."

# Chapter One

"I am so late," Piper Ryan muttered irritably. Her grip tightened on the steering wheel as she stared at the endless lines of cars sitting bumper-to-bumper in all three lanes going in her direction. She hated morning rush hour.

Especially on Mondays.

Particularly when she was already late.

The never-ending construction in this swiftly growing area of downtown Atlanta only magnified the undesirable situation. The fact that it was nearly ninety degrees at 9:00 a.m. didn't help. August dog days were as hot as Hades in the good old South. A little much-needed rain would be nice about now. Anything to cool things off. She had to admit that the one saving grace of this time of year was the beautiful blooming crepe myrtles. And the glossy-leafed magnolias, she added on second thought. They were still lovely, too. A few blooms managed to hang on here and there.

She glanced at her rearview mirror in search of a much more unattractive feature of her life these days. The dark, nondescript sedan that shadowed her every move was three cars back and in the right-hand lane. Piper doubted she was the only one complaining about traffic this morning. The two FBI agents assigned as her security detail were likely less than happy at the moment, as well. Knowing they were there was definitely a comfort, even if she didn't want to admit it.

Puffing out a burst of frustration, she relaxed more fully into her seat and watched the stalled cluster of disorganization in front of her. Life in the big city, she mused. Wasn't it just the other day that she had boasted on how she thrived on the excitement and energy of living in one of the fastest growing cities in America today?

Discounting traffic, she should have qualified.

Maybe she would finally get to inch forward when the flagman snapped out of his trance. Assuming he ever did. Piper was relatively certain it was past time for this side of the street to have a turn at moving forward. Anytime now, horns would start blowing and angry shouts would erupt among the sweltering, impatient drivers. Engines weren't the only things heating up on days like these.

The sound of someone attempting to open her car door jerked Piper's attention to the driver's side window. Her gaze collided with the black barrel of a pistol. She blinked, uncertain for a moment that she was actually seeing what her brain told her she was. Seemingly in slow motion she lifted her gaze up to the cold, determined eyes of a man who stared at her with complete, unadulterated hatred.

Before the scream could rip from her throat, a big body, unidentifiable but decidedly male, slammed into the man holding the gun. The loud report of the weapon and the shattering of glass echoed around Piper. Fear wrapped around her and squeezed the air out of her lungs.

''Go!'' a male voice commanded.

Without thought, her foot slammed onto the accelerator and her car lurched forward. Expecting to hear the crunch of metal as she plowed into the next vehicle, Piper snapped her attention to the cars in front of her. They were moving. Thank God.

Her heart pounded so hard she could hardly catch her breath. Blood roared in her ears. She glanced down at her side mirror and saw the two men struggling on the pavement's center line between the two lanes of moving traffic. What if the man who saved her was hit by a car? And who the hell was he? He definitely wasn't one of the Feds who shadowed her. Just as she reached for her cell phone to call 9-1-1, a charcoal-gray sedan screeched to a sideways halt a couple of cars behind her, stopping the flow of traffic in the two inside lanes.

The FBI agents, easily recognized by their trademark dark suits and sunglasses, bounded out of the car and moved in on the men still rolling around on the pavement.

It was okay now. Piper released a long, shaky breath. *You're okay,* she told herself as she drove on. *Damn, that was too close.* Her uncle Lucas would have a cow when he heard about this.

She wanted to scream. She couldn't even drive to work without someone approaching her. Of course, if there hadn't been so much construction and such a lack of organization, she wouldn't have been stalled in that spot long enough for the incident to occur.

The image of the flagman who'd held up her side of the street so long, and the possibility that he'd been a part of it broadsided her.

"Stay calm, girl," she said aloud, reaching for any remaining inner strength she could find. But the last month had taken its toll on her ability to face this insanity. There was no way to recognize her enemy. It could be anyone. She shivered. "Don't let them win," she murmured fiercely, and clenched her teeth against the fear. She would not fall apart now. Later, when she was at home and alone she would let it out. But not now. She had a job to do.

As she slowed to turn into WYBN-TV's lot, Piper felt the rage begin to boil inside her, temporarily burning away her gripping terror. She would not let them win. She would not be a prisoner in her own home or in some safe house the way her uncle wanted.

No one was going to take her life away from her.

*No one.*

The blistering anger fueling her shaky bravado, Piper parked in the secure parking garage beneath the station and emerged from her car. She sighed, disgusted, at the shattered window. She did love her little red sports car. Calling the insurance company and a repair shop would be the first order of business this morning. But at least she wasn't in an ambulance on her way to the emergency room. The memory of her unknown savior filled her mind. She hoped he wasn't hurt.

Now, if only there was a way to keep this harrowing event from her uncle and her boss, she considered as she strode toward the stairwell and the security guard waiting there.

But there was no point in trying to keep it a secret. One of her relentless FBI agents had likely already called in the incident to her uncle. Dave probably already knew, as well, considering the guard waiting patiently for her.

Smiling, the man politely opened the door and then followed her in. Defeat weighed heavy on her shoulders as she climbed the stairs leading into the newsroom. Three of the reporters who had attended the doomed press conference were dead already; she and two others remained. Maybe Uncle Lucas was right. The image of that long black barrel flickered before her eyes. Maybe she should go into hiding until it was over.

"No way," she muttered. Piper lifted her chin and squared her shoulders. "No damn way."

"STOP RIGHT THERE," Piper instructed as she studied the images on the monitor. "Now go to the skyline and fade."

"You got it." Ned's nimble fingers flew over the keys and the scene ended just as Piper had envisioned it, complete with her voice-over. The story was timed and ready for broadcast.

"Perfect." She pushed out of her seat, satisfaction sighing through her. "Dave wants to run that package at noon today. Kind of as a teaser for tonight's prime-time spot."

"I'll get it to him ASAP." Ned smiled up at her. "Great job, Piper. The audience is going to eat it up."

"Thanks." She gave Ned an appreciative pat on the shoulder. "I'll tell Jones you approve. I couldn't have done it without him."

"Jones is definitely top-notch," Ned agreed. "And so are you."

Pride welled in Piper as she strode across the WYBN-TV newsroom. Jones was the best cameraman, videographer, he would remind her, in the business. They had worked as a team since her first day as a naive but hungry reporter almost four years ago. Dave, the news director, had made a good choice when he'd teamed the two of them, and Piper would be forever grateful. No matter how hard a good reporter worked, if she and her cameraman weren't in synch or if they simply didn't mesh, the results could be disastrous for a fledgling media career.

If this piece on the problems with the ever-growing local gangs garnered the attention she felt certain it would, Piper would owe Jones dinner at Ray's. She smiled. A table at Ray's with a view of the Chattahoochee River would be a far cry from the drive-through cuisine they usually grabbed on the run to a breaking news scene. There was never time to waste in this business. Dave's motto was News Happens Now, and he was a firm believer in not allowing the moment to pass.

Ringing telephones and the buzz of conversation underscored the steady hum of newsroom activity. Several twenty-four-hour news shows were currently showing on the overhead monitors. The new desk assistant raced around with his notepad delivering phone messages and instructions from the news director. Reporters shuffled papers around on their desks to find a clean space on which to write the passed-on information. Piper felt herself smiling again. This was the heart of the station. No matter what the prime-time anchor would say, or anyone in any other department, the lifeblood of WYBN flowed right here in this room with the beat reporters.

And Piper Ryan was incredibly grateful to be a part of it. According to her agent, her recent notoriety beyond the local viewing area was the first step in moving up the ladder. Dave wouldn't be able to keep her much longer. And she would surely miss this place. Her agent was already feeling out larger markets. But she would not go anywhere that Jones couldn't go with her. They were a package deal. She might be Atlanta's "sweetheart," but Jones was the one who captured it all on film for the world to see. Dave Sullenger would just have to be prepared to lose them both.

No two ways about it.

"Piper!"

Speak of the devil, Piper glanced toward the news director's office. He waved from the open door, motioning for her to join him. They'd already had their Monday-morning staff meeting; surely nothing had changed in the last hour. She hadn't mentioned why she'd been late, and was more than a little surprised he hadn't questioned her. She supposed that the Feds had decided to follow their own chain of command. And she could see no point in sending Dave's blood pressure into the red this early in the morning. He'd hear about it soon enough, she felt certain. As soon as the Feds had relayed the event to Lucas, he would call Dave and rant at him again for allowing Piper to continue working the territory.

She pushed the thought away. She had to find Jones and head out. She had an interview set up with several families residing in Hope Place, the area currently suffering from serious gang problems. Next week it would be another block near that same area. It was an ever-evolving situation. But this time someone was trying to make a difference, trying to break that never-ending cycle.

Thus, a serious, in-depth look into the increasing gang problems in Atlanta's less fortunate areas had been born. Piper planned for the story to include about five segments. And hopefully, call enough official attention to the issue to get something done. In an effort to help themselves, the families in the area now hit with the most strife had formed a neighborhood watch, which was good, but they needed far more help from local law enforcement. If telling the ugly truth on the news would get the residents that attention, Piper would take it as far as she could.

"What's up?" Piper paused at her boss's door and waited expectantly for whatever it was he wanted to say.

"There's a situation we need to discuss that I didn't want to bring up in this morning's staff meeting."

Dave looked too serious. He had that *you're-not-going-to-like-what-I'm-about-to-tell-you* air about him. Tension raced up Piper's spine. "What kind of situation?"

"Jones had to take an emergency leave. He'll be out of town for a couple of weeks."

Piper blinked, taken aback. "But I just talked to Jones last night. He didn't mention anything to me then."

"He didn't know until this morning. It's a personal family issue that he didn't want to discuss at length. So he left for Detroit on the first available flight this morning."

It must have been really urgent for Jones to leave without so much as a quick call to Piper. She couldn't remember him ever doing that before. They were more than co-workers. They were friends. "I should call and see if there's anything I can do," she said more to herself than to Dave.

"I'm—I'm not sure that would be a good idea," Dave hemmed and hawed. "Jones gave me the impression that it was a very private matter and that he would call us when he could."

Piper flared her hands in a gesture of bewilderment. The whole thing sounded entirely too clandestine and made absolutely no sense at all. "Well, okay, if that's the way it has to be."

"In the meantime I've got a new cameraman for you," Dave went on. At Piper's distressed expression, he added, "Don't worry. He's only temporary until Jones gets back."

"I didn't know we had any new temps." Piper tried to stay on top of personnel changes at the station. It made life easier when you needed something in a hurry. And she was relatively certain that no new faces had appeared recently. Well, other than the desk assistant, but he'd been there a couple of weeks already. Tech support personnel were usually replaced by temps who had understudied to the point that their ability to do the job could be counted on. It was the first rule of the station's manager.

"I interviewed the guy just a few minutes ago," Dave explained. "Here he is now." The news director shifted his gaze beyond Piper. "Martinez, I'd like to introduce you to Piper Ryan."

Great, just what she needed, some hotshot off the street. Piper turned to greet WYBN's newest staff member. She felt her mouth drop open the moment her gaze lit on the guy in question, but she was too stunned to snap it shut again. A tall, extraordinarily handsome man walked slowly toward her. His hair was short and raven's-wing black. A square jaw and chiseled features lent masculinity to a face that was most accurately described by the word *perfection*. And then there was that body. Piper felt the air rush out of her lungs as her gaze moved over that awesome body. Broad, broad shoulders were covered in one of those black silk shirts that wasn't tucked into his black, loose-fitting trousers, the cutting edge of fashion. The man looked as if he'd just stepped off the cover of *GQ*.

He definitely did not look anything like any cameraman Piper had ever met. To make matters worse, the closer he came to her, the more convinced she grew that he knew just exactly how handsome he was, too. Confidence screamed in every move that lithe, muscular frame made. His walk, his posture, every part of him exuded blatant, cocky male attitude and a kind of smooth rhythm that made her mouth go dry. But it wasn't until he stopped directly in front of her that Piper was certain of her assumption. It was right there in those dark, devastatingly alluring eyes that said, *Close your mouth, baby, 'cause I already know just how good I look*.

This man didn't belong behind a camera, Piper protested silently. He belonged in front of one decked out in Ralph Lauren's latest. Either that or on MTV belting out a Latin pop song and showing off that to-die-for body and the seductive moves he could no doubt execute. But he damned sure didn't look like a cameraman Piper wanted to drag around Atlanta for the next two weeks. And if his ego in any way compared to the attitude that emanated from every square inch of his unbelievable body, she wasn't sure it would fit into the WYBN-TV news van.

"Ric Martinez," the Latin hunk said smoothly, then extended his hand. "It's a pleasure to meet you, Miss Ryan." Just a hint of south-of-the-border flavor accented his rich baritone.

Several seconds passed before Piper had the presence of mind to place her hand in his, and when she did, she lost whatever ground she had gained. Long fingers curled around her hand, sending a shiver through her, followed immediately by a flash of heat.

"Could you excuse me, please, Mr. Martinez?" she said abruptly, yanking her hand back with equal suddenness. Swiping her tingling palm against her hip, Piper rounded on her boss and ushered him backward into his office. She waited for the door to close behind them before she spoke.

"You can't be serious," she demanded in a stage whisper.

Dave frowned, then glanced at Martinez who waited outside the glass walls of his office. "I don't see the problem," he countered as his concerned gaze came back to rest on Piper's. "Hell, he's more than qualified. I called every single one of his references before I even interviewed him."

Piper immediately suppressed the ridiculous quivering her insides seemed determined to do at the mere thought of that…that…Martinez. "Look at how he's dressed." Piper stole a glance at the tall, handsome man waiting patiently outside the office. "He looks like he's about to stride down a fashion runway or pick up a hot Saturday night date, but he definitely doesn't look like a cameraman.

At least not *my* cameraman.'' Jeans and T-shirts were Jones's favorite fashion statement.

Dave's brow furrowed with impatience. He hated conflict. Especially among the members of his staff, temporary or not. ''You know I've never dictated dress unless you're in front of the camera. So the guy's a little flashy. What's the big deal?''

''Flashy?'' Piper lowered her voice an octave. ''He looks like…a high-priced gigolo.'' A heart-stunningly good-looking one, she had to admit. She squared her shoulders, her irritation building as the possible complications related to her new cameraman piled one on top of the other in her whirling thoughts. ''This isn't going to work. Can you see me walking around Hope Place with him strutting along beside me? How will I ever get anyone's attention? They'll all be looking at Lover Boy as if he were the last loaf of bread on the shelf before a winter blizzard. *This isn't going to work.*''

Instantly, as if she'd said something completely hilarious, a broad grin spread over Dave's thin face. He glanced Martinez's way once more, then settled a knowing gaze on Piper. ''Don't tell me you're afraid this slick guy will get more attention than you?''

Piper seethed at his remark. She bit back the first retort that came to mind. After all, Dave was her boss. And her friend. ''I'm going to pretend you didn't say that. You know that isn't what I meant.''

Dave narrowed an accusing gaze at her then. ''If you think you can't handle yourself around him…'' He shrugged noncommittally. ''I mean, if you think there's some sort of unprofessional attraction that might—''

Her drop-dead glare stopped him cold. ''You don't want to go there,'' she warned. She had a contract and a high-powered agent. For that matter, she had definite seniority.

She shouldn't have to do this if she felt uncomfortable. She definitely wasn't going to be accused of...whatever Dave had just accused her of.

A weary breath huffed from her boss as he passed a hand over his face. "Look, it's only for two weeks. Besides it's out of my hands." Dave sagged onto the arm of a nearby chair. "Martinez must be related somehow to the station manager since he *instructed* me to hire the guy."

Piper rolled her eyes. This just kept getting better and better. "Great. So I'm supposed to baby-sit the Casanova for two weeks while he learns the ropes of his long-lost relative's business." She threw up her hands. "That's just perfect. It isn't bad enough that I've got the Feds tailing me everywhere I go, now I have to entertain Mr. Too Sexy." She glowered at Dave, some of her resolve crumbling as the memory of this morning's episode nudged at her. She refused to think about it. If she let that slip back into her thoughts now she would definitely lose it. She had to be strong. "He's just not going to work, Dave. His whole—" she searched for the right words "—persona just isn't right, especially the attire."

Dave tugged at his tie. "He looks fine to me. What do you want him to wear? A three-piece suit? It's August, for Pete's sake."

Piper fell silent as the unbidden image of Martinez wearing an elegant suit filled her mind. Another wave of heat that had nothing to do with anger and everything to do with sexual awareness washed over her, irritating her all the more.

"Just try to get along with him, okay?" Dave pleaded. "I'd like to keep my job a little longer."

Banishing the infuriating images from her head, Piper straightened her lightweight rayon jacket and adopted the "calm in a storm" attitude for which she was known. It was only for a couple of weeks. She could deal with it. There was no point in making Dave miserable, too.

"Fine. I'm sure he'll do an adequate job until Jones returns," she relented.

"His credentials are impeccable," Dave reiterated hopefully.

Piper manufactured a halfhearted smile for her boss. This wasn't his fault. As long as he made sure Jones got his job back when he returned, she would be happy. She could do anything for two weeks. "Well, we'll just be on our way then."

"Piper."

She hesitated before turning to the door. "Yes."

Dave's gaze searched hers. "I really want you to be careful out there. Martinez has been briefed on the situation, but I'm worried about you. You know it would make me feel a lot better if you stuck close to the station until this is over."

If he heard about this morning...

"Who's to say it'll ever really be over?" she argued. "I'm not going to stop living my life or stop being who I am because some scumbag terrorist has decided to sentence me to death." She smiled, a genuine smile this time. Dave cared and she appreciated that. They were like family here at WYBN. "Don't worry, boss. That's what the Feds are for. Let them worry about keeping me safe. Lord knows they're never far away." Of course they had been a little too far away this morning, but it wasn't their fault.

Piper frowned. Who the heck was the guy who'd saved her? Just a passing Good Samaritan? That seemed a little too unlikely. She dismissed the question. Probably another federal agent, or maybe one of her uncle's friends. She was quite certain Lucas was leaving nothing to chance.

After giving Dave a quick pat on the arm, Piper started

for the door again. "Everything's going to be fine," she assured him. All she had to do was stay alert. This morning was a perfect example of not keeping up her guard and allowing too much distance between herself and her designated protection.

"Don't give Martinez too hard a time," Dave tossed out, again slowing her departure. "I have a feeling there's more to him than that flashy exterior."

"Let's hope so." She hated that Martinez was now privy to her personal situation, but she supposed it was only fair. As if fairness had anything to do with *any* of this.

RIC BREATHED a sigh of relief when Piper exited the news director's office and actually made eye contact with him. He'd been worried there for a minute that she was going to put up a fuss about accepting him as her new partner. But he doubted she could be any more upset than her regular cameraman. The guy had been royally ticked off at having to take this little unplanned vacation. Ric checked the smile that twitched his lips. Lucas Camp could be a very persuasive man.

Piper glanced at her watch, then at Ric. "We have a ten-o'clock shoot. We'd better be on our way."

"My equipment's in the van already."

She just looked at him for a moment, then said, "Fine."

Okay, Ric decided, time for him to turn on some of his own persuasive powers. He wasn't about to risk screwing up this assignment. If Piper Ryan thought he couldn't do the job her regular cameraman did, he'd just have to prove her wrong. And he would win her over. Ric allowed the smile to slide across his lips then. Oh, yeah, he hadn't met a woman yet he couldn't charm. This one would be no different.

His course of action settled, Ric followed Piper through the newsroom and down the stairwell into the parking garage. The two FBI guys assigned to her moved ahead of them to check the garage and the WYBN news van. To his surprise, Piper had carefully masked any lingering fear from this morning's little drama. Ric couldn't help but wonder if she was as tough as she pretended to be. It took one tough cookie to face death and then walk away as if nothing had happened.

He also decided that Piper looked even better in person. The sway of her hips was seductive in a very elemental way, as was her manner of dress. She didn't exploit her feminine assets, yet she couldn't hide the exquisite attributes that had no doubt helped along her television career. That conservative suit did little to hide her sexuality. She was definitely hot.

And her hair, almost as dark as his own, hugged her neck in one of those swingy styles that looked sophisticated yet sexy. But the eyes were the most notable of her features. As blue as a clear summer sky. The kind of startling blue that you never expected on a brunette. When she looked at him, heat went right through him. Which was intriguing but most definitely out of bounds. Ric felt with a fair measure of certainty that that little point would prove the most difficult to keep in mind. The attraction was there, but he couldn't act on it. Not the way he wanted to anyway. This was an assignment, and even if it wasn't, Lucas Camp would probably kill him for thinking even remotely carnal thoughts about his niece if he ever found out.

End of subject.

"Hope Place is just off Memorial Drive." Piper pulled the passenger side door open as she spoke. "If we hurry we'll get there in time to get some footage before the interview."

"Just tell me which way to go." He started to close the door after her.

"You don't know the way?" A surprised and openly accusing gaze collided with his.

"This is my first day in Atlanta," he said with a confident smile. "But I'm a fast learner."

Piper blinked those amazing eyes, but failed to conceal her utter disbelief. "You are kidding, right?" She laughed, a kind of startled sound. "Surely you can't mean that you don't know your way around this town." The disbelief turned to something resembling outright panic when he didn't immediately respond. "Oh, God, you're serious. You're completely lost."

Ric delivered one of the megawatt smiles that usually got him anywhere he wanted. "Don't sweat it, *querida*. I won't let you down."

Outrage kindled in her eyes, searing away the panic.

Before she realized his intent, Ric reached up and traced the line of annoyance marring her smooth forehead. "You're much too pretty to frown like that, *querida*."

He moved back a step when she bounded out of the van to stand toe-to-toe with him. Fury blazed in those blue eyes now. She jabbed him in the chest with her finger. "Let's get this straight right now, Martinez. I am not your *querida* or any other pet name in your vast 'charm' vocabulary. You will refer to me by name or you won't refer to me at all. And you will keep your hands to yourself. *¿Comprende?*"

Ric braced one hand on the open door and the other on the van, effectively trapping her. Then he leaned in close. Very close. He smiled when she held her ground in spite of the flicker of uncertainty he saw in her eyes. The emotion was banished behind that slick, professional veneer she wore as swiftly as it appeared.

*"Comprende,"* he said softly.

He didn't miss the little hitch that disrupted her breathing. Before he drew back, Ric took his time studying her eyes, her cute little turned-up nose and then her lush velvety lips. He could smell the barest hint of perfume, something subtle and entirely too enticing. This close he could see the tiny, almost imperceptible scar on her delicate chin. He wanted to know what caused it, and even more, he wanted to touch it. But that would be a big mistake. Reluctantly he drew back from her personal space.

"After you." He indicated the seat she had abandoned.

Piper blinked then turned away from him. Once she had climbed back into her seat, Ric closed the door firmly behind her and headed to the other side of the van. Miss Ryan might think she was tough, but she wasn't. Ric had her number already. Spoiled little rich girl. She might be the hottest thing going on local television here in Atlanta, but outside the state of Georgia she was just another wannabe. And if he had her pegged right she usually got her way. But then she'd never tangoed with Ric Martinez.

He grinned as he climbed behind the wheel of the WYBN-TV news van. He had every intention of keeping the upper hand. Just like he told her uncle, this assignment was going to be a walk in the park.

He started the van and turned to his silent companion. "Which way?"

She settled back into her seat but kept her gaze straight ahead. "Left out of the parking lot." She turned to him then and smiled sweetly—too sweetly. "I'll tell you the rest on the way. You have twenty minutes."

"Don't sweat it, boss lady. I'll get you there."

Ric stomped the accelerator, burning rubber as he exited the garage. This was going to be a walk in the park all right, but definitely not the park he'd had in mind.

Once he merged with the flow of traffic on the street, he stole an assessing glance at his assignment. If it was a war of wills Miss Ryan had in mind, Ric could teach her a thing or two about perseverance. This was one time the pretty lady was not going to get her way.

And he was going to enjoy every moment of teaching her how to compromise.

## Chapter Two

As her new cameraman snapped on his utility belt and then gathered his equipment, Piper scanned Hope Place to determine which shots of the housing area she wanted Martinez to take. Unlike her relationship with Jones, she would likely have to tell this guy each and every pan of the camera. Piper tamped down the irritation that wanted to bubble up inside her yet again. She had promised Dave that she would get along with this guy and she would. If only he wasn't so damned cocky. Martinez obviously had his share of testosterone and someone else's, too.

Her two G-men shadows stayed in the background, but still close. For the first time since this whole thing started, she was immensely grateful for their presence. Although it had been a stranger who saved her this morning, she knew the two federal agents were highly trained and dedicated. Piper was at fault for not taking their presence more seriously. She should have been more careful not to get too far ahead of them. The way she darted in and out of traffic, how could she expect them to stay on her tail where they belonged?

She pushed away the memory of staring into the business end of that handgun. She couldn't think about that right now—it would only undermine her sense of control.

And currently it was tenuous at best. The Feds would take care of the police report, relieving her of the hassle and still satisfying the requirements of her insurance company. Sometimes it paid to have an uncle in the right place.

Martinez pivoted and hoisted the camera onto his shoulder. The turn drew Piper's gaze to his rhythmic movements. She frowned as she considered what exactly it was that captured her attention. There was something vaguely familiar about the way he moved. But that was impossible. She didn't know the man, had never even seen him before their introduction outside Dave's office only an hour ago.

Still, something niggled at her. Piper dismissed the distraction and turned her attention back to the business at hand. She had an interview to do. Six residents had agreed to speak out on camera against the increasing violence in their neighborhood. And that was no small thing, as Piper was well aware. Retaliation was a definite possibility. She knew it and so did the half-dozen people who had asked for the opportunity. Piper would never have asked anyone to purposely put themselves in danger. Her last segment had been based on what she referred to as anonymous tips. But the people of Hope Place had decided it was time to stand up for their rights and make their intentions known.

Hope Place had been built just over ten years ago in a goodwill effort by the city's mayor at the time to offer affordable housing to low-income families. It had been well received and had helped numerous families. In Piper's opinion, the mayor's appointed planning committee's one oversight had been not proposing strong clean-up steps for the nearby crime-ridden neighborhoods. Eventually those problems had crept into the new housing area, a seemingly unstoppable epidemic.

"Tell me how you want it, boss lady," Martinez said

smoothly, his smile quick, the flicker of insinuation in his eyes even quicker as he moved in her direction.

He made the request sound intimate…sexual.

"My name is Piper," she reminded him firmly.

"Piper," he acquiesced, adding emphasis and a sultry tone to the one word so that she shivered at the sound. "I'll try to remember that."

He was too handsome, too close and too darned infuriating. Piper stepped back. "Why don't you tell me how you would do it, Martinez?"

He inclined his head in acceptance of her clear challenge. "My pleasure."

She wanted to rant at him. She wanted to hit him. Piper blinked. But mostly she just wanted to touch him and see if he felt as hot as he looked.

Damn. She hated this crazy attraction.

"Sweep the block," he suggested solemnly with a wave of one massive hand. Junked automobiles and battered trash cans lined the street. "Zero in on the run-down highrises, and the laundry hanging from the lines outside the windows, then the cluttered alleyways." He took his time surveying the area once more. A scrawny cat peeked from behind one of the dead cars and then scurried away. "That about sums it up, I think."

Gone was the easy smile and the teasing glimmer in those dark eyes. Piper saw the glimpse of sadness before he closed his expression. She frowned. Surely Mr. I'm-too-sexy-for-my-own-good wasn't the sentimental type. Before Piper could make a decision on that possibility, the voice of Mr. Jackson, one of her interviewees, called out to her as he and the other residents he'd rounded up ambled closer.

"That sounds good, Martinez," she told him before turning away. It actually sounded better than good; it was precisely what she would have said herself. But she wasn't about to admit it and give him one more thing to enlarge that already-overblown ego.

"Whatever your heart desires, *querida*."

Piper ignored the extrafoolish beat of her heart that invariably accompanied his persistent use of the Spanish endearment. She absolutely would not let this cocky Casanova get under her skin.

"THE SITUATION IS under control, Mr. Camp." Ric kicked off his shoes as he crossed the living room of his temporary apartment to lower the volume on the television. "No, man, I'm telling you I was on top of the situation."

Ric blew out a breath as Lucas Camp continued to rehash this morning's events on the other end of the line. Jack Raine had been poised from his point position to take out the guy with the gun, but Martinez had gotten to him first. Which was okay with all concerned since it left Raine in an anonymous position and the would-be shooter alive to be interrogated. But Lucas Camp hadn't been happy that the bastard had gotten that close to his niece without encountering resistance. Outside of forcing Piper to ride in a bulletproof vehicle, there wasn't any way to prevent the same thing from happening again. And she refused to change her routine. Allowing the Feds to follow her around was the extent of her concession.

If she discovered that her dear old uncle had not one, but two, additional personal protectors in place, she would likely go berserk. The woman had no intention of making Ric's job easy. She was dead set on maintaining her normal routine. As much as he hated to admit it, Ric respected her for her courage.

Most, male or female, would have cowered in fear under much less threatening circumstances. But not Piper Ryan.

She didn't intend to let the bad guys win. As risky as it was, she wasn't backing down in the least. A smile slid across Ric's face. She was one tough lady for a spoiled little rich girl. He suddenly wondered what events in her life had given her that much backbone. He doubted she would ever share anything that personal with him, but his respect for her had grown somewhat today. She wasn't just another pretty face on the television screen.

"She doesn't know it was me," Ric assured him when Lucas asked if Piper had recognized him outside her car that morning. "My cover is intact. She thinks I'm some sort of Casanova."

Definitely the wrong thing to say. Ric regretted using the term immediately. "No, man, I am not flirting with your niece," Ric lied. As far as he could tell, flirting with Piper Ryan was the only way he'd found to throw her off guard, to make real contact. She clearly did not allow anyone close. He wondered about that. She was young, beautiful and wildly popular with the viewing audience. But on a personal level, an introvert if he'd ever seen one.

"Yes, sir, I won't take my eyes off her," he said in response to Camp's final warning. Ric punched the off button on his cell phone and tossed it onto the sofa. The man Ric had tackled this morning had no previous record, and he wasn't talking. Since he didn't sport the usual shield tattoo on his right bicep, there was no way to know if SSU had sent him, or if he was somehow related to the gang series Piper was doing. Or, hell, he could just be a nut case trying to make the evening news. Whatever his motivation, the threat had been neutralized. Lucas was royally ticked that he couldn't talk Piper into going into seclusion. Prior to calling Ric, he had apparently spent the last thirty minutes trying to convince her to take a leave of absence from her work.

"You're one headstrong lady, *querida*," Ric murmured distractedly as he unbuttoned his shirt. He'd ruined one of his favorite shirts this morning, and had to change before he got to the station. He shouldered out of his shirt and tossed it onto the back of the sofa, then started to unfasten his slacks when Piper's face on the screen grabbed his attention. The segment lasted less than four minutes but it was very good. Ric gave himself a mental pat on the back for his videography. He unzipped his pants and headed for the bathroom. He supposed he could always be a cameraman if Lucas Camp got him fired from the Colby Agency for flirting with his niece. A vision, including her pretty face, especially those lush lips, instantly loomed large in his mind.

Ric needed a shower. If he couldn't keep his thoughts away from the woman next door, it might be in his best interest to take a cold shower. The signal was set loudly enough that if Piper decided to leave her apartment while he was in the shower, Ric would hear the alarm. But she wasn't scheduled to go anywhere for another hour. He had time. And since he couldn't keep his eyes on her every waking moment without blowing his cover, he'd had to wire her apartment to ensure he knew her every move— or anyone else's who might try to go through the Feds and enter the premises.

Considering his sore shoulder, he opted for the hot shower after all. The pavement had been hard, and his shoulder had taken the brunt of the fall when he'd slammed into the guy with the gun aimed at Piper. Ric scrubbed his hands through his hair and allowed the relaxing spray to flow over his tense muscles. The image of Piper Ryan, all five feet four curvy inches of her, filled his head once more. He had not expected the physical attraction between them to be so fierce. He'd thoroughly read her file. She'd grown up in the lap of luxury, was educated at a fancy private college and had all but been an overnight television success. *Atlanta's sweetheart.*

The complete opposite in every way with Ric's upbringing. He'd grown up in the Projects on the south side of Chicago. He'd had to fight his way out of that barrio, and only the kind of drive and fortitude borne of desperation and alien to the likes of Piper Ryan had saved him. In her world she stood head and shoulders above the rest when it came to determination and courage, but she wouldn't last five minutes in the world he'd known as a kid.

Ric leaned against the cool tile wall and forced that old bitterness from his thoughts. He wasn't envious of people like Piper, only impatient with their way of thinking. He knew what she probably thought about him. Though she was physically attracted to him, she saw him as a lesser person somehow because they hadn't attended the same Ivy League schools, because he wasn't the refined gentleman with whom she preferred to associate.

He swore at his foolish reverie and shut off the spray of water. It wasn't Piper's fault she'd had it all as a kid, no more than it was his that he hadn't. And Ric had no intention of letting that old chip climb back onto his shoulder. He had a job to do. Protecting the princess next door. This was an up-close-and-personal assignment and he would simply have to get over the social differences between them. He could be judging her too harshly. He knew better than to fit her into the same mold with the types he'd been forced to tolerate in his youth. It was just as wrong as those who'd lumped him in with every bad boy in his neighborhood.

Ric shook his head. Hell, he thought he'd gotten over that inferiority complex long ago. The past was just that; he couldn't change it…didn't want to really. Those tough

years had made him a better man. He didn't like being
judged based on how others from the barrio had failed, no
more than he was certain Piper would want to be held
accountable for what some of her royal crowd had turned
into.

The high-pitched tone of the motion detector warned
him that the subject of his contemplation had just opened
her door. Ric hissed a curse and quickly wrapped a towel
around his waist. She wasn't supposed to make a move for
at least another forty-five minutes. Piper's neighbor had
worried that he'd promised to attend some sort of charity
function with her tonight. Camp had told him he would
take care of informing Piper of the sudden change in plans.
It would be just Ric's luck that Piper had decided she
needed a pair of panty hose or something, which would
require her to leave early.

Before he could consider what the hell he would say to
stop her from going anywhere without him, he had
bounded to the door, unlocked it and jerked it open. To
his surprise Piper stood directly in front of him wearing a
tight little black dress that barely hit midthigh. Very sexy
high-heeled shoes and definitely no panty hose. Whatever
he'd decided to say left him the moment his brain assim-
ilated all that he saw.

For the second time today, Piper stood gawking at Ric
Martinez. Only, this time he wasn't wearing that slick mix
of silk and rayon attire. This time he was naked, save for
the towel carelessly slung around his hips. Water droplets
clung to his golden skin, some slipping down muscled terrain that did strange things to her insides. His hair was
damp too, she noted, when at last she could tear her gaze
away from that truly incredible bare chest.

The shower. He'd been in the shower. But she hadn't

even knocked on his door. Had she? Piper shook her head to clear the fog there.

Reality abruptly kicked in. What was he doing in Mr. Rizzoli's apartment?

And why was he staring at her like that?

When his gaze finally connected with hers, desire flashed in his eyes. The bottom dropped out of her stomach, then flip-flopped when she considered that he must see the same thing in her eyes. Piper blinked and squared her shoulders in an attempt to mask her runaway response to the man.

"What are you doing here? Where's Mr. Rizzoli?"

Why hadn't she noticed before the perfect cut of Martinez's nose in proportion with his chiseled jaw? Or that sexy cleft in his chin?

Her cameraman. They worked together. She wasn't supposed to notice things like that about a co-worker. She wasn't supposed to feel this way about a man she had absolutely nothing in common with, and didn't even like for that matter. Especially one that infuriated her to the extent Martinez did. But those unbelievably wide shoulders and that amazing face...mercy, she was losing her perspective altogether. A plausible excuse bloomed in Piper's mind, sending relief soaring through her.

*Sex.* It was about sex. She hadn't...in, she concentrated hard, in almost a year. Her eyes widened. A whole year? Had it really been that long? No wonder she was drooling over Mr. Latin Lover here. It was nothing personal. Just hormones. She'd been too busy for a social life lately, and her body was simply overreacting to the first attractive man under fifty who got too close.

"Mr. Rizzoli's in Hawaii on vacation," Martinez finally responded, jumping into her strange reverie with both feet, his tone tense and slightly clipped as if he'd sensed her epiphany and realized he'd drawn the short straw in her opinion because of it.

*Hawaii?* A frown knitted its way across her forehead. "Mr. Rizzoli didn't mention a vacation."

"It was sudden," Ric offered. "He won the trip and had to leave right away."

Suspicion wiggled into Piper's muddled thoughts. This was too coincidental. Too much had happened in her life during the past few weeks for this sudden turn of events to leave her anything but wary. "That doesn't explain why you're in his apartment. And just how do you know Mr. Rizzoli?"

Martinez licked those incredible lips and Piper almost jerked with reaction. Silently she cursed herself. She had to get a grip here. She'd worked with Jones for over three years and he'd never once had this effect on her.

"I'm apartment-sitting." Martinez lifted one shoulder in the hint of a shrug. "Watering the plants, feeding the fish, you know, holding the fort down. My aunt and Mr. Rizzoli met in a gardening class of some sort."

Piper felt herself nod, though she didn't understand at all. Had Mr. Rizzoli ever mentioned attending a class? Nothing came to mind. But even so, this wasn't like Mr. Rizzoli. He never went anywhere, not since his wife died anyway. The few occasions he left the apartment other than as dictated by necessity were when Piper coerced him into attending some function at which she needed an escort.

Like tonight's charity art auction.

Oh, God.

Her eyes rounded and this time it had nothing to do with Martinez's naked body, her hormones or her suspicions. She had no escort for tonight's function. And it was definitely too late to call anyone else. She'd RSVP'd for two.

No one—*no one*—came unescorted to these affairs. And if she did, it would be the gossip of every local television as well as radio talk show host tomorrow.

"Was there something you needed?" Martinez was watching her closely now, as if he expected her to faint or make some unanticipated move.

Piper felt certain all the blood had drained from her face at the thought of all the possible ramifications of attending the art auction alone. Maybe she would be lucky and faint; then she could claim she'd fallen ill and unable to attend tonight's goodwill mission.

"Mr. Rizzoli was supposed to be my—my escort at a charity function tonight," she finally stammered. "I suppose he forgot," she said.

A devilish grin lifted one corner of Martinez's sexy mouth. "No problem," he said smoothly. "I'll be more than happy to stand in for him."

She shook her head, then realized he wouldn't understand unless she said the words. "It's a black-tie affair. You don't have time to—" He leaned close, the fresh scent of his soap tickling her senses, cutting off her next words and sending a shiver through her. Mr. Rizzoli certainly never smelled like that.

"Don't worry, *querida.* You think I can't dress the part?" he teased softly. "Give me five minutes." He winked, then pivoted and strode away, leaving her standing, stunned, in the open doorway.

Any air still remaining rushed out of Piper's lungs as she watched him stride across the room and disappear down the hall. The white towel hung low on his slim hips, and stood out in sharp contrast to the smooth, dark skin that made him the perfect candidate for a sexy body oil commercial. She could just imagine that muscular body slathered in exotic-smelling oil. Piper sucked in a burst of

much-needed air at the unbidden image of her smoothing
it over his skin. She shook her head to dislodge the ludi-
crous picture and forced one foot in front of the other until
she'd gotten inside far enough to close the door. She
sagged against it. Another deep breath and she felt somewhat rational again. All she had to do was stay composed
on the outside. He didn't have to know what havoc he
played with her inside.

Piper swallowed with immense difficulty and surveyed
the familiar environment. She had played cards many times
with Mr. Rizzoli since his wife died last year. Brought
dinner to him even more often. He was a kind, good-
hearted man. He would never ask someone to watch his
apartment if he didn't trust that someone completely. And
if he knew Martinez's aunt…

Surely that meant that she could trust Martinez.

Piper paused next to Mr. Rizzoli's antique desk. His
ancient manual typewriter looked lonesome without a
piece of paper and a half-finished letter hanging out of it.
He was always corresponding with a friend or relative he
hadn't seen in ages. Mr. Rizzoli wrote letters like most
people these days used the telephone. Piper smiled, remembering the man's rare smile and even rarer laughter.
Maybe he would find a fun companion in Hawaii. The
name of an island resort hotel along with a telephone number was written in Mr. Rizzoli's bold strokes on the desk's
notepad. For Martinez to contact him in case of an emergency, she supposed.

To ensure Martinez was taking his job seriously, Piper
walked across the room and surveyed the aquariums. All
looked well, as best she could tell. The setup was pretty
much self-maintained in that the fish were fed automatically. She guessed that Martinez's job was to make sure
the food reservoir was kept filled and that nothing went

wrong with the water's chemical balance. The slow gurgling sound was somehow soothing to her frayed nerves. The urge to collapse on Mr. Rizzoli's comfortable old sofa and sleep until her life was back to normal was almost overwhelming.

"Don't be ridiculous," she chastised softly. "You are not going to hide." Piper strode determinedly to where the orchids sat on their glass shelves beneath their special light and she studied them closely. No sign of wilting…yet. It appeared that Martinez was doing what her neighbor had asked of him.

She still couldn't understand why Mr. Rizzoli hadn't left her a note or something. Frowning, Piper turned away from the lovely flowers just in time for her gaze to collide with a fully dressed and completely elegant Martinez.

"Where exactly are we going?" he inquired as he crossed the room in slow, deliberate strides designed to enhance the overall picture of sheer sophistication. "I hope this is acceptable," he added as he indicated his attire with one broad sweep of his hands.

It was her turn to speak. "That's—" she cleared her throat "—fine." Piper clutched the small purse in her hand until the beads felt like tiny needles. "Fine" was nowhere near an adequate description as was generally the case with Martinez. "I requested that the limo come a little early," she continued around the rock lodged in her throat. "I'd thought we—Mr. Rizzoli and I—would have time for dinner, but…" She jerked her gaze away and tried to banish the image of Martinez in a tux. If she'd thought he looked handsome in flashy street garb, she now knew why the word *devastating* was often used to describe the way the right man could look. The tux fit like a glove. The contrasting black and white only served to set the classic frame for his model-perfect build. "We should just go straight to the Exhibit Hall. There's a charity art auction," she finally remembered to say in answer to his original question.

He shrugged easily. "Sounds interesting."

For the first time in her entire life, Piper knew what it was to be totally blown away by the way a guy looked.

She had to get a grip. Things like this didn't happen to her. She was too logical, too professional. She didn't have time for this kind of distraction.

Somehow she had to convince Dave that this new cameraman would not do. No way was she going to allow years of hard work to go down the drain because she lost her head and got involved with a guy like Martinez. She knew nothing about him and he probably liked it that way. Dave hadn't even told her where he'd come from, only that he was somehow related to the station manager. She had learned only this morning that he wasn't from Atlanta.

Her chest tightened at her next thought. Maybe Martinez thought the best way to ensure his place at the station was to have something on Piper. She had a squeaky-clean reputation. The last thing she needed was some hunky guy like Martinez going around saying he'd slept with her.

She would not let that happen. She would never, ever trust her future or her heart to any man. That lesson had been hard learned. She'd watched her mother's life fall apart around her. Piper's father had been gone for months before her uncle Lucas had come bearing the news that he'd died on a secret mission in some place that Piper had never heard of. Her father's career had always been top priority. He'd loved and died for his government, leaving his wife and daughter to find their own way without him. Lucas had always been there for them. Piper was grateful for her uncle, but still resentful of her father's selfishness.

All that was in the past. She had accepted it and moved

on long ago. Still, the scars kept both her and her mother from fully trusting again.

Piper's gaze moved back up to the man offering his arm to escort her to the ordered limo. She wouldn't change now. Especially not now. Why should she trust her heart to any man? And she wasn't about to trust her career to anyone except her bought-and-paid-for agent.

"Just so you know, Martinez," she said as he opened the door, "Mr. Rizzoli's orchids are more than mere plants, they're like his children. You'd better take good care of them," she warned.

"Don't worry, *querida*," he replied wryly and with a quick grin. "I inherited my aunt's green thumb."

As HE AND PIPER ENTERED the hall outside her apartment door, the waiting agent descended the stairs in front of them. Ric's bodyguard mode moved to a higher level of alert. Going out at night definitely entailed more risk. Though Piper didn't know it, Raine was their driver tonight. There would be no chances taken with a regular driver and the Bureau boys would be in the chase car right behind them.

Ric paused, keeping Piper close to his side, and allowed the agent to play pushman. He exited the building and scanned the perimeter. Once the okay was given, Ric escorted Piper outside and across the sidewalk toward the open limo door. He didn't miss the shaky breath she inhaled just before settling into the vehicle. This had to be extremely difficult for her. From what he'd gathered, from research and personal observation, Miss Piper Ryan was a very independent young woman. Since leaving home and starting her own life, she had never once gone to her mother for help. She intended to make her own way as an adult. Having to admit she needed protection and couldn't protect herself had to be a huge blow to her confidence.

As she scooted across the seat, her black dress slid to the tops of her thighs and Ric almost stopped thinking at all. He quickly diverted his gaze and settled into the luxurious seat beside her. This was not the time to dwell on those shapely legs or those firm breasts outlined by the well-fitting dress. He wouldn't even go into the way she had her dark hair twisted up on top of her head in a sexy hairdo that left wisps hugging her delicate neck.

When the door closed, Ric met Raine's gaze in the rearview mirror briefly before the limo left the curb. Ric silently cursed himself. He would not make a foolish mistake during this assignment. Piper's life depended upon his doing the job right. No matter what this chemistry brewing between them turned out to be, Ric could not and would not cross the line that would surely endanger her wellbeing. He might flirt a little to throw her off balance when he felt the situation warranted his having the upper hand, but he wouldn't go beyond that. His errant gaze swept over the beautiful woman sitting silently beside him. No matter how damned hard it proved.

"We'll be taking an alternate route," the "driver" announced.

Ric jerked his attention forward. "Problems?" He knew the answer. Raine would have driven directly to the Exhibit Hall otherwise. Ric rested his arm across the back of the seat and glanced at the dark gray sedan carrying the two federal agents that followed close behind them.

"Unexpected traffic delays, sir. Nothing major."

They had a tail. Ric glanced behind them once more, but resisted the impulse to stare. The unidentified tail was right on the bumper of the sedan.

Piper looked concerned.

"I'm sure it's nothing we should worry about. Probably an accident or some sort of construction," he offered in hopes of defusing the mounting anxiety clear in her pretty blue eyes. She was too smart not to understand that something was going on. "How about some champagne?" He reached for the complimentary bottle chilling in an ice bucket.

"That would be nice," she murmured as she looked away to stare out the tinted window.

Ric met Raine's gaze in the rearview mirror once more as he filled a fluted glass. The look that passed between them left Ric with a bad feeling in his gut. He and Piper couldn't risk emerging from the car with an unidentified vehicle nearby. An evade maneuver would be necessary. Ric glanced at Piper and hoped like hell she wouldn't go ballistic on them and demand to know exactly what was going on. He sure didn't want to have to deal with an irate female, especially one as perceptive and headstrong as Piper Ryan. And blowing his cover at this point would be a major mistake. She could and likely would dismiss him. She intended to maintain dominion over her own life— risky business or not.

Raine made a sudden right, almost sloshing champagne on them both. The sound of squealing tires told Ric that the agents behind them had made a tactical move against the tail. Piper drained her glass, set it aside, then twisted around to see what was happening, but Raine moved too quickly. Before she could piece it all together and ask what was going on, the limo stopped in front of the Exhibit Hall. Raine was out of the vehicle and had opened their door curbside in less than five seconds. Ric scanned the area, though he knew Raine already had, then reached down to assist Piper out of the vehicle.

"I'll be standing by, sir."

Ric nodded to Raine and ushered Piper up the steps and into the building as quickly as he could without alarming her further.

The moment they entered the grand entry hall Ric felt immense relief. Those SSU jokers were getting braver and braver. They did not intend to back down. They just kept pushing, hoping for an opening to get close enough to assassinate one more news reporter. Ric gazed down at the woman at his side. Anger unfurled inside him. One thing was certain—they'd have to go through him first.

And Ric had no intention of making it easy for them.

## Chapter Three

Ric scanned the room once more, ever alert for any abrupt move or new face. He would feel a lot better when he had Piper safely back home in her apartment. It was evident that she was under twenty-four-hour surveillance by both the good guys and the bad guys.

Agent Townsend had managed to get a partial license plate number before the unidentified car disappeared down a side street. Now, an hour later, the only thing Ric knew was that the license plate could have come from one of two vehicles from the Atlanta area. One was owned by an elderly woman who was out of town, car included, and the other had been reported stolen earlier that evening, then found abandoned only minutes ago. Whoever had stolen it and used it to tail Piper was long gone.

Another dead end unless forensics found a usable set of prints, which was highly unlikely. SSU had proven too smart in the past for a mistake that simple, and he doubted they would suddenly grow so stupid.

His gaze instantly sought out Piper. She had relaxed immediately, or at least pretended to, when they entered the crowded Exhibit Hall. She mingled among the elegant and elite society attendees with an unparalleled grace and confidence. She introduced Ric by name only, not mentioning that he was her cameraman, and going quickly to another subject when the required formality was out of the way. Though the women seemed inclined to take special notice of him.

Ric had been given more private telephone numbers in the last hour than he could remember getting on his best night when he had been actually looking to pick up a woman.

He studied a watercolor by a local artist that was currently up to a twenty-eight-hundred-dollar bid. This was Ric's first experience with a silent auction. A register stood on an ornate stand where guests could peruse the latest bid and up the ante, if they so desired, by simply signing their name and an amount they wished to bid.

Personally, Ric couldn't see the attraction in this particular piece, but then, he wasn't the artsy type. The closest thing to art he'd known growing up was the graffiti that marked the area as low-rent, possibly dangerous to anyone from the better side of town who happened to get lost there.

A tall, slender blonde approached him and Ric shifted to attention and smiled a greeting. He was pretty sure she had arrived with the new, hotshot sheriff of Fulton County.

Ric definitely did not want to be seen accepting anything that might even appear remotely like her number. He doubted the sheriff would be too happy about a move like that.

"A lovely piece," she said, flicking her gaze from the watercolor to him in a furtive move. "Have you placed your bid?" She sipped her wine and licked her lips slowly, suggestively, then leaned closer. "The artist who painted it died recently. I'm sure the bids will go much higher." She moved closer still. "And higher."

"Actually," Ric explained, angling his head so that he

looked directly into her assessing eyes, "I'm not here for the art."

Her smile was feline, and blatantly sexual. "I was relatively certain you weren't." She offered her hand. "I'm Sally Carter. I do *Atlanta Live* on Channel 9. And they tell me that you're Ric Martinez. I've been dying to get the inside scoop on Piper Ryan for ages." Miss Carter tilted her chin upward and whispered in his ear, "I would love to interview you for my 'Kiss and Tell' segment. The audience would eat you up."

*And so would you,* Ric guessed. He eased back a step, putting some distance between them. So, this female barracuda wanted to get some trash on Piper.

She plucked a card from her dainty purse. "Give me a call when you have some free time, Mr. Martinez." She gave him a thorough once-over and then a smile of approval. "I'd love some one-on-one."

Before Ric could recite his polite, practiced response, she turned and drifted toward the other side of the room, ensuring that she gave him the full treatment as she walked away. He shook his head and tucked the card into his inside jacket pocket along with the rest.

"What did *she* say to you?"

The sharp demand jerked Ric's attention to his left. Piper stood, seething, only a few feet away. Could that be jealousy blazing in those gorgeous blue eyes?

It sure looked like it to him.

Taking slow, calculated steps, Ric moved in on her. Her eyes widened slightly, but she recovered quickly and schooled her expression. "She said she wanted to have sex with me," he offered candidly.

Wide-eyed, Piper demanded, "She didn't?"

He shrugged noncommittally, a smile itching to spread

across his lips. "But first she wanted to know if I'd had sex with you and what it was like."

Piper's mouth dropped open. She snapped it shut, then exhaled the outrage, which had just synapsed into word form, "That bi—"

He held up a hand to halt her outburst of indignation. "Don't worry, I set her straight." He leaned down so that he could whisper his next words. "I told her we hadn't had sex…yet."

The grin overtook his lips at the startled expression on Piper's lovely face. Realization quickly dawned in her eyes, and her gaze narrowed accordingly. "You did no such thing."

"No." He tasted the wine he'd been nursing all evening. His fingers curled around the stem, his thumb smoothed over the warm glass. How would it feel, he suddenly wondered, to caress that silky smooth cheek of hers? His gaze drifted down to Piper's mouth then quickly darted back to her eyes. "I didn't tell her that," he admitted, trying his level best not to allow what he was thinking to filter into his tone, "but she did give me her card and suggest we share some 'one-on-one' time in the near future."

"That woman has been out to get me for the past year," Piper grumbled, surveying the crowd for the transgressor in question. "She loves to smear images and ruin reputations. You stay away from her, Martinez. She's not a nice person."

"Don't worry, *querida*," he soothed. "I put her card with all the rest. I have no intention of calling any of them."

"All the rest?" Piper looked properly mortified. "You mean all these women I've seen chatting with you have been giving you their numbers?"

"Not all." It amused him that she'd noticed other women talking to him. Or, he admitted reluctantly, maybe it pleased him. "But most."

She rolled her eyes and huffed a sound of impatience. "I knew it. I told Dave this wouldn't work." She drained her glass and thrust it at Ric. "And I was right. Women have been trying to pick you up all night. Excuse me," she snapped, then pivoted and stormed away.

Ric quickly deposited their glasses on the tray of a passing waiter and followed.

Piper stamped down a dimly lit, deserted corridor and disappeared into the first door on the left. Ric paused in front of the closing door, noting Ladies emblazoned on the wood plaque. He stepped to one side to wait. She would come out eventually. He folded his arms over his chest and leaned against the wall. And then he would demand that she explain herself. His smile widened to a grin. He was going to enjoy this.

In thinking back to her incensed outrage, he supposed that Piper's tantrum had more to do with propriety and appearances than anything else. It didn't look proper for her date, escort or whatever, to accept the cards of any of the other female guests in attendance. But, he thought with another slow grin, he could pretend that it was more than that. He could pretend that Miss Perfect, Proper Piper Ryan saw him as a man, rather than as simply "her co-worker."

Ric immediately dismissed that line of thinking. This was an assignment, nothing else. And Piper was the principal. He had to remember that, no matter how much he wanted to forget it for just a little while.

He was her personal protector.

It was his job to keep her safe.

And he would do that above all else.

PIPER TOOK ANOTHER deep breath and stared at her reflection in the gilt-framed mirror. She was a complete idiot. How could she be jealous of Martinez?

Sure, he looked amazing in that tux. The fact of the matter was that he looked pretty damned amazing naked, too. But *she* wasn't supposed to notice that. *She* had purposely avoided overly handsome men in the past. They were trouble. That's what her mother said, and Piper herself knew it to be true. Her father had been extraordinarily handsome. And every friend she'd ever had had a story to tell about how some good-looking guy had done her wrong.

Piper squared her shoulders and adopted a "no prisoners" expression. She would not be another conquest in Martinez's memoirs. So what if he was cute and sexy...as well as nice and funny? Her fierce expression wilted. The people at Hope Place during today's interview had loved him. He'd fit right in, connected with them on a level Piper hadn't been able to. And then tonight, when she was in the very element her mother had trained her to fit into, he was at home there, as well. Chatting knowledgeably and intelligently. Smiling that killer smile that made all the ladies take notice. And taking their cards, yet!

Piper squeezed her eyes shut and wished for Jones. She didn't like it when she felt confused, and Ric Martinez confused her. Somehow she had to block his effect on her. Dismiss his overpowering persona. One week and six days. That's all she had left. She could ignore him for that long, couldn't she? Jones would be back and so would Mr. Rizzoli. And then her life could go back to normal. All she had to do was get her emotions back under control.

Still holding her eyes closed tightly, she counted to ten. She had to go back out there and face Martinez...and all the rest.

"Hello, Piper," a distinctly male voice whispered.

An arm instantly closed around her neck. Piper's eyes snapped open. The lights were out. The room was pitch-black.

Fingers of steel closed over her mouth before she could scream. "No screaming," the voice told her.

Piper struggled to identify the voice. Had she heard this man's voice in the crowd tonight? Was he someone she knew? Her heart slammed against her rib cage. Fear ignited inside her. No. She didn't know him. He was not a friend or acquaintance.

SSU had sent this man. She was going to die now. It was her turn, she realized. The image of the three dead reporters flashed in vivid Technicolor before her eyes. She would be the fourth victim. She should have listened to her uncle.

"Someone is going to die tonight, but it isn't you," the voice assured her as if he'd just read her mind. "You still have time, Piper. Time to promote our cause and undo some of the harm your kind have done."

Her fingers clamped instinctively around the arm tightening on her throat. An agonized moan echoed in the darkness. The sound came from her. Tears spilled past her lashes. She never cried. Not even when her uncle had told her that her father was dead. She hadn't cried even once. The salty droplets slid down her cheeks now only to stall on the fingers held tightly over her lips. She didn't want to die.

"Every move we make is deliberate. Those protecting you believe they are foiling our attempts, but, as you can clearly see—well, maybe *see* is not the right word," he mused sardonically. "As you can feel—" his arm tightened to the point of cutting off her breath "—you are quite vulnerable to us. We could kill you, just as we have the other three, at any moment. *Now* if we so desired."

His arm loosened. Air surged into her burning lungs. She needed to gasp...to cough, but his hand was still on her mouth holding her silent and right where he wanted her.

He hummed a note of sympathy in her ear. "It's such a relief to be able to breathe, isn't it? Every day we take that simple, yet life-giving ability for granted." He jerked her head back hard against his shoulder. "Know this, Piper Ryan, you will die when the time is right." He laughed softly, menacingly. "No one can protect you from us. No one can save you. *No one.*"

Ice-cold dread strummed through her veins. The urge to scream, to fight, was overwhelming. Before she could act on the impulse, his fingers pressed into her throat, against her carotid artery. She needed to get away! All thought ceased as she slumped against him.

RIC GLANCED at his watch once more. Seven full minutes had passed since Piper disappeared behind that door. Seven minutes too long. And what about the other woman? The blonde who'd walked in maybe five minutes ago? He straightened and turned back to the door technically off-limits to the male species.

He rapped firmly against it. "Piper, are you all right in there?" If she was chatting with the other woman, she would just have to be embarrassed. He had to know that she was safe. He didn't really put a lot of stock in propriety anyway. He never had.

No answer.

Frowning, he considered his options. Knock again or open the door and find out for himself. His palm flattened on the door just as something at the edge of his vision snagged his attention. The crack under the door was dark.

His frown deepened as his pulse kicked into overdrive. That meant the room beyond was dark.

*Damn.*

Withdrawing the weapon tucked into the back of his waistband, Ric leaned against the door but met firm resistance. It was locked. Adrenaline slid through his veins. He swore under his breath and readied himself to force the door open. He slammed hard against it once, twice, then pushed into the darkness.

The room was thick with silence. He felt for the switch on the wall with his left hand and with one flick of his thumb filled the room with light. He blinked as his gaze adjusted to the brightness.

A sitting area. It was empty. Listening intently, he eased across the small room and listened for several seconds. Nothing. Holding his weapon with both hands, he swung into the tiled area where the fancy stalls and elegant sinks lined both sides of the walls.

Piper lay on the floor.

Fear surged into his throat. Keeping an eye out for any movement, he knelt beside her just as she tried to push up into a sitting position. She made a sound, half sob, half whimper, as he closed his arm around her and pulled her close.

"Are you all right?" he demanded, surveying her for damage. Her hair was mussed, but that appeared to be the extent of the external damage.

"What happened?" he asked when she didn't answer quickly enough to suit him. Where the hell was the blonde? Was she the one who did this? And where the hell did she go? Anger rushed through his veins. Dammit, he should have checked the place out before she came in here. But she hadn't given him the chance. Could he have kept the blonde out without causing a scene?

"He...he—" Piper touched her throat "—did something to my neck and I blacked out." Her eyes rounded with remembered fear. "Did you see him?" She whipped her head from side to side. "Where is he?" Before Ric could stop her, she tried to scramble up.

"You're sure it was a he?" As he helped Piper to her feet, Ric considered whether the blonde could have been a man in disguise. He didn't see how, but...

"It was a man," Piper insisted, her voice sounded raspy. "He was wearing a wool mask, like a ski mask. I felt the roughness of it against my cheek." Now that she was vertical again, and despite the visible shaking, anger was quickly replacing the fear in her eyes.

"Don't move," Ric instructed. No one came back out of the door, not even the blonde. And, unless she was dead inside one of the stalls—he quickly scanned the bottom of each and decided that wasn't likely—she was in on it. Ric pushed each door inward just to be certain, ready to fire if anyone moved.

The stalls were empty.

"He was here," Piper insisted. "I'm telling you he turned out the light and tried to choke me to death. I didn't imagine it."

"I didn't think you did." He glanced at her, still concerned that maybe she was hurt and he just didn't know it yet. "You didn't hear a woman?" Ric scanned the ceiling, his gaze jerking back to the corner above the row of fancy basins. One of the acoustic tiles was angled slightly, not resting in the frame, as it should.

"What woman?"

Ignoring her question, he reached into his pocket and removed his cell phone. Without taking his eyes off the ceiling he punched the speed dial number for Townsend.

"We're in the ladies' room in the east corridor." Ric didn't wait for the agent's response.

"Where the hell did you get that gun?" Piper demanded, only now noticing the weapon in his hand.

*"De donde vengo no se toman chansas."* He'd definitely learned not to take chances where he'd grown up.

Piper looked at him for a long moment before she responded. Ric couldn't quite read what he saw in her eyes. *"Yo comprendo eso,"* she finally said, her words too knowing.

Her response surprised him. *I can understand that.* How could she know that he'd had to learn to protect himself as a kid? That he hadn't been able to take chances and hope to survive. The smart ones like him and his brother learned early on to cover themselves.

"Get against that wall over there," he ordered, breaking the suddenly awkward moment and refocusing his attention. He indicated the other side of the room. "Townsend is on his way."

"What are you going to do?" she asked as she moved swiftly to obey his instructions.

Ric didn't take the time to analyze the foreign concept that she had actually done what he'd told her without arguing. He climbed onto the counter and pushed the large, rectangular tile to the side. He shook his head at what he saw. A small hoist attached to an overhead steel beam. The perp was long gone, Ric was certain.

"Is that how he got in?"

To his supreme annoyance, Piper was peering up at the dark opening in the ceiling from the floor right next to where he stood. Ric hopped down beside her. "Looks that way," he said tightly. "And there were two of them."

She shook her head, then rubbed at her throat. "I don't understand. I didn't hear anyone else. In fact, I didn't hear anything. And the lights went out in the space of a couple of seconds. How did he get from here to the switch and back to me that quickly?''

''A woman came in a few minutes after you.''

''What woman?'' Confusion reigned supreme in her eyes.

Ric nodded toward the sitting area. ''The woman who stayed over there and turned out the light. The same one who had probably shadowed you all evening and warned him when you headed in this direction so that he could get into position.''

''But there wasn't anyone here when I came in.''

''He was probably hiding in one of the stalls, waiting for just the right moment.'' Ric tucked his weapon back into his waistband at the small of his back.

''This is crazy. I can't even go to the bathroom,'' she murmured, then faltered, her vertical position in serious jeopardy.

Ric pulled her back into his arms. She didn't protest and her arms went around his waist.

Townsend burst into the room, weapon drawn. His partner followed. ''What happened?'' Townsend demanded.

Ric pointed upward. ''Miss Ryan was attacked. There were two of them, a man and a woman, and that appears to be the exit point. I saw the woman, but neither of us got a look at the man.''

Green, Townsend's partner and the smaller of the two, scrambled onto the counter and pulled himself up into the darkness above the ceiling.

''Are you sure you're okay?'' Ric murmured against Piper's hair. ''He didn't hurt you?''

She shook her head, then pressed her cheek to his chest. ''He just scared the hell out of me, that's all.''

''What did he say to you?'' Townsend demanded.

Ric glared at him. She was badly shaken. Those kind of questions could wait until later.

She turned to Townsend, drawing slightly away from Ric. "He said no one could protect me from them, that I would die when the time was right."

She began to shake and Ric tightened his hold on her. "I'm not going to let anything happen to you," he assured her quietly. "I promised Dave I'd watch out for you."

"He said—" she pushed back so that she could look directly in Ric's eyes "—that none of the attempts so far were real. They want the Feds to think they're foiling their attempts on my life, but they're not really. It's all a game of some sort." She shook her head. "They're going to kill me, Martinez, just not tonight."

Before Ric could promise her that he would personally see that that didn't happen, terror filled her eyes and she spun around to face Townsend.

"Call whoever you have to and warn them!"

Townsend instantly went into a higher state of alert just as Ric did. "Warn who about what?" Townsend asked slowly as if he didn't really want to know the answer.

Piper moistened her lips, then bit her lower one for a moment to stop its quivering. "He said that someone was going to die tonight, but it wasn't me."

The other agent dropped back down to the counter. All eyes moved to him. "They used a steel beam to cross over to the men's room on the other side of the hall. They probably walked right out of there as if nothing had happened while we were all gathered in here trying to figure out what they'd done."

Ric's gaze connected with Townsend's. "Where are the other two reporters tonight?" Ric asked, hope warring with the undeniable instinct that they were probably too late already.

Townsend immediately started punching buttons on his cellular phone.

"I'd like to go home."

Ric stared down at the woman in his arms. Fear had taken its toll. He had a feeling that Piper Ryan had never felt this vulnerable before. She looked very fragile at the moment, as if she might break if he said the wrong thing.

"We'll leave right now," Ric said calmly. He turned his attention back to Townsend. "Any reason why we can't get out of here?"

Townsend shook his head. "I don't see any need to stay. I'll call the local authorities later to see if they can lend us a sketch artist for a few hours. We need an ID on the woman if possible. But first we have to make sure Weaver and Sorrel are okay."

PIPER LAY in her bed, feeling numb and completely drained of energy. She touched her tender throat. That man could have killed her tonight, but he hadn't. She closed her eyes and battled the tears that wanted to fall once more. She would not cry again.

They wanted to scare her…to make her hide. But she would not hide. Tomorrow she would be right back on the streets reporting the news just like always. To hell with those bastards. She would not cower to their tactics and give up for them. She'd heard her uncle say hundreds of times that terrorism feeds on fear. If you give in, then you've lost the game before you've started. Of course, that had been before one of the targets was his niece. Now her uncle Lucas just wanted her to be safe. To hide.

Piper pushed up to a sitting position on the edge of her bed. She combed her fingers through her hair and considered tonight's episode. She should have fought back. Instead, she'd been paralyzed with fear. She clenched her teeth. That would not happen again. Next time she would definitely fight back. She would not play the part of victim so well next time. She would kick, bite and scream at the top of her lungs.

The telephone rang, making her jump. Piper took a long, deep breath. How could she be prepared to fight back when even the unexpected ring of the telephone startled her? It didn't ring twice; Martinez must have answered it. He had insisted on staying the night—on her couch, of course. She had been too shaken to argue with him. She wondered if the sketch artist was still working with him.

A soft tap sounded at her door, followed by Martinez's accented voice. "Piper, we need to talk."

She started to speak but had to clear her throat first. God, she was still rattled. "Come in."

Martinez, sans the elegant jacket and cummerbund, strode across her room and sat down on the bed beside her. His crisp white shirt was open at the throat, revealing a breathtaking view of the sleek skin beneath.

Piper felt suddenly naked. Though she was wearing a fairly conservative nightshirt, he was in *her* bedroom, sitting on *her* bed. When that dark gaze settled onto hers, a wave of heat washed over her, making matters considerably worse.

"The sketch artist is gone. But that call was from Townsend," Martinez said softly. The hesitation that came next made her tremble. "Edgar Sorrel is dead."

The journalist from Savannah. *Someone is going to die tonight....*

Piper's stomach roiled. The heat that had suffused her only moments before was gone now, replaced by a bone-deep chill. Tears burned in her eyes. Edgar Sorrel had a wife and two kids. And now he was dead.

"Townsend thinks you should consider going into protective custody now—tonight."

Sorrel had been in a safe house, Piper remembered, and still they'd gotten to him.

She met Martinez's worried gaze. Even her new cameraman was afraid for her. She moistened her lips and held his gaze steady so that there would be no misunderstanding her words. "Tell Townsend I said *no way*."

There was only one way to stop a madman. And next time Piper would be prepared for him. The next terrorist son of a bitch who came for her would be the victim, not Piper.

# Chapter Four

"Piper Ryan." Piper cradled the telephone between her ear and shoulder as she continued to surf the Internet for any new information she could find on the SSU. According to the FBI, each time the SSU Web site was shut down, it instantly sprang up again on some other URL. It always amazed her at just how flagrant these groups could be, regarding their cause. Of course, their courage dissolved when it came to listing names and showing faces.

Spineless bastards.

Piper frowned when no response sounded from the caller; her fingers stilled on her keyboard. "Hello," she said into the eerie quiet emanating from the receiver. It wasn't a no-one's-there lack of sound, either; it was that make-the-hair-on-the-back-of-your-neck-stand-up kind of silence. "Hel-lo," she repeated slowly, emphasizing each syllable with growing irritation.

"Are you afraid, Piper?" whispered the male voice from last night's ladies' room encounter.

The stark fear she had experienced less than twelve hours ago rushed up her spine and exploded inside her chest. Her hand went instinctively to the scarf tied at her throat, hiding the bruises he'd left there. This was the man who'd held her life in his hands for those few short, yet seemingly endless minutes. He was one of those faceless enigmas who called themselves the Soldiers of the Sovereign Union. And they had killed Edgar Sorrel less than an hour after terrorizing her. Maybe the very man who'd warned her of her impending demise was the one who'd done the deed.

"Go to hell," she spat, her fingers tightening around the receiver with white-knuckle intensity. She wanted to kill this man. The near overwhelming sensation was both instant and palpable. At no other time in her life could she recall wanting to murder someone with her bare hands. As she started to hang up, he spoke again.

"We have more in common than you know, Piper, much more than you could ever imagine." He chuckled, a sinister sound, then continued before she could deny his sickening accusation. "But I promise you'll know everything before you die. I wonder if you'll beg for your life the way Sorrel did. A most pathetic way to die." Another sick laugh. "But then, most members of the media are rather pathetic creatures, aren't they, Piper? They bravely boast their opinions when looking into the camera, but put them face-to-face with real life and they fall completely apart."

Like when she'd looked into the barrel of that weapon.

Piper slammed the receiver back into its cradle. Her heart bumped painfully against her sternum. She slowed and lengthened her respiration to fight the emotions clutching at her. She would not panic. They wanted her to be afraid, and she definitely was. But they could not make her give up. Sorrel had. He had hidden away in fear and he was dead anyway. She would not give those maniacs the satisfaction.

She gathered her composure around her like a protective

shield and forced her attention back to the screen in front of her. She had work to do.

She needed a gun.

The abrupt thought startled her and her fingers slowed once more in their work.

*Martinez had a gun.*

Her thoughts turned to her temporary cameraman. She understood now why Martinez had connected so well with the people at Hope Place. He had obviously spent some or all of his youth in a similar environment. But she'd seen a different side of him at the art auction. He was clearly well educated, and had certainly fit in, yet on the inside he was not like the society-column types who had reveled in outbidding each other last night. Piper couldn't quite place Martinez in a particular category. He was tougher, more streetwise and cockier than any man she had ever met. Generally those macho attributes would be a huge turnoff to her…but there was something about Martinez that somehow made them all look good on him.

Heat instantly chased away the chill her caller had produced. The image of Martinez wearing nothing but that towel materialized in her mind, made her heart beat faster. Maybe Dave was right. Maybe there was more to him than what she could see on the outside. The memory of Martinez in that tux filled her mind next.

"And maybe you've lost your mind," she grumbled, and focused her wayward thoughts back to the search engine on the waiting computer screen. Terrorists were trying to kill her and here she sat fantasizing about a man she had no intention of getting involved with.

And who, she added firmly, would be out of her professional life in a few short days. Jones would be back and then everything could get back to normal. The telephone rang again. Piper jumped at the sound. Her hand flattened on her chest and she tried her level best to draw in a steady breath.

"This is certainly a hell of a start," she scolded. How could she even put life and normal in the same thought if each ring of her office phone would send her into a cardiac episode? Before she could lose her nerve altogether, she snatched up the receiver.

More heavy silence.

"Look, if you don't have anything interesting to say, stop calling me." She was going to have to talk to that switchboard operator about screening her calls. Piper was about to slam the receiver down again, but an angry voice stopped her.

"Yo, news lady, I have somethin' to say."

Piper reached for calm. She was relatively sure this call wasn't from any SSU members. "All right," she agreed as she gathered her scattered composure.

"You got nerve comin' down here, makin' Hope Place look bad." The caller was young and male. "We do what we gotta do to survive. Somethin' you don't know nothin' 'bout."

"You're right. I don't understand." She searched her desktop for a pen or pencil. "Are you suggesting that you would like to give our viewing audience your side, Mr…?" Piper allowed the question to dangle in the silence that lapsed between them.

"Maybe," he countered eventually, rising to meet the challenge she'd offered.

Pen in hand, she shoved aside research notes to clear a spot on her blotter pad. "I'm a firm believer in showing both sides of any story. Give me your name, a time and place we can meet. I'll be happy to provide you with the opportunity to tell your side of things."

Piper quickly wrote down his name and meeting specifics. "All right, Mr. Taylor. I look forward to speaking with you." Adrenaline surged through her at the prospect.

"Don't bring no cops wit' you. I ain't talking wit' no suits hangin' 'round."

"No cops then," she assured him. "I want you to be completely comfortable, Mr. Taylor."

Without another word, he hung up.

Piper placed the receiver in its cradle and stared at it for a long moment. Fear trickled through her as she considered the promise she'd just made. In the past she wouldn't have thought twice about going alone, with no one but Jones for backup. She always did whatever it took to get the job done...to get the story. But terrorists had stolen into her life and attempted to take two things near and dear to her very being—her trust and confidence.

And they'd almost succeeded.

Renewed anger flamed inside her. "To hell with SSU," she muttered. She had a job to do and she damned well intended to do it. Martinez had a gun. And maybe she'd get one of her own. She knew the places to go to avoid the legislated waits. She glanced around the newsroom until her gaze landed on Martinez. He was busy with his camera equipment.

All she had to do was convince him to go along with her plan. She definitely couldn't do this without her cameraman.

"Here's your coffee, Miss Ryan."

Piper jerked her gaze to the smiling young man offering a cup of the steaming brew. The new desk assistant. What was his name? Kyle...Kevin...no, it was Keith. "Thank you, Keith," she said as she took the cup.

"If you need anything else, just let me know." One last quick smile and he was gone.

She'd started out that way herself. Doing everything

from pouring Dave's coffee to picking up his dry cleaning. Piper frowned. Had she been as enthusiastic as Keith about that crappy job? Yeah. She smiled. She had been. She was just so darned glad to be a part of the news team, she didn't care what she had to do to be there.

Her attention shifted back to the problem at hand. *No cops.* Her gaze sought out Martinez once more. Now, if her powers of persuasion were just good enough, she could make this happen.

"ARE YOU OUT of your mind?" Ric glared at Piper. *"Mierda."* He shook his head at the insanity of her proposition. He had grossly underestimated the lady. She wasn't just independent, she was reckless. "You think I'm going to take you to this place so you can buy an illegal handgun?"

"Keep your voice down," she snapped as she glanced around and made sure no one was listening to their hushed, yet heated, conversation. "I don't want anyone else to know about this. Not even Dave," she added pointedly.

Ric pinned her with a gaze he hoped conveyed the finality of his next words. "There is nothing to know because we aren't going anywhere without Townsend and Green. And we sure as hell aren't going to the pawn shop you suggested. If you want a weapon, you can apply for a license and buy one just like everybody else."

"Dammit, Martinez, I don't have time to wait. I need protection now." She edged closer, putting herself nose-to-nose with him. "I will not run from these people, but I'm also not stupid. I need to be able to fight back."

She was serious. This spoiled little rich girl, who probably still had the silver spoon she'd been born with tucked away in her hope chest, intended to take control of her personal safety like a vigilante. Why was he not surprised?

"I have a weapon, *querida*," he reminded her. "I will use it if necessary to protect you."

Piper rolled her eyes. "Well that's just great, Martinez, but what about at night when I'm in bed? Who's going to protect me then if those maniacs sneak into my apartment?"

The beginnings of a grin motivated by a very wicked thought kicked up one corner of his mouth. "I don't have a problem sleeping with you, *querida*, if it would make you feel safer."

She adopted an expression of outraged disbelief. "Get real, Martinez. Like I'd sleep with you under any circumstances." She looked away, folding her arms firmly over her chest.

But she didn't look away quite quickly enough. Ric saw the flash of heat in her eyes. She'd thought about sleeping with him. He was certain of it. His grin widened in pure male satisfaction.

Ric felt the blood rushing away from his brain as his gaze skimmed her lithe body. Though she wore her usual conservative pantsuit, this close he could feel her vibes— confident, feminine heat that stirred the need inside him. The sweet, subtle fragrance she wore didn't help, either. It made her seem soft and fragile when he knew she was as tough as nails, otherwise she would have agreed to go into hiding after last night's too-close-for-comfort encounter.

He leaned forward, his lips almost touching the delicate skin at her temple, and murmured, "Not to worry, *querida*, I don't intend to let anything happen to you."

She drew back and looked up, directly into his eyes, the barest hint of vulnerability in her own. "And why would you do that, Martinez? You don't even know me...." She shrugged halfheartedly and ran a hand through her silky hair. "Of course, I suppose it would look rather bad for you if you allowed the station's star reporter to get maimed or worse on your watch. I imagine your uncle or whatever would be somewhat disappointed.''

"Cousin," he corrected, playing along with the cover he'd been given as a relative of the station manager. "And you're right. He wouldn't be too happy. And neither would I.'' Ric tapped her on the nose, but resisted the urge to drag his fingertip down and over those lush lips. "Besides, Jones would probably have it in for me if I let anything happened to you while he's gone.''

Her face brightened at the mention of her regular cameraman. Ric suddenly wished she would light up like that for him, but he quickly pushed away the foolish thought.

She was his assignment.

His first Colby Agency assignment...a very important assignment.

Besides, Piper Ryan would end up with a man like one of those guys he'd seen escorting Atlanta's society princesses to the charity art auction last night. Anything he and Piper felt at the moment was only physical...and definitely not meant to be acted upon. Not if Ric wanted to live anyway. Lucas Camp would have his hide if he learned that Ric had so much as looked at Piper the wrong way.

"Gun or no gun, I can't have Townsend and Green blowing this interview for me, *partner,*" she countered. "What do you propose we do about that?"

*Partner?* She was putting the ball in his court. Whatever he came up with, it would be a hell of a lot safer than her suggestion that they lose their Bureau tail and meet with her caller.

"Don't worry, *querida,* I'll think of something."

MARTINEZ DROVE the news van slowly along the street toward the rendezvous point. Townsend and Green had gotten into position forty-five minutes early as Martinez had instructed. He hoped this damned meeting went down without a glitch. He didn't like taking chances like this, but he had a feeling that if he hadn't set it up, Piper would have figured out a way to do this on her own.

Hope Place reminded Ric of his old neighborhood. Run-down housing, cluttered streets and kids playing stickball and running around as fearlessly as if they were at Disney World rather than in a place where drive-by shootings and drug deals took place regularly.

"That must be him," Piper said, wading into his trip down memory lane. She nodded to the young caucasian male who'd stepped out from the alley and now leaned nonchalantly against the side of an abandoned building that had once been a local market.

Ric pulled the WYBN news van over to the curb. Although clearly young, the kid looked as mean as a junk-yard dog, with his worn-out jeans, leather boots and chains. The color of his bandanna marked him as a member of the gang that currently ruled over this territory. The same one Piper had reported on in her two previous segments on life in the forgotten side of Atlanta. While Ric sized him up, the kid took a long drag from his cigarette then flicked the butt away. As he exhaled a cloud of smoke, he met Ric's gaze for about three seconds.

This guy was trouble.

"I have a bad feeling about this, Ryan," Ric said quietly, his gaze never leaving the kid's movements as he lit another cigarette. "I think we should leave now. Townsend and Green aren't nearly close enough to be effective if this goes sour."

Piper turned to face him, those blue eyes brilliant points of fierce determination. "I want this guy's story, Martinez.

*¿Comprende?* Don't give me any grief here. Just do your job and your cousin and I will both be happy.''

Ric was going to regret this. He had that feeling. The one that he'd cultivated as a kid living on one of the meanest blocks on the south side of Chicago. His gut tied into knots and his heart kicked into overdrive.

He grabbed her by the arm when she would have opened the van door. "I go first," he told her, his tone deadpan. "No arguments. You don't get out until I open your door."

She tried staring him down but quickly realized the futility of her attempt. "Fine."

Ric opened his door and slid from behind the steering wheel. He automatically adjusted the weapon tucked into his waistband beneath his shirt as he carefully surveyed the immediate area, then moved around to the passenger side of the van and opened the sliding door to retrieve his camera.

Townsend was positioned in a second-story apartment belonging to one of Piper's previous interviewees who lived directly across the street. Green was at the end of the block in a deserted Laundromat. Both men were watching every move he and Piper made. But would it be enough?

Raine was around. He wasn't the kind of guy who divulged his plans unless he wanted to. But he would be close—that was certain. He wouldn't interfere, of course, unless it became necessary.

Ric hoisted the camera from the van and turned to the teenager waiting a few yards away. "You Taylor?"

"That's right," the boy shot back, then spit as if the words had left a bitter taste as they rolled across his tongue.

"You alone?" Ric watched for eye movement and other

body language in the kid's answer. He needed to get a fix on whether or not the kid was telling the truth.

"That's right, but I ain't got nothin' to say to you, *amigo*."

He was lying. Adrenaline rocketed through Ric's veins. He'd noted the way Taylor had shifted his gaze, the subtle change in his posture. The sound of a door opening behind Ric jerked his attention toward Piper. She was out of the van and striding toward Taylor. Ric swore hotly. He'd told her not to move until *he* opened her door.

She stuck out her right hand, microphone already plugged in and held confidently in her left. "Hello, Mr. Taylor, I'm Piper Ryan." She shook the kid's hand firmly. "I'm pleased you want to share your story with WYBN-TV."

Left with little other choice, Ric hoisted his camera and slid into character. He watched through the viewing lens as Piper effectively questioned the guy, gently guiding him where she wanted him to go. The kid had no clue that he was following her lead so well. Ric smiled in spite of his irritation with her. The lady knew her business, but, damn, she was cocky. He almost frowned at his next thought. A little too much like him. This was definitely a first. Ric had, apparently, met his match.

Taylor suddenly bolted from his casual stance. He shot an arm in the direction of the Laundromat. "Hey, you said there wouldn't be no cops," he shouted.

Ric glanced toward the Laundromat. Green must have shown his face somehow. Ric hissed a curse. Just what they needed, the kid going ballistic on them. Piper was trying to calm the situation by assuring Taylor that everything was fine, but her tactic wasn't working.

Ric lowered his camera and reached for her. "We're out of here," he said tightly.

She ignored him. "Mr. Taylor, I wish you'd consider continuing. This interview could explain a great deal of what you and your followers stand for."

"You lied to me, *bitch*."

The camera hit the ground and Ric pulled Piper out of Taylor's reach just in time. Before Ric could shove her into the van, three of Taylor's friends poured out of the abandoned building. One grabbed the camera and ran, the other two, along with Taylor, closed in on Ric.

"Get in and lock the doors," he ordered over his shoulder, hoping like hell she would obey him for once.

"But—"

"Do it!"

Ric heard the door slam shut, then the distinctive click of the power locks. "Okay, Townsend," he said under his breath, "anytime now."

Piper frantically searched the van for the weapon Jones kept. She couldn't leave Martinez out there on his own. Townsend and Green obviously weren't going to get there soon enough.

The sound of fists colliding with flesh jerked her attention out the van window. "Oh, God." She grabbed the equalizer, a three-foot piece of steel pipe Jones kept in the van behind the driver's seat for just such an emergency. Piper shoved the sliding door open and bounded out. She swung at one of the gang members, slamming the pipe into his upper back with all her might.

"Get in the damned van!" Martinez shouted, then grunted when an elbow connected with his abdomen.

Absolute fear surged inside her, but rather than paralyzing her, it empowered her. She swung blindly at another of Martinez's attackers. She connected with his shoulder. The blow rattled her bones. The guy dropped like a rock, screaming in agony.

Townsend barreled straight into the middle of the battle, pushing Piper back as he went. Before she had time to react to the sudden move, Green was at her side ushering her back into the van to safety.

"I'll take that," Green said as he took the equalizer from her. He closed the door and immediately swung the pipe, taking down another of the gang members that suddenly appeared out of nowhere.

Martinez landed a right hook, and the last of the bunch dropped. Piper jumped back out of the van and ran straight up to Martinez to inspect the damage. She cringed at the blood seeping from his split lip and his battered cheek.

"Back in the damn van, Ryan," he barked, then dragged in a gasping breath.

Motivated by his lethal glare, Piper obeyed.

MARTINEZ DIDN'T SAY one word the entire trip back to her apartment building. To say he was extremely angry would be putting it mildly. But then so was she, Piper decided as she folded her arms over her chest and clenched her jaw. He'd dropped the camera and one of those hoodlums had absconded with it. She shot Martinez a threatening look, for the good it did with him staring straight ahead.

"You know, the station's insurance will replace that camera, but there's no way to replace the interview." Her anger gained momentum as she spoke, as did the pitch of her voice. "I needed that video footage and *you* threw it away."

Martinez parked the van in her reserved slot. He glared at her then, the damage beginning to show on his handsome face, making him look all the more dangerous. "Do I look like I care?"

She jerked at the deadly tone of his voice. Determined not to allow him to get the better of her, she squared her shoulders and glared right back at him. "Well, you should." She snatched up her purse and yanked on the door handle to open her door. "It is your job, you know."

She turned away from his hot glare and strode toward the entrance of her building. Townsend was already going inside, having scouted out the landscape.

Fury boiled up inside her. Her whole life was a mess. If the SSU weren't threatening to kill her, then Green wouldn't have been there to interfere with her story today. Martinez wouldn't have dropped the camera and lost the video...and he wouldn't have gotten beaten up. She swallowed against the lump of emotion forming in her throat. He was hurt and it was her fault. It infuriated her all the more that she felt this way about him—not the regret that he'd gotten hurt, but those other feelings that she couldn't quite label.

She stormed up the stairs, Martinez right on her heels. And did he have to live next door to her, as well? She lengthened her stride. She couldn't get away from him and these crazy feelings fast enough.

Townsend stepped out of her apartment and gave the all-clear sign. Her apartment—her home—was safe for her to enter. She hated living like this. She hated that a bunch of madmen had reduced her life to this level. The renewed burst of outrage sent her common sense scurrying into those rarely used recesses of gray matter.

"You know—" she pivoted on Martinez, knowing he was right behind her "—Jones would *never* have lost that camera." Their gazes locked for several long seconds, the fury simmering between them like molten lava. When Piper could tolerate the dark heat of his eyes no longer, she turned on her heel and stamped into her apartment.

The door slammed loudly behind her a few seconds later, a deliberate warning that Martinez had followed.

She whipped around to face him and threw her purse onto a nearby chair. "Get out of my apartment, Martinez. I don't have anything left to say to you."

If the glitter in his eyes was any indication, he was beyond rational speech. She felt a twinge of apprehension. The battered cheek and split lip only made him look fiercer. "I asked you to leave," she repeated with a good deal less conviction.

He looked away from her, then blew out a harsh breath. *"No seas pendeja."*

A fresh wave of irritation washed away the lingering hint of apprehension. "What did you say?" she demanded. Though she spoke Spanish fairly well, she hadn't quite caught that remark. Something about not being stupid maybe. Whatever he'd said, she was more than certain that it wasn't the least bit flattering.

He stepped closer, his hands braced on his hips. "I said that you shouldn't be stupid, Miss Ryan. You would risk your life and mine for a story that two weeks from now won't matter."

Every ounce of rage drained from her as if she'd been stabbed and it had bled from her open wound. She blinked away the hurt she knew rose instantly into her eyes. "You don't know what you're talking about."

Realization seemed to dawn on Martinez then. "You're right." He plowed his fingers through his hair, disheveling it further. "I was out of line. I understand how much your work means to you."

Piper let out a breath and closed her eyes. She pressed her fingertips to her closed lids and tried to think rationally. It had been a long day. Neither of them was thinking clearly at the moment. She pressed her fingers to her lips a moment before she spoke. "I was out of line, too, I guess." Her right hand fluttered in midair a moment as she tried to figure out a way to explain what she felt. Finally she dropped her arms to her sides and admitted the truth, "I was scared, Martinez. I really thought they were going to hurt you."

God, why did her admission have to sound so...personal?

"Me?" He reached out and traced her cheek. The smile that spread across his handsome face was mesmerizing. He grimaced at the pain that move cost him. "I can take care of myself. But you took me by surprise wielding that pipe."

Heat stained her cheeks. She really had done that, hadn't she? Jones would be proud. "Jones calls it the equalizer."

"I'd say he was right." Martinez rubbed at his bruised jaw. "Things could have gotten a lot worse really fast. You did good, Ryan, even though I did tell you to stay in the van."

She clasped her hands together in front of her to keep from fidgeting. "I've never been very good at following orders," she offered contritely.

"So I've noticed."

Her gaze collided with his once more. The heat there made her tremble inside. "You..." She cleared her throat and tried again. "You need some ice for that." She gestured to his jaw, afraid to touch him, but wanting desperately to do just that. Her heart started to pound at the mere thought of what his skin would feel like beneath her fingertips.

He captured her hand and drew it to his face as if he'd read her mind. The hitch in his breathing at her touch sent a spear of desire straight through her. His skin was smooth and warm, the feel of it making her tingle.

Martinez slid one arm around her waist and pulled her close against his lean, hard body. He tangled the fingers of his free hand in her hair. "I know I'm going to regret this."

Before she could protest, his mouth covered hers. His lips were hot and firm, yet soft and gentle somehow. Her heart seemed to stop beating all together only to jolt back into an erratic rhythm. Her hands slid over the silky smoothness of his shirt, around his neck, and forged into his short hair. Her body went bonelessly soft, contouring to his hard, male terrain. A blast of need, of pure desire, mushroomed inside her. His tongue traced the seam of her lips and Piper gladly opened for him. The feel of that part of him inside her banished any inhibitions she might have had left. She tiptoed, kissing him harder. He groaned when she pressed her hips more firmly into his. The coppery taste of blood reminded her of his injured lip, but she couldn't bear to draw away from the escape, the pleasure he offered.

Her telephone rang. Martinez started to draw away but she pulled him back to her, hungry for more of him. She thrust her tongue inside his mouth and any thoughts of retreat apparently left him since his arms went tight around her once more. He picked her up, moving until he could press her against the wall. His hands moved over her body now, touching, learning, tantalizing. Her fingers found their way to the buttons of his shirt. She wanted to touch more of that hot, smooth skin.

The answering machine picked up, playing her outgoing message as her palms flattened against his bare chest. He growled savagely, grinding his hips into hers. The feel of his arousal made her shiver, made her weak. Her feminine muscles clenched in protest of the long months without release.

"Piper, this is Lucas. We need to talk *now*," emanated from the answering machine and echoed around them.

Martinez's mouth stopped moving over hers. He released her instantly and stepped away. Piper blinked, confused. Her whole body cried out at the sudden denial of his nearness.

"I have to go," he said, his voice still thick with the lust burning between them. Desire still clouded his gaze, but he turned away all the same.

Before she could even utter a reasonable protest, he had walked out the door.

Humiliation seared through her. She was a complete idiot. She had kissed Martinez like a starved nympho, and he'd walked out like nothing had happened. Fury quickly quenched her humiliation. Well, she might have let her guard down this once, but it wouldn't happen again. In fact, if she had anything to do with it, Martinez would find himself working with another reporter.

# Chapter Five

"This just isn't working." Piper stood before her boss's desk staring down at him, her hands on hips, her expression the sternest she could muster. She remained standing rather than taking a seat, a blatant attempt at intimidation that she already knew wouldn't work, but she was too angry to care.

Dave leaned back in his leather executive's chair and studied her for a time before speaking. She hated when he did that. It was a sure sign that he had no clue what he was going to say, and even less idea of how he was going to handle the situation. More often than not it meant that he wasn't going to do a thing in the world to solve the problem except to deny its existence.

"Personally," he finally began, "I don't see the problem. Martinez appears to be doing a good job."

Piper resisted the impulse to pat herself on the back for seeing that one coming. "But he abandoned his camera," she refuted.

Dave cocked an eyebrow. "To save your neck, as I heard it," he countered.

Piper huffed out an impatient breath and dropped into the closest chair. "You know as well as I do that the story comes first. Good reporters put themselves in dangerous situations all the time. That meeting with Taylor was no different." She leveled a gaze on her boss that carried a clear rebuke. "We're in the news business, not the hero business."

Dave planted his feet on the floor, leaned forward and matched her chastising gaze. "Piper, I've been in this business for thirty years and no one knows what we're about better than I do. But—" he paused for effect "—my perspective has changed recently. Sometimes I think maybe we sacrifice too much in the name of the news and to keep the people informed. Maybe the people don't need to know some of the things we show them."

She couldn't believe her ears. Dave Sullenger, the hardcore newsman who'd taught her everything she knew, was obviously going soft. This didn't add up. She knew him too well.

"What's going on, Dave?" She searched his gaze, her own more than a little suspect. This didn't sound like him at all. "Has Lucas been talking to you?"

Her boss released a heavy breath. "Yes, he has." Before Piper could rail against the injustice of her uncle's interference, Dave pressed the intercom button. "Keith, bring us some coffee in here, would you?" An instant "Yes, sir" reverberated through the speaker. Dave settled his solemn gaze back on Piper. "Look, I know it's not fair, but I agree with your uncle." He held up a hand to stay her protests. "I just don't think it's safe for you to be on the streets. So, I'm going to ask you one more time to take a vacation until this is over."

She shook her head. "No way." She blinked back the wall of hot tears burning behind her eyes. She refused to cry. "I admit that this SSU business makes me as nervous as hell, because I don't see it coming when they strike. It's not like I'm consciously choosing to walk into a hot

zone. But I won't let them win. I've thought long and hard
about this, Dave, and I will not back down. What good
did it do Sorrel to hide from them?''

Keith breezed in, carrying two cups of coffee. Knowing
which side his bread was buttered on, he placed Dave's
cup before him first, then, with a wide smile, he offered
the remaining cup to Piper. ''With cream, just the way you
like it, Miss Ryan.'' He smiled as if this mundane task
were an immense pleasure.

''Thanks, Keith.'' She took the cup and sipped from it.
She needed something, anything, to soothe her nerves at
the moment. And a little caffeine boost wouldn't hurt, considering the meager amount of sleep she'd gotten last
night.

When the desk assistant was gone, Dave continued.
''All right, Piper, I won't push the issue.'' He sipped his
own coffee, looking thoughtful for a time. ''I've been
keeping some pretty exciting news from you for the last
three days in hopes that you'd change your mind, but it's
apparent now that you don't intend to. So I see no reason
not to tell you.''

Piper almost burned her mouth with a gulp of hot coffee.
''Tell me what?''

''You're aware that a few months ago the President set
up his own antiterrorist organization specifically designed
to focus on fighting terrorism in this country.''

She nodded. ''Of course. You know I did the informa-
tive piece on it shortly after the announcement was made.''

''They've selected Senator Rominski from right here in
Georgia to head up this new organization.''

Piper nodded. That was old news. The announcement
had come more than a week ago. Why was Dave rehashing
that now? If it didn't happen today it wasn't news.
''And?''

"Senator Rominski is going to be in Atlanta next week speaking to the law-enforcement groups regarding his plans for involving the authorities at the local level."

Piper sat up a little straighter. Anticipation zinged through her. This could be big...really big. "Do we have an inside track?"

That old sparkle she recognized and loved twinkled in Dave's eyes. "We have the only track. Senator Rominski has agreed to an exclusive interview with our station and he asked for you by name."

The cup in her hand was suddenly too heavy to hold, and she plunked it down on Dave's desk. "He asked for me?"

"The senator feels that since you were invited to SSU's secret press conference, you're the only logical choice." Dave pegged her with his most authoritative gaze. "But I haven't given him my decision yet."

"Don't even think about trying to keep me from doing this," Piper warned. Though she loved her uncle Lucas, she was plenty angry with him for interfering with her career. In the past, Dave would never have hesitated like this.

"The interview will be in the studio under heavy security. But there's still a risk that SSU will come after you, and maybe even the senator. Think hard, Piper. You're sure you want to do this?"

"You know I do."

Dave nodded, a slight smile creeping into his otherwise concerned expression. "I knew you would. Since that's settled, there's one more thing. I can't make any promises just yet, since all the details haven't been worked out, but there's a good chance that it'll be picked up by one of the networks."

"National? It could go national?"

He nodded. "It's a strong possibility."

Piper drained the rest of her coffee. She was going to need all the caffeine she could absorb today. She had a ton of research to do on this new organization. Chances like this didn't come along often in this size of market. She fully intended to make this interview one no one would forget.

"Miss Ryan!" Keith burst into Dave's office just as she stood to leave. The desk assistant bubbled with excitement, his face flushed, his eyes wide.

"What's up?"

"I took this call for you." He flashed a lengthy message. "I wanted to put the woman on hold and pass her to you, but she couldn't wait and insisted I take a message."

Piper frowned when she noticed SSU in the text of the message. "Slow down and tell me what she said."

"She's the mother of an SSU member. She wants to talk to you. She's worried about her son." Keith pointed to an address on the note. "This is where she lives. She said she's ready to talk, to give her story to the press to see if she could stop this from happening to other mothers."

Renewed anticipation scorched through Piper's veins. This could be a huge break. "Where's Martinez?"

"He's going over the location with those FBI guys to see if they think it's safe to take you there."

Piper took the note from Keith. "Like he has any say in the matter," she muttered.

"Piper." Dave interrupted the interview strategy already in motion inside her head. "You listen to Martinez. He has your welfare in mind."

She chewed her lip to prevent the sharp retort as to just what Martinez had had in mind yesterday afternoon. The kiss she'd struggled to keep out of conscious thought all morning slammed into her like a speeding bus. His taste...the feel of his lips on hers. The fit of her body against his. Need and desire whirled instantly inside her as remembered pleasure cascaded over her. She'd hardly slept last night for reliving that mind-blowing moment. Piper closed the door on those thoughts. She couldn't think about that now.

And she darn sure would not allow anything like that to happen again. She was a professional. Martinez was her cameraman. In just over a week Jones would be back and Martinez would be assigned to someone else. She wasn't about to jeopardize her position at the station or her reputation with her constituents for a night of hot sex with the man. Automatically her brain conjured up the image of Martinez's lean, golden body moving over hers. She clenched her teeth and forced the unbidden fantasy away. She definitely would not go there. No touching, no kissing. From now on their relationship would be strictly business as it should be. What happened last night would not happen again.

No matter how much her traitorous body wanted it to.

"MRS. OLSEN, I'M NOT SURE I'm following you," Piper said, interrupting the older woman's lengthy monologue.

Ric stood only a few feet away from the sofa where Piper sat. The woman had insisted the interview not be videotaped. She'd been so adamant, in fact, that Ric had stored the camera back in the van to make her more comfortable. The entire interview had taken an unexpected direction. Whatever the lady had said on the telephone, she was singing a totally different tune now.

"You just don't understand, Miss Ryan," Mrs. Olsen

insisted. "We stand for what this country should have been all along…what it still could be."

Ric could see the surprise and supreme annoyance in Piper's expression. This had been a complete waste of time. Townsend and Green had checked the place out. There was no one here but the woman. Still, Ric had a bad feeling about the whole setup. And this had definitely been a setup.

"But when you called the station you suggested that you were concerned for your son."

"I am concerned," Mrs. Olsen insisted evenly. She sat ramrod straight on the edge of her chair. Her hands folded neatly on her lap. "But my fears lie with those hateful reporters." Something malicious flickered briefly in her gray eyes. "They make it sound like my son is a criminal for standing up for what he believes in." She cocked her head and studied Piper in a way that fell somewhere close to insane. "You're not going to say anything bad about him, are you?"

Ric readied to hurl himself between Piper and the woman if Mrs. Olsen suddenly became violent.

Piper placed her hand on the other woman's for a couple of seconds in a gesture of assurance. "You have my word that I won't say anything at all negative about your son. I'm only trying to understand what motivates the men with whom he associates. What is it they expect to accomplish by killing innocent people?"

Piper grimaced. Ric tensed. What had that look been about? When the pained expression deepened, he started to step forward, but Mrs. Olsen started talking again.

"We have plans, Miss Ryan. Plans that include you," the woman said knowingly. "We had hoped that you and the others selected so carefully would portray our cause in a better light, but you didn't."

"I reported what I heard with my own ears and the actions I observed firsthand," Piper explained carefully. "The SSU seems determined to wipe out anyone who doesn't see things their way. What happened to freedom, Mrs. Olsen? In this country we're supposed to be free to believe as we choose. But those who support the SSU would take that freedom away from the rest of us. Where's the democracy in that?"

The woman only smiled patiently. "But they would give us so much in return. No one would want for medical care or the basic necessities of life as they do now. When was the last time you didn't have enough to eat, Miss Ryan? This country has lost itself by embracing too many outsiders. Why should refugees from another country have food in their bellies and free medical care when many of those born and raised here don't? It's time for the pure ones to take back what is rightly theirs."

"By pure ones, I would assume you mean those of your own persuasion?"

Mrs. Olsen flicked a glance at Ric. "Of course, dear. Who else would I mean?"

Ric ignored the dig at his Latin heritage. This woman was not the first, nor would she be the last bigot he encountered. He'd learned a long time ago that he couldn't change the way people thought and acted, but he could definitely control his reaction.

"I think—" Piper stalled abruptly. The color drained from her face right before Ric's eyes. She stood suddenly. "May I use your rest room?" she asked stiffly.

"Why, of course." Mrs. Olsen gestured to the hall behind her.

Piper rushed in that direction. Ric resisted the urge to follow her and make sure she was all right. He doubted she would appreciate it. Maybe she'd eaten something this morning that didn't agree with her. They hadn't bothered to stop for lunch before showing up here.

Mrs. Olsen flicked another of those disapproving glances in his direction but Ric ignored her. He shifted, suddenly remembering the incident in the bathroom he'd thought was safe at the art auction.

Thankfully, Piper appeared just when Ric had decided he had to go after her.

"I appreciate your time," Piper announced, still looking pale. She extended her hand. The other woman stood and, somewhat hesitantly, accepted the offered gesture that indicated the interview was over even before Piper spoke. "Thank you, Mrs. Olsen, but I think I've heard all I need to."

The woman held on when Piper would have turned away. "Don't be foolish, Miss Ryan," she warned, her tone and expression stone cold. "You should make your final days on this earth count. Take up our cause, and perhaps mercy will be shown for you."

"This isn't about what I believe or don't believe," Piper insisted as she tried to pull away once more. "I report what I see and hear. It's up to the viewing audience to form their own opinion."

Mrs. Olsen jerked Piper close and embraced her. "Bless you, child, for you know not your true destiny."

Ric pulled a stunned Piper from the woman's clutches. "Let's go." Piper didn't resist as he tugged her toward the door. This old lady was nuts and he had no intention of hanging around another second.

Piper stalled. "Wait." She shouldered loose from Ric's firm hold and turned back to Mrs. Olsen. "What is my true destiny?"

"We don't need to listen to this," Ric insisted.

The woman smiled, her eyes glazed with a strange mixture of hatred and glee. "You will be instrumental in showing our strength and commitment."

Piper shook her head, confusion and a hint of fear evident in her expression.

"Let's go," Ric murmured to her. "We don't need to hear any more."

Piper started to say something, but suddenly stiffened. She took a halting breath, grabbed her stomach and doubled over with a harsh cry of pain.

Startled, Ric crouched down next to her. "What's wrong?"

She cried out again. "I...don't...know," she gasped. "The pain..." Anguish streaked across her face. She squeezed her eyes shut and bit down on her lower lip.

*"Mierda."* Ric shot to his feet. "I have to get you to a hospital."

"There's a small private hospital very close," Mrs. Olsen said, concern marring her features. "Two blocks up the street on the right."

Ric didn't bother thanking her. His mind kept replaying the way the woman had grabbed Piper and embraced her. Surely this loco lady couldn't have done anything that would have caused this. Piper cried out again as he lifted her into his arms. Before he got halfway down the sidewalk, Townsend was out of his car and sprinting in their direction.

"Open the van door," Ric ordered.

"What the hell happened?"

"I don't know." Ric settled Piper into the passenger seat and snapped her seat belt into place. Tears were streaming down her face and she literally writhed with the pain. "I'm taking her to a hospital a couple of blocks up the street."

Townsend swore. "We're right behind you."

AFTER WHAT FELT like a lifetime later, Ric skidded to a halt in front of the hospital's emergency entrance. Piper was still holding her abdomen and alternating between moans and sobs. When he lifted her from the seat, she cried out in agony, crushing him with the knowledge that he was adding to her pain, but there was no other way.

Ric rushed to the emergency room admissions desk. "I need help," he demanded, his voice sounded raw and harsh to his own ears.

The stern-faced attendant shot to her feet and called for an orderly. "What seems to be the problem, sir?" she asked then, surveying Piper as she spoke.

Ric shook his head helplessly. "I don't know. She just doubled over in pain."

The orderly wheeled a gurney next to the counter. Ric carefully laid Piper onto it. She cried out, and curled into a fetal position. His heart hammered so hard, he could barely think. What the hell was happening?

"Just calm down, sir. We'll take good care of her," the orderly assured Ric before wheeling Piper away.

"I have to go with her."

"Wait, sir," the desk attendant called out behind him. "I'll need you to help me with the admissions forms."

Ric watched Piper disappear through the double doors, torn between going with her and doing what he knew had to be done.

"I'll take care of the paperwork," Townsend said, seeming to come out of nowhere. "You stay with her. What about her insurance?"

"Her purse is still in the van," Ric shouted over his shoulder. Not waiting for the attendant's okay, he barreled through the double doors just in time to see which room the orderly wheeled Piper into. A nurse was taking Piper's vitals when Ric entered the room.

"I'm sorry, sir, but you'll have to wait in the lobby."

The orderly indicated the door with an impatient gesture, but Ric looked him dead in the eye and said, "I don't think so." There was no mistaking the challenge in Ric's tone or posture.

The orderly threw up his hands and backed off. "Work it out with the doctor."

He left the room. Which was good. Ric didn't really want to have to fight him right now. He felt relatively certain that his current, slightly battered face lent credibility to his willingness to do just that, however.

"Can you tell me if she's taking any medications or is allergic to any?" the nurse examining Piper asked.

"No medications. No allergies." Lucas had insisted that Ric know all there was to know about Piper. The only thing he hadn't read in her file was how she got that little scar on her chin. "Is she going to be okay?" he ventured hesitantly, his defiance dissolving.

"The doctor will have to answer that question for you," she told him flatly. "All I can tell you is that her BP and pulse rate are a little high."

"Martinez."

Ric's gaze went instantly to Piper at the sound of her weak voice. "Everything's going to be okay, *querida*." He smoothed her silky hair back from her damp face. "They're going to take good care of you."

She closed her eyes and groaned as a fresh wave of pain hit her. "That woman," she managed to mutter.

Ric leaned closer. "Did she hurt you somehow?" Though he couldn't see how that was possible, he had to ask.

Piper shook her head. "She was trying to tell us something. Send Townsend—" Piper screamed in agony.

Ric's heart shuddered. Dammit, there had to be something they could do. "Can't you give her something?" he demanded of the nurse still monitoring Piper's vitals.

"Not until the doctor sees her," she told him patiently.

Piper grabbed Ric by the shirt and pulled him to her. "You have to listen to me," she whispered hoarsely.

"Don't try to talk now, *querida*," he urged. "You can tell me later."

She shook her head, then licked her lips as if she were thirsty.

"I think she needs some water," he snapped. Ric shot an accusing glare at the nurse. Why the hell was she just standing there? Doing nothing!

"The doctor has to see her first," the nurse repeated.

"Send Townsend," Piper groaned. "Send him to talk to her."

"I will," Martinez assured her. He had a few questions for the crazy old lady himself. But right now he had to make sure Piper was all right.

"I'll need you to wait outside, sir." A tall, thin man, Dr. Petersen, according to his name tag, stepped into the room and paused next to Ric, a folder in his hand. He offered a pleasant smile, then added, "I'll let you know what's going on as soon as I know."

Ric nodded. He didn't know what else to do. He'd never felt this helpless before in his life. He stared down at Piper for a moment, then pressed a kiss to her temple. Without looking back, he turned away and forced himself to leave her.

He stood in the empty corridor and grappled for composure. He wasn't supposed to fall apart like this. Piper was counting on him. The sound of her cries taunted him through the closed door. He squeezed his eyes shut and tried to block out the images that accompanied the sounds. She was in terrible pain. A cold sweat had broken out over her skin. He'd felt it when he touched her. He had never seen anything happen so fast. Every instinct told him that this was somehow connected to the SSU. But his more rational side kept asking how that could be possible.

Finally, when he felt certain his legs would give way under him any moment, he braced his hands on the wall for support to wait for the doctor's report. Ric pressed his forehead against the cool painted surface and replayed every second of every minute of their day. Nothing struck him as out of the ordinary...or as a possible contributing factor to Piper's sudden illness.

"Mr. Martinez."

Ric looked up to find the doctor standing in the hall next to him. "Yeah." He scrubbed a hand over his face, and to his surprise found it damp with the emotions careening out of control inside him.

"My first guess at Miss Ryan's condition would be appendicitis. But I can't be certain without further testing." Behind the doctor, the orderly, who'd attended to Piper before, hurried into her room. "So, we're going to take her up for an ultrasound and the necessary blood work to try and confirm that diagnosis." The nurse and the orderly wheeled Piper from the room and down the hall, away from Ric.

"Is she going to be all right?" He had to know now. He couldn't survive another minute of not knowing.

The doctor offered a curt smile. "I'm sure she'll be fine. We just have to locate the trouble and take care of it."

Ric nodded, too emotionally drained to speak.

"When I know more, I'll give you an update."

Ric watched him disappear down the hall just as Piper had.

He supposed that he should go back out to the lobby and tell Townsend, then call the station. And he'd have to notify Lucas, if Jack Raine hadn't already. But somehow he couldn't make his feet take the necessary steps. So he simply stood there, waiting.

And hoping with every part of his being that she would be all right.

# Chapter Six

The waiting room was empty except for Ric. Townsend had gone to further question Mrs. Olsen, for the good it would do. And Agent Green paced back and forth outside the emergency entrance, puffing one cigarette after the other.

Ric glanced at his watch again—1:22 p.m. Two hours had passed since their arrival. He swallowed hard. No one had bothered to keep him informed of Piper's condition. Each time he asked the attendant at the desk for a status, she only repeated her practiced answer in that annoyingly hushed tone that there was no word yet. "Be patient," the woman had advised, "I'm sure we'll hear something soon."

He didn't want to be patient. He wanted to know now how Piper was doing. The sound of her agonized cries echoed inside his head. Ric blew out a weary breath and forced the haunting memories from his mind. He hadn't been able to reach either Dave or Lucas. Both men would probably go ballistic when they got the messages Ric had left for them.

Restless and frustrated, Ric stood. He paced the carpeted floor, back and forth, his step keeping time with his thoughts. He couldn't stand to just sit there a minute longer. Frowning, he considered the green-and-brown up-holstered chairs that lined two walls of the waiting room. The empty chairs only enhanced his feeling of desolation. A wide wall of windows, blinds closed, faced the street. Current issues of several magazines were fanned across the top of a fake-wood table. His brow furrowed as he surveyed the desolate room once more.

Ric tried to think what it was that bothered him about the place. It was nothing he could put his finger on. But some indiscernible something nagged at him.

He glanced at the lady behind the admissions desk. He supposed her shift didn't end until three. Maybe he'd be lucky and get somebody with a little more personality and ambition. He sure as hell hadn't seen anyone else to ask anything of. The place felt deserted. But maybe it was just his restlessness that had him off kilter. It was a private hospital and it wasn't as if one-thirty on a weekday afternoon was prime business time for injuries anyway.

Ric shoved his hands into his pockets and rolled his neck, releasing the tension knotting there. With his eyes closed, the vivid memory of holding Piper in his arms...of kissing her captured his senses. Her scent, the sweet taste of her lips. Her tentative touch. The feel of her body pressed firmly against his. He licked his lips, almost tasting their brief but fiery kiss. He knew better than to become personally involved with a case. And if he'd forgotten, the sound of Lucas Camp's voice had been a better reminder than a hard slap in the face or an ice-cold shower.

Victoria would be more than a little upset with him if this assignment got screwed up—if he lived through what Lucas did to him. Ric opened his eyes and stared at the stained beige carpet. It was more than that. It was the difference between daylight and dark.

Ric had loved his parents. They'd died younger than

they should have, both working hard in deplorable factory conditions to make a better life for their two sons. He'd grown up poor and with a distinctly jaded outlook on life. Then, when he was just twenty, he'd fallen in love with a woman ten years his senior. He'd thought she loved him, too, but the fact of the matter was they were from different worlds and the relationship was doomed from the beginning. He had nothing to offer a woman like that and she'd soon realized that undeniable truth and moved on to bigger and better things. The last he'd heard she was engaged to some hotshot lawyer. She was probably married to him by now. Maybe even with a couple of kids.

Ric rubbed at his neck and kicked those unpleasant memories from his head. He'd gotten over the raw deal life had dealt him and his brother as orphaned teenagers. And he'd had his share and more of female company. He was only twenty-eight. There was plenty of time for life-time commitments and settling down. But he had learned one very powerful lesson: never fall in love with a woman out of your league.

Like Piper Ryan.

She was a rising star. Her upbringing was so different from his that it seemed impossible that they were even from the same planet. Though she was definitely attracted to him, she didn't like him. Or, at least, she didn't want to like him. Ric had been down that road before. He wouldn't consciously take that journey again. He had learned the hard way that love does not conquer all. Some gaps are too wide even for love to fill. The one that yawned between Piper and him was mammoth in size.

Ric scrubbed a hand over his face and swore at himself for even mulling over the ridiculous thoughts. This was an assignment. As soon as it was over he'd never see Piper Ryan again except maybe in the news. Forcing that thought from his mind, he located the men's room and splashed some cold water on his face. He needed a clear head, and worrying about things that would never be wasn't the way to get it. Ric stared at his reflection in the mirror. His lip was healing but still hurt like hell. He swallowed hard when the taste of Piper's sweet mouth popped into his mind. She'd felt so good in his arms.

He shook his head, banishing the memory. That kiss had been a stupid move and he knew it. Piper had been royally ticked off at him for getting so close—even though she'd liked it. She'd responded to him, even pulled him closer when he would have stopped. Ric exhaled a heavy breath. "You're not her type, Martinez," he told the slightly worse-for-wear reflection staring back at him. "Get over it."

Ric walked back into the waiting area at the same time that the sliding door opened to allow someone entrance. Townsend strode straight up to Ric.

"Any word on Miss Ryan yet?"

Ric shook his head. "If I ask the lady at the desk again, she's probably going to kick me out." Man, he was tired.

Townsend looked a little down in the mouth. "Mrs. Olsen split on us. The place was clean. I'd be amazed if we could even lift a print."

Worry and irritation made Ric's tone sharper than he intended. "Did you really expect her to hang around? It was a damn setup. Those *bastardos* are playing head games with us. They've got us chasing our tails. And scaring the hell out of Piper in the process."

Townsend nodded. "You're right. But we have to follow every lead."

Ric glared at the admissions desk once more. Why the hell didn't someone call? "Yeah, well, I know that. But I don't have to like it."

"Weaver has agreed to go into protective custody."

Weaver was the only other remaining journalist besides Piper. Ric cocked an eyebrow in clear skepticism. "Any chance he'll survive it?"

"I resent that," Townsend snapped. "It's not like you've been faring any better. Think about it," he ground out. "They got to Miss Ryan in the ladies' room while *you* stood right outside the door."

Ric wanted to kick himself for being a complete ass. "You're right, man. That was way out of line." He plowed a hand through his hair. "I'm just worried about Piper."

Townsend shrugged wearily. "We're all a little touchy right now."

Ric chucked him on the shoulder. "Let's get some coffee, man. I think we both need a shot of caffeine to revive us."

Townsend followed Ric back down the hall toward the men's room. Ric remembered seeing a lounge. When he stepped into the deserted room labeled Lounge, that annoying feeling that something wasn't quite right swamped him again. Two tables, each surrounded by metal-and-plastic chairs sat in the middle of the room. But absolutely nothing else. No vending machines of any kind.

"Well, this sucks," Townsend griped.

"Yeah, big-time," Ric agreed.

"Mr. Martinez."

Ric whirled toward the voice. The doctor stood in the doorway. Ric tried without success to read the man's expression. He supposed doctors were like poker players, trained to keep their emotions hidden. "How is she?"

Dr. Petersen's expression remained impassive. "Miss Ryan's going to be fine."

Ric sagged with relief. Damn, he'd never been so glad to hear anything in his life.

"We didn't find anything on the ultrasound and her blood and urine tests were fine," the doctor said, now directing his comments to Townsend. "And just to be certain it wasn't an atypical appendix, I performed an exploratory laparoscopy." He shrugged. "I didn't find anything. I can only speculate that the episode was a viral infection that mimicked a hot appendix."

"What happens now?" Ric asked, anxious to see Piper, but a little irritated that the doctor seemed to want to ignore him.

"We've been watching her in recovery for about an hour and everything is as it should be," he answered, his attention still directed toward Townsend as if he'd asked the question. "I don't see any reason not to send her home. Of course, I'll send along a mild pain reliever in case she needs it, but I don't think she will. She does have a couple of stitches where we performed the exploratory, but other than that, she appears to be doing well."

Ric didn't give a damn what the doctor's problem was, nor did he bother to ask why the hell someone hadn't let him know an hour ago that she was in recovery. All that mattered to him at the moment was that she was going to be fine.

"Thanks," Ric said tightly, garnering himself more of a grimace from the doctor than a smile. To his credit, Townsend stayed out of the conversation. "I appreciate everything you did."

"Just doing my duty, Mr. Martinez. If the two of you would follow me to the lobby, the orderly is bringing Miss Ryan down."

A frown creased Ric's forehead at the doctor's choice in words. The headache that now pounded fiercely in the back of his skull didn't help. Maybe the guy was ex-military. He supposed it was a doctor's *duty* to help his patients.

"What's his problem?" Townsend said quietly as he and Ric followed the doctor as instructed.

Ric shrugged. *"Cabrón."*

"Whatever you said—" Townsend chuckled "—I agree."

Ric didn't smile. The strange doctor aside, the whole situation still bugged him.

The same orderly who had taken Piper away brought her into the lobby, only this time in a wheelchair. She looked dazed and entirely too vulnerable.

"I'll get the vehicles ready to go," Townsend said quickly before starting for the door.

Ric only nodded, all other thought faded into insignificance. He couldn't take his eyes off Piper. He didn't like seeing her like this. "Anything else I should know?" He glanced at the doctor, an edge in his voice. "Any symptoms to watch for or possible problems?"

"I would suggest that someone keep an eye on her tonight in case she needs anything. Rest is the best medicine under the circumstances." His gaze locked with Ric's as he completed his recommendations, something less than friendly clear in his eyes.

"I'll personally see that she gets plenty of rest," Ric assured him, his tone clipped. He had no intention of leaving Piper in her apartment alone. He turned his attention back to her then. He fully intended to make sure nothing else happened to her.

"Yes, Uncle Lucas, I'm well aware of that." Piper bit her lip as she tugged at the tape holding the plastic over her bandage. She felt immensely better after her shower. Martinez had insisted that she go straight to bed, but she wouldn't listen. She needed a shower. All she had to do was keep her bandage dry. She ripped the last section of tape loose and barely stifled a yelp. She flung the sticky tape and piece of plastic into the trash.

"Yes, I'm resting exactly like the doctor said," she lied when her uncle demanded to know what she was doing. "Yes, Martinez is here."

Piper frowned when Lucas asked if Martinez was being nice to her. "What do you mean, is he being nice? Of course he is. Taking care of me isn't exactly in his job description. I'd say he's going way beyond nice." But she didn't have to tell Martinez that. His ego was overblown as it was.

"I know you're only worried about me." Piper smiled. Lucas had been like a father to her. She probably should show a little more appreciation for his concern. "I told Dave I would take the next couple of days off." Piper shook her head when Lucas took that inch and ran a mile with it. "No, that doesn't mean I'm going to lay low until this is over. It means a couple of days, that's all."

Piper rolled her eyes and mouthed the words that followed. Her uncle's personal safety speech. She'd heard it so many times, she knew it by heart. "I promise," she vowed. "I love you, too."

Glad to have that conversation out of the way, she pressed the off button and tossed the receiver onto the bed. She needed something comfortable to wear. Though the incision in her belly button wasn't large, it was definitely tender. She frowned when she considered how bad this virus or phony appendicitis attack had hurt. She'd never had anything grab her so fast with such intensity. She licked her lips and swallowed. She supposed the bad taste in her mouth was from the anesthetic.

She tugged on a pair of blue silk panties, suddenly wishing that she owned just one pair that wasn't a thong. She didn't usually think about it, but knowing that more than six feet of hot Latin male waited on the other side of that door made her a bit apprehensive. An oversize T-shirt and a loose-fitting pair of sweatpants with the waistband shoved beneath her bandage was about the best she could do since she couldn't comfortably lounge around the apartment with Martinez hanging around.

Piper pulled the T-shirt over her head and allowed it to drop down her body. Her stomach growled. She hesitated as she reached for her sweatpants. Her brow creased with the effort of concentration as she tried to remember if she'd eaten today. No, she hadn't. And she was starved. Careful of her incision, she dragged on the baggy sweats. She needed food. She combed her fingers through her damp hair, then headed for the living room. Takeout from Mario's down the street would be good and fast.

A heavenly aroma met her the moment she opened her bedroom door and stepped into the hall. She inhaled deeply, nearly buoyant with the appetite-arousing scent.

Martinez couldn't be cooking.

Could he?

Intrigued and damned hungry, Piper followed the enticing smell into her kitchen. She paused at the door and did a double take. Martinez, with Piper's only apron draped around his waist to protect his slacks, stood in front of her stove stirring something in a rather large pot. She would have laughed out loud had the picture not been so thoroughly awe inspiring.

He looked…domestic and way too handsome. How could a guy so cocky, so incredibly male, appear perfectly at home in a kitchen? *In an apron!*

Piper squeezed her eyes shut and then looked again just

to make sure she hadn't somehow conjured up a Freudian slip of her imagination. Nope, he was still there.

"What are you doing?"

Martinez looked up from his work and smiled. "Dinner." He pointed to the pot he was conscientiously stirring.

Piper's heart dropped to her stomach under the force of that brilliant smile. How could a man wearing an apron and wielding a wooden spoon look so...so sexy?

Piper mentally cursed herself.

It had to be the drugs. She wasn't thinking straight.

"You feeling better?" That dark gaze skimmed her body. "You look really good."

*Drugs.* Oh, yeah. She didn't look good. She looked like death warmed over. She was imagining this entire scene. That explained everything.

"Would you like something to drink before dinner?"

"Dinner?" She stared at him, completely dumbfounded. Maybe she needed to go back to her room and lie down.

He nodded, indicating the steaming pot once more. "I wasn't sure what you would feel up to eating so I rummaged around in your cupboards and found enough ingredients to make soup." He stopped stirring and covered the pot. "It's ready if you're hungry."

"I'm starved." Okay, so it was real. He'd cooked soup. But his comment about her looking good was obviously just an attempt at being nice. Because she looked like hell. Felt like it, too.

"Make yourself comfortable." He gestured to the living room behind her. "And I'll bring it to you."

Piper didn't respond; she just turned around and walked to the couch. She eased down into the overstuffed cushions and got as comfortable as she could—considering. The television was on and tuned to WYBN and the evening news.

There sure wouldn't be a report from Piper Ryan on there tonight. She'd lost the taped interview of Taylor, and the meeting with Mrs. Olsen had been a bust. Then she'd spent a nice trip to the hospital in horrendous pain, and the kind people there had proceeded to poke, prod and suture her until she felt like a pincushion. She was batting a thousand here.

Surely tomorrow's agenda would be better.

Martinez, a loaded tray in his hands, appeared next to her and placed her dinner on the coffee table. The soup smelled absolutely wonderful. There were crackers, grapes and an ice-cold glass of water.

What else could a girl want?

Her gaze collided with Martinez who had crouched down next to her to slide the table closer to where she sat. His handsome face was intent on his task. The healing lip drew her attention to his mouth. His lips were full and well shaped, especially for a man. The lines and angles of his face were well defined and perfectly proportioned. This close she noticed that his nose wasn't as straight as she'd thought. She wondered vaguely if he'd ever broken it. That would explain the ever-so-slight imperfection.

He turned to her then, those dark, alluring eyes tugging at her feminine senses. "Can I get you anything else?"

Piper blinked and forced herself to breathe. "This is fine," she replied, and to her supreme chagrin, somewhat breathlessly.

He touched her chin, tracing the tiny scar from her fall down the stairs when she was a small child. Piper couldn't say precisely what it was at that moment, but something in his touch warmed her…affected her on a level that she couldn't quite understand. He straightened and walked back into the kitchen. She watched, losing her breath all over again, simply watching him move.

She scrubbed her hands over her face and through her hair. *Snap out of it,* Piper, she railed silently. *He's only being nice. Lucas probably coerced him into staying and doing all this.* There was no telling what her uncle had said to him before asking to speak with her. Piper had heard the series of "yes, sir's" Martinez had belted out. Lucas had already recruited her boss and most everyone else with whom she worked closely as guardians. Martinez would be no different. She imagined all those macho genes he had made for an inflated sense of protectiveness anyway. And she was certain Dave had ordered Martinez to keep a close watch on her.

Ignoring the little prick of pain caused by bending forward, she reached for her soup. Gingerly she tasted it. She almost moaned out loud. It was marvelous. A lightly seasoned chicken broth that was thick and smooth. *She* couldn't make soup like this. Especially with nothing but a half-dozen or so bouillon cubes and milk, which was about the only thing in the house. She couldn't even remember what kind of seasonings she had on hand. Obviously enough for him.

She suddenly wondered what else the man could do?

The sound of running water reached her ears, then the clanging of pots. Confusion inched its way across her forehead. He was cleaning up the kitchen. The man cleaned, too? Piper took another sip of soup and banished the image of Martinez cleaning her kitchen.

Then she remembered the gun he carried. She stilled, the spoon halfway to her mouth. He was quite adept at defending himself, as well, she remembered from the brawl with Taylor and his friends. He carried a gun that he no doubt knew how to use. She stared at the bowl in her hand. He cooked. She glanced toward the kitchen. He cleaned. She moistened her lips. He kissed like no man she'd ever been kissed by before.

Piper quickly gulped down the soup. She needed to focus on anything other than Martinez. After she'd finished her soup, she made herself drink the water. Just as she set the tray aside and reached for the grapes, Martinez came into the room and dropped into the chair directly across from her. He leaned forward and braced his forearms on his knees, his hands dangling between his spread thighs.

"Can we talk?" he asked, his expression suddenly serious.

And now he wanted to talk?

This hallucination had gone entirely too far.

"I don't think so." Piper shot up from the couch, grimacing at the pain generated by the abrupt move. "I'm tired. I think I'll take a nap."

He was on his feet and at her side before she could escape between the couch and the coffee table. "You're sure there's nothing else I can get for you?"

Piper backed away from him, her hands held up in a defensive maneuver. "No. You've done more than enough."

She strode straight to her door and closed it behind her. Sagging against it, she considered how he could know all the right things to do.

He couldn't. It had to be coincidence. No man was that perfect. Certainly not *the* man she'd described in her diary when she was a college freshman. She and her roommate, Darlene, had laughed for hours about what they required of their future mate: handsome, built, loyal and sensitive.

And he had to be able to cook and clean, Piper had added, laughing until she cried. Because she never intended to play housewife to any man. And then, of course, the final item she had secretly added to her own diary entry: he had to be an incredible lover.

That was one thing about Martinez she had no intention of learning.

Piper would not be ruled by the silly notions she had entertained as a teenager. No matter how much her traitorous body seemed to want to.

## Chapter Seven

Ric lay on Piper's sofa staring at the digital clock on the VCR—2:35 a.m. He'd tossed and turned for the past two hours and still, sleep would not come. He kept replaying the events surrounding Piper's sudden and unexplainable illness. She had acted fine until they were at the Olsen woman's house. Piper had not been out of his sight at any time except for her one trip to the bathroom. But he'd noticed her strained facial expressions just prior to her leaving the room, so whatever went wrong had to have started before she left his sight. And Townsend had checked the place out before they entered the Olsen residence. There was no one else in the house and the woman had seemed harmless enough to proceed with the interview.

Ric sat up and jammed his fingers through his hair. It didn't make sense. Sure, the doc had a reasonable explanation, but Ric wasn't satisfied. He hadn't liked the condescending doctor. He hadn't liked the place…and he sure as hell didn't like the way the whole event nagged at him now. Something just wasn't right. He wanted to talk to Piper about his uneasiness, but she'd blown him off when he tried. She'd disappeared into her room and hadn't come out since. He knew she was exhausted. He'd read the fatigue in the tiny lines etched in her face, but he'd wanted to get her take on what had happened.

At least she'd eaten and appeared to be resting comfortably now. He had heard the television until around eleven, then the sound had ceased and the light spilling from beneath the door had disappeared. He considered sneaking into her room to check on her, but decided against it. He doubted she would appreciate his concern if she awoke and found him hovering over her bed for whatever reason.

Ric clasped his hands behind his head and relaxed into the thickly padded sofa cushions. He wanted desperately to pretend that his restlessness was related to nothing more than his job and the hard driving way in which this assignment appeared determined to go south on him. In the three days he'd been working Piper's case, she had been attacked by SSU, then gang members and now some sort of weird virus. And he always seemed a step behind. He realized that in the bodyguard business it was his job to react and protect, but he wanted to do more. He wanted to keep Piper away from risk. Period.

But she had no intention of allowing him to do that. Ric wondered if a prerequisite to being a reporter was fearlessness. Piper wasn't afraid of much as far as he could tell.

*I was afraid they were going to hurt you.*

Well, she had admitted to being afraid for him. But that was exactly what she didn't need to worry about. Ric could take care of himself. He'd grown up in a rough neighborhood, learning to fight before he learned his ABCs. Ric closed his eyes and tried not to allow the belief that her fear for him was anything other than basic human compassion. But no matter how hard he tried, his self-deprecating mind kept dangling that kiss as evidence that there was more to her concern. She had responded with a great deal more than worry.

The distinct creak of a door opening at the far end of the hall jerked him to attention. The barely audible whisper of bare feet on carpet sounded next. Ric sat perfectly still as Piper, her white nightshirt reflecting the dim light from the hall, shuffled through the living room on her way to the kitchen. Ric's gaze slid down her shapely legs, instantly noting that the baggy sweatpants were now missing. Awareness kicked his heart into a faster rhythm.

She was either looking for a drink or a midnight snack. The fridge door opened with a rattle of plastic and glass. Ric stood, then moved silently in her direction. He wondered if she had forgotten he was here or simply assumed he was asleep. He paused in the doorway and opened his mouth to speak, but any words he might have uttered took a hike when she bent down to reach into the fridge. The shirt rose to the tops of her thighs, teasing him with just a hint of the curve of her firm behind. His throat went dry.

"Hungry?" he asked, unable to stand that tantalizing position one moment longer without doing something else he would regret.

She jumped, bumping her head in the process. A spicy curse echoed from inside the fridge. She turned around, rubbing the back of her head. "Dammit, Martinez, you scared the hell out of me."

Ric winced in empathy. "Sorry, *querida*." He crossed the room and studied her irritated expression. She actually looked better already. Maybe he was just being paranoid about Petersen and the hospital. "Can't sleep, or just hungry?"

She stared at his chest for two endless beats, a quart of orange juice in her hand. Ric looked down at himself to see what had snagged her attention. He'd taken off his shirt. His gaze instantly sought hers. She didn't blink quickly enough for him to miss the pure feminine appreciation in her eyes. She was attracted to him even now, after all that had happened. Before the moment could turn any more awkward, she shooed him away so that she could step out and close the fridge door.

"Go back to sleep. I only came in here for a drink." She reached for a glass in a cupboard near the sink and filled it with juice. "I don't know why you didn't go back to Mr. Rizzoli's. I'm perfectly capable of taking care of myself. I'm not a child."

"The doctor said someone should stay with you tonight." Ric strode over to the cupboard and retrieved a glass for himself. He picked up the carton she had abandoned on the counter and poured his glass full. He took a deep drink from the juice, then licked his lips. "You have a personal physician, don't you?"

She stared at him, as dumbfounded as if he'd spoken in a foreign language. "What?"

"A doctor," Ric repeated. "You have someone you prefer when you need medical treatment, right?" What was up with her? She usually composed herself more quickly than this. He was pretty sure he didn't have that much of an effect on her. Maybe the anesthetic was making her slow to process responses to his question.

Piper sipped her juice, her gaze carefully averted from him. Finally she shrugged. "Sure, I have a doctor. Why do you ask?"

Ric set his glass down on the counter and leaned against it. He wasn't sure how she would take his suggestion. She'd probably think he was loco, but that was a chance he'd have to take. This whole scenario still didn't sit right in his gut. "I think you should get a second opinion."

She looked surprised, then frowned. "That's ridiculous.'' She plunked her own glass down and busied herself by putting the orange juice away. ''What would be the point in a second opinion? They didn't find anything. Who knows? Maybe I ate something bad. And besides, I feel fine now.''

Before Martinez could say anything else, Piper hurried out of the room. Other than being a tad groggy, she'd felt fine when she awoke, just thirsty and in need of a bathroom break. How could she have forgotten that Martinez had bunked on her couch? She supposed that she was groggier than she'd thought. He'd scared the life out of her. And, as if that wasn't bad enough, he'd blatantly flaunted that bare chest right in her face, making her feel…odd somehow. She rolled her eyes in self-disgust. Who was she kidding? She knew exactly how he made her feel. Hot. Wanton. She wanted to flatten her palms against that awesome chest and push him to the floor so she could climb aboard right now.

Damn. What did that make her? *Desperate.* He was her co-worker. She never slept with co-workers. No matter how damned good they looked. Or how horny she was.

''Wait, Ryan,'' he called out before she could escape to her room. Piper stalled. ''Give me a chance to explain my concerns,'' he added then.

Why didn't he just go back to sleep? She did not want to talk to him right now. He was half-naked and she was…susceptible. Piper gulped at the knot lodged in the back of her throat. Why did she have to be so fiercely attracted to the man? A year—that's why.

Slowly she turned to face him. ''What concerns?''

The dim glow of the hall light only enhanced what she wanted so to ignore. His navy blue slacks were the typical loose-fitting style he appeared to prefer. His feet were bare, long and well formed. Piper shook herself. Why the hell was she staring at his feet? Admiring them, at that? Because being celibate for a year wasn't natural? She was young; she should never have allowed her career to take over her social life—at least not to this point.

Dreading the reaction she knew would slam into her with breath-stealing force, her gaze slid slowly up his lean body. From his long legs, to the rippled abdomen and on to those perfect pecs and mile-wide shoulders. His skin was smooth, stretched taut over bulging muscles that made her feel undeniably restless.

Her gaze settled on his face. The full effect of his extraordinary good looks hit her then. She felt flushed and needy. Her entire body went on alert. Her nipples rose to attention and her pulse pounded. Those hypnotic dark eyes drew hers like light to the dawn. And when she stared directly into them she found that he was assessing her with the same avid interest.

She couldn't let this get out of control.

Dave wouldn't like it. And the station manager had a strict policy about this sort of thing…especially considering Martinez was his cousin.

"I'm not going to have sex with you, Martinez." The words, strangely emotionless, sounded as if they had come from someone else.

"I didn't ask you to have sex with me," he said slowly, but the naturally seductive quality of his voice only tempted her all the more despite his rather flat denial.

The flame that kindled to life in his eyes further belied his words and made her ache in places too long neglected. "Yes you did."

He moved a step nearer to her. "There are some things a man just can't control, *querida,* no matter how hard he tries. I didn't ask. I won't ask." There was no mistaking the added layer of huskiness in his voice.

''Don't come any closer,'' she warned, though her words were impotent since she couldn't possibly bring herself to move, much less run away.

He stopped, maybe three feet away. ''Don't worry, *querida.* I have no intention of starting anything neither of us wishes to pursue.''

Oh, but she did wish to pursue—that was the whole problem. She wanted desperately to do just what she said she wouldn't do. Piper struggled to keep her gaze locked with his. At this point, looking into those eyes proved more disturbing than gawking at his bare chest. ''I wish you'd stop calling me that. I don't like it.'' She lied for good measure. The word, when he said it, made her tremble inside. Made her feel some sort of crazy bond with him.

''We do have to talk.'' His gaze dropped to her mouth.

Instinctively she licked her lips. A tiny hitch disrupted his breathing and sent anticipation surging through her veins. She liked it that she did that to him. ''About what?'' she asked, as if she cared about talking. Those dark eyes moved lower, studying the outline of her breasts and the nipples his nearness had turned into hard, jutting peaks.

''I want you to see your regular doctor, just to be sure everything is all right.'' His gaze traveled back to hers. With one flutter of his thickly lashed lids, he blinked away the haze of lust and pinned her with a serious look. ''Humor me. It's just a hunch I have.''

What was it about this man that made Piper suddenly want to lean on him and allow him to take charge of the insanity she called her life these days? How could she be so vulnerable to his many charms when no one else in her personal or professional life had ever made her feel this way?

One last look into those tempting eyes and Piper knew what she had to do to save herself.

"News flash, Martinez. The only hunches I follow are my own, and—" she marshaled her sternest glare "—for future reference, I also decide when I should go to the doctor." She lifted an eyebrow to punctuate her declaration. "Do you understand me?"

"Completely," he acquiesced in a rich, smooth tone emphatic with that sexy accent he so rarely allowed to surface.

A shiver twirled up her spine. "Good." Piper turned her back on him, determined to stalk away.

"Just one last thing," he urged, ruining her determined exit with a sinfully exotic tone that beckoned her as effectively as if he'd crooked his finger in a hypnotic summons she couldn't resist.

Her defenses slipped another notch as she shifted to face him once more. She inclined her head in silent question, afraid if she opened her mouth, she'd say what she wanted to hide. That she wanted to do a great deal more than simply have sex with him. That almost healed lip and just the slightest hint of discoloration on his left cheek reminded her of how he'd stepped between her and danger, only enhancing the irresistible picture. She couldn't recall ever wanting anyone this badly.

"Call me Ric," he suggested, oozing more charm than Antonio Banderas in his finest role. His alluring gaze raked her body so thoroughly that she gasped in spite of herself. "I think we're definitely past formality," he added in that too-cocky tone.

Irritation burrowed its way through the heat and attraction. He knew exactly the effect he was having on her and he was enjoying it. "Ric? Is that short for Richard? If so, why don't I just call you *Dick?*" Sugary sweet, her words dripped with sarcasm.

As fast as lightning, and just as abrupt, he wrapped the

long fingers of one hand around her arm and pulled her close. Close enough to feel his citrusy sweet breath on her lips. "I've answered to worse," he murmured, then sealed her lips with his own.

Ric knew damn well he shouldn't have. But he did anyway. He kissed her hard, punishingly. She resisted for about two seconds. She had asked for this. His fingers threaded into her silky hair and angled her head. Her lips parted with surrender and he was inside. She was hot and sweet, and he kissed her harder still. His whole body hummed with white-hot desire. He wanted to make love to her, no matter that he shouldn't. No matter…

He pulled back. If he didn't stop now… He released a slow, shaky breath. "You should go in your room and lock your door, *querida,* because I'm not sure I can trust myself."

His hands dropped to his sides and he started to back away, but she stopped him. "Like hell you will. You started this." She went up on tiptoe, grabbed him by the ears and pulled him back down to her and kissed him until he couldn't think.

Unable to deny himself the pleasure of touching her, he slid his arms around her slender waist. Gently he tucked her yielding body closer to his. Her nipples rubbed against his chest, the thin cotton proving no barrier. She sucked on his tongue and Ric growled. Instinctively he squeezed her buttocks, wrenching a groan from her.

She pulled free of his mouth, her breath as ragged as his. "If not Richard, what, then?" she murmured thickly, as if she really cared at the moment what his full name was.

She was beautiful.

He nipped her bottom lip, then licked the softness of it. "Ricardo," he murmured. He made a path to her ear with the tip of his tongue. "Juan Jose Ricardo Martinez," he whispered against that sensitive flesh.

She shivered in response. "Hmmm. Why—" she gasped when his tongue traced the perfection of her delicate ear "—so many names?"

He angled her head once more so that he could plant a trail of kisses down the slender column of her throat. "My mother," he explained between moist, lingering kisses, "had four brothers she loved very much. Juan and Jose are two of them." He drew a slow, languid circle around the fluttering pulse at the base of her throat with his tongue, then blew on it. Piper shivered again. "And my father's name was Ricardo."

She tilted his chin up to cover his mouth with her own. Her kiss was frantic, hungry and was driving him insane. His groin grew heavy with arousal. The need to make love to her was a raging force inside him. He knew he should stop…but he couldn't. Not with her soft fingers tracing his flesh. Every place she touched felt alive and on fire. He trailed his fingers down her neck, over her shoulder and lower still until he found her breast. Those firm mounds filled his hand, firm and warm. He squeezed gently; she moaned into his mouth. His thumb flicked one ultrasensitive nipple and she shuddered in his arms. His body hardened to the point of pain.

She rubbed her thigh along the length of his. He cupped her bottom and lifted, aiding her move to better align their bodies. Her legs went up and around his waist. His arousal throbbed in anticipation of her moist heat. The hot feel of her singed him, even through the fabric barriers standing between them.

Piper pulled her mouth free of his and made a tiny sound of distress. It took Ric a moment to realize that the sound

was from pain not pleasure. Realization made him stagger.
The tiny incision at her belly button.

"Damn." He gently lowered her feet back to the floor,
his eyes searching her face. She bit her lip to quell the
wince, but not before he saw the depth of it. "I didn't
mean to hurt you, *querida*."

Her cheeks stained with color. She backed away a couple of steps. "You didn't hurt me," she said, staring at
the floor. "I didn't think. It was me. I…" She shook her
head. "I didn't think," she repeated.

Ric passed a hand over his face and let go a heavy
breath. "I don't believe either of us were thinking."

She straightened her oversize T-shirt, still looking anywhere but at him. "You're right. We both got a little carried away."

Ric gestured vaguely. "You're sure you're okay? I
didn't…" He should have remembered. Where was his
mind? Below his belt, that's where.

She nodded, finally meeting his gaze. "Really, I'm
okay."

"And you're sure I can't talk you into checking this out
with your doctor?" Why not give it another shot? Whatever had happened between them was over now. And that
was good, even if his throbbing body didn't think so. He
licked his lips and savored the taste of her.

She sighed. "I'm okay, really. Stop worrying. The doctor said everything was fine. The pain is gone except for
the soreness related to the stitches." She forked her fingers through her hair and angled her head toward her
shoulder in a shrug of sorts. "If I have even the slightest
twinge that doesn't feel like healing stitches, I promise
I'll go straight to my regular doctor." She smiled. Ric's
heart thumped at the sweet gesture. She was so beautiful.

''I'll even let you take me there if it'll make you feel better.''

Unable to help himself, he reached out and brushed her cheek with his knuckles. She didn't quite welcome the contact. She stiffened, but didn't move away. He trailed his fingers down her arm until he found her hand, then he squeezed it gently. ''I'll hold you to that, *querida*.''

''I should—'' she hitched a thumb in the direction of her room ''—get some sleep. And so should you. It's late,'' she added quickly.

Before Ric could say good-night, she pivoted and strode toward her door. As he turned to head back to the living room, she suddenly spoke, drawing his attention back to her.

''Do me a favor, would you, Martinez?''

Ric resisted the urge to shake his head. So they were back to Martinez. She was one hardheaded lady. ''Name it,'' he encouraged with as much innuendo as possible.

She blinked rapidly to cover her surprise at his blatantly suggestive tone. ''Keep your shirt on, would you?'' She gave him one of those no-nonsense, all-business looks that could make a man wonder if ice water ran through her veins. ''It's—'' she flared her hands and indicated his bare chest ''—very distracting.''

He smiled widely, wickedly, at her, then smoothed a palm over his chest. Her gaze followed the movement. ''I've been known to have that effect on women.'' He winked. ''I'll try to remember to keep my shirt on in the future since you're having trouble with control.''

Her eyes rounded and her mouth dropped open, but Ric gave her his back and walked away before she could say anything.

He smiled to himself as he settled back on her sofa. It

was nice to know he wasn't the only one having a hard time maintaining control.

But one of them would damn well have to, and it might as well be him.

He just had to figure out how.

# Chapter Eight

Piper stood in her bedroom and contemplated facing Martinez this morning. She pressed her palms and forehead against the cool flat surface of her door and chastised herself once more for allowing that second kiss. She made a disparaging sound in her throat. "Right, Ryan," she muttered. It wasn't the kiss that had been so bad, it was the way she'd tried to climb right inside his skin.

Disgusted, she whirled and sagged against the door. There was nothing like making a fool of oneself to bring a girl's self-esteem down a few degrees. She'd all but attacked the guy like a horny teenager. The only thing that had stopped her from really screwing up was the stinging reminder of her recent trip to the hospital. Reality had crashed down around her then. Big-time.

Piper straightened and squared her shoulders. It was simple. She'd just tell Martinez he had to go home—to Mr. Rizzoli's—where he belonged. He couldn't stay all night with her again. His being this close in the middle of the night would likely prove too tempting for even a saint. Anyway, she felt fine now. Just a little tenderness around the stitches, which was expected.

Except she was obviously losing her mind. It had to be that stupid diary entry coming back to haunt her. The memory of her and Darlene's silly proposal of the necessary male qualities had obviously planted some silly notion in her subconscious. Between that and the fact that she hadn't had sex in a year, she was vulnerable to Martinez's numerous charms.

That had to be it.

The only thing she had to do was get rid of him.

Decision made, Piper took a deep breath and faced the door with the intention of putting her plan in motion. The telephone rang as she reached for the doorknob. Grateful for any sort of reprieve, however temporary, she hurried to her bedside table and snatched up the receiver.

"Ryan."

"Miss Ryan—" the voice was male, and there was a slight hesitation "—this is Keith at the station."

She instantly went into reporter mode. "What's up, Keith?" She glanced at the clock on the bedside table and winced, 10:00 a.m. She never slept this late. She supposed she wouldn't have this morning if she'd been able to sleep after that kiss. It had been almost 5:00 a.m. before she'd finally fallen back to sleep. Those tantalizing fantasies featuring Martinez had taunted her both before and after she'd finally dropped off into a fretful sleep. She had to find a way to get this guy out of her system. Piper never, ever had this kind of trouble staying focused.

"Look, I know you're supposed to be off today, and Mr. Sullenger would probably have my hide if he knew I was calling you." Keith fell silent then…as if realizing the truth in his own words.

Impatient, Piper frowned. "Don't worry about Dave. What's the problem?"

"Well, you know that open house Mrs. Carlisle is having to showcase the proposed new hospital wing?"

Piper massaged her forehead with the tips of her fingers.

The open house was scheduled for next week. Today was Thursday; surely they hadn't canceled at this late date. "Has it been rescheduled?"

"No, it's still on," Keith explained quickly. "But dear old Mrs. Carlisle called this morning and invited you to an impromptu luncheon with the hospital board of directors and a couple of the new wing's benefactors."

Only Mrs. Carlisle could have a whole board of directors and assorted wealthy businessmen scrambling to reschedule their days at the drop of a hat.

"Where and when?" Piper asked automatically. One didn't tell an influential lady like Mrs. Carlisle "no" or offer excuses. Not if one wanted to stay on the top of the food chain in this town anyway.

"Mr. Sullenger's going to be upset that I called." Keith stalled, hesitant again.

"Just tell him that Mrs. Carlisle called me at home. He'll never know the difference."

"Okay. I just don't want to get into trouble." The desk assistant sighed. "But I knew you wouldn't like it if I didn't tell you."

"You're right." Piper was already at her closet shuffling through her wardrobe possibilities. "Whether I'm taking a day off or not, Keith, I'd like to have *all* my messages. Understood?"

"Yes, ma'am."

Piper listened as Keith relayed the time and place of the luncheon. She glanced at the clock and, grimacing, noted that she had less than an hour. The location, a ritzy restaurant that catered to the Atlanta elite, cinched her attire decision. The lavender sheath. She'd bought the dress a month ago, but hadn't worn it yet. Once she'd gotten it home and actually tried it on, she'd realized her mistake. She hated the buttons up the back. From collar to hem, one little annoying button after the other. But she looked good in it and it was pretty classy. Mrs. Carlisle would like it. In television, impression was everything, though it was one of Piper's least favorite parts of the job. Her mother had, admittedly, attempted to mold Piper into the perfect, confident female, but she hadn't been totally successful.

Deep inside, where it counted most, Piper didn't feel so confident. But if she was smart, no one would ever know that little secret but her. In this cutthroat business of shifting power and colliding egos, it didn't pay to let anyone see your soft side.

Piper quickly shed her slacks and blouse and stepped into the dress. She'd discarded her gauze bandage and replaced it with a Band-Aid this morning. The incision was no more than half an inch long, the stitches barely visible. She'd forgotten to ask if she had to have them removed. Maybe she would call her regular doctor about that.

The telephone rang again.

Struggling with the frustrating dress buttons, Piper scooped up the receiver and tucked it between her shoulder and ear. "Ryan."

"Miss Ryan, this is Dr. Petersen."

Speak of the devil, Piper mused. "Good morning, Doctor. I hope you haven't decided to change my diagnosis." She didn't have time to be sick. The interview with Rominski was only a few days away.

"Not to worry, Miss Ryan." The doctor chuckled. "You're quite well, indeed. I only called to make sure you remembered that your stitches deteriorate after a week or so. Removal won't be necessary. You may clean away any fragments that linger, but don't be too hasty about it. Give it about ten days before you attempt any scrubbing of the immediate area, just to be safe."

"You must read minds, Dr. Petersen," Piper teased. "I was just thinking about that."

"I can assure you I'm not a mind reader. Just experienced at dealing with patients. Oftentimes patients don't remember their orders. That's why we give them written instructions." A female voice in the background informed the doctor that they needed him in exam room two. "However," he continued a little more briskly, "the man who whisked you away so abruptly left too quickly for the nurse to give him the final paperwork. I thought it best if I called personally."

Piper thanked him and, as she placed the receiver back in its base, she wondered what Martinez's problem with Petersen was. The doctor seemed exceptionally nice to her. Dismissing the thought, she fastened the final button on her dress and checked her hair, then stepped into a pair of matching lavender heels.

"All set," she told her reflection. She stared at her closed door for a second before moving. All set except for facing Martinez.

Piper smoothed her palms over her dress. She might as well get it over with. All she had to do was keep reminding herself that this was business and Martinez was her co-worker.

His tall, dark and handsome image suddenly loomed large in her mind. She wasn't supposed to think of him as a sex object. Though he definitely made her think about sex. Just to prove her point, her skin instantly heated and her pulse throbbed impatiently.

Had she ever met a man as utterly sexy as Martinez? Piper shook her head. She hadn't. From the man's coal-black hair to his handsome feet, he was awesome. She wondered when he found the time to work out. No one had muscle definition like that without working at it. And those eyes. She shivered. So dark, so mesmerizing. Then there was the way he moved. Rhythm and grace all wrapped up in one breath-stealing, heart-pounding package.

She sighed and banished those thoughts from her mind. Time was wasting. She had thirty minutes to get across town. Piper opened her door and breezed out of the room, chin set defiantly against her own desires. She would not get involved with the guy.

No way.

She was on the verge of bigger things careerwise right now.

Her career had to be top priority.

When she reached the end of the hall, her breath fell short of filling her lungs and her feet bogged down as if suddenly mired ankle-deep in the carpet. On the far side of her living room, the French doors leading onto her balcony were thrown open. Unaware that he was being watched, Martinez, his arms folded over his wide chest, leaned in the open doorway that looked out over the woods and man-made lake behind her building. An oatmeal-colored ribbed knit shirt molded to every impossibly sensual contour of his torso. His slacks were khaki, a bit snugger fit than usual. He must have gone next door sometime this morning to shower and change.

Piper swallowed with extreme difficulty as her gaze moved to his face. Those classic features were a study in concentration, his full lips drawn downward by his musings. That silky black hair glistened in the morning sun, a perfect contrast to his golden skin. It was at that precise moment that she realized the depth of the danger Martinez represented to her. He drew her like no one else ever had…made her feel things she didn't want to feel. No one had ever held that much power over her.

She couldn't let this happen. It wasn't only her career that motivated her caution; it was her heart. Piper closed her eyes to block the distracting image he made. She never wanted to fall in love, no matter how perfect the man appeared to be. Especially not a man like her father.

Her eyes drifted open at that last thought. But then, Martinez was nothing at all like the man she'd called Daddy. He had been one of those cloak-and-dagger types for the CIA. His job meant more to him than his family. His allegiance had always been to his government. And, in the end, he had died for it.

Martinez was a videographer. He seemed to like his work, but it didn't appear to be everything to him. After all, he'd dropped that camera to come to her aid. Her safety meant more to him than the interview. Piper chewed her lower lip. He was so cocky.

She smiled.

And she liked him.

Her smile faded.

She liked him too much.

"It can't be that bad, *querida*. Such a pretty face should never frown so."

Piper snapped her gaze to the Adonis now speaking to her. He smiled a slow, sensuous gesture that made her heart shudder. She would not like him that way. She lifted her chin and pinned him with a firm look. "I don't know why you're still hanging around here, but I have to go." She gestured to the front door. "I'm sure you have other things to do."

He straightened, closed and locked the doors, then started toward her, stealing her breath yet again. How did he move like that? So deliberately, yet so fluidly. The man's body was incredible. Piper felt her blood heating in her veins. Where on earth was that big gun he carried? she wondered fleetingly. His gaze roved the length of her with equal slowness, pausing at strategic places. He stopped directly in front of her and peered down into her eyes. His scent, a subtle musk, surrounded her, making it difficult to think.

"Very nice." He skimmed her body once more. "Do you have a date, *querida?*" His low voice rasped along her skin, making her tingle.

She moistened her lips and resurrected her determination. "I asked you not to call me that."

"*Perdon,* Miss Ryan. I'll try to remember that."

He was watching her, analyzing his effect on her. It infuriated her that he knew just what he did to her. And if he hadn't, he certainly did after that little show she'd put on last night. She cleared her throat. "I have a luncheon engagement with Mrs. Carlisle. But I appreciate your staying with me last night."

He angled that handsome head and studied her face. "And you don't need a cameraman or an escort?"

The vision of him at her side, his arm draped possessively around her instantly filled her mind. The security of knowing he was there nudged at her, made her want to admit she needed him. The widow Carlisle did enjoy a good-looking man, Piper rationalized. Surrounded herself with them, in fact. It was a kind of whispered joke among the people who knew her. Mrs. Carlisle only did business with what she considered beautiful people. Maybe taking along Martinez was a good idea. Piper was reasonably sure he would go a lot further at impressing Mrs. Carlisle than this new lavender dress. And she could use some video footage.

"You'll need a jacket," she said in invitation. This was probably a mistake, but she just couldn't help herself.

"No problem." Martinez extended his hand toward the front door.

Piper picked up her purse from a nearby chair and headed in the direction he'd indicated. She paused at the door and waited as Martinez picked up a lightweight navy blue jacket he'd obviously left on the sofa. How had he known he would need a jacket? He couldn't have. The dark color accentuated the lighter colors beneath.

"Being prepared is my motto," he explained in a gently teasing tone.

Ric followed Piper through her apartment door and paused to lock up while she informed Townsend of their destination. Raine, who was monitoring Piper's calls, had already called Ric on his cell phone and passed along the pertinent information from the desk assistant's call.

Green was waiting near Piper's little red sports car when they exited the building. Her expression brightened instantly.

"They brought my car back!" She rushed to examine the repairs. She glanced at Ric. "You didn't tell me."

"The guy from the body shop just dropped it off this morning." He didn't bother to mention that Raine had gone over the car with a fine-tooth comb, and even added a few things Piper didn't need to know about, such as a tracking device. Lucas had ensured that the body shop insisted on taking her car in for replacing the glass, rather than sending a glass company out to do it on-site.

Piper took her time surveying the shiny automobile, inside and out. Ric had to admit, the woman had good taste when it came to a snazzy ride. This baby was one he would have chosen for himself. In fact, it was every bit as racy as his Camaro, only newer. While she appraised the work the body shop had done, Ric took the camera and the supplies he would need from the news van.

Piper opened the driver's side door and slid behind the wheel. "Let's go, Martinez," she urged.

Mentally preparing himself for the ride, Ric placed the camera into the back seat and dropped into the passenger seat. He snapped his seat belt into place. Townsend had already warned him about her driving habits—fast and furious. Ric had noticed she was an aggressive driver that first day he'd been tailing her, but the rush-hour traffic had kept her pretty much in line.

Piper rocketed onto the street like a speeding bullet. Ric eased back fully into his bucket seat and pretended not to notice. They made the trip across town in record time. He was amazed that Townsend had managed to stay on their bumper for most of the trip. It wasn't until Piper eased up to the curb where the valets waited that Ric realized his jaw had been tightly clenched the entire trip.

Piper was out of the car before Ric could round the hood. He continually scoped the area. He didn't like being out in the open like this. It was too risky. Townsend and Green had parked right behind them and were emerging from their sedan. Raine would be close. But the numerous shops and towering skyscrapers offered an endless supply of sniper cover.

Ric placed his hand at the small of her back as much to reassure himself as her. He had that feeling again that something wasn't as it should be, and he didn't like it. Green was inside already; Townsend was still surveying the block and bringing up the rear.

The doorman offered a polite greeting and opened the elaborate wooden door. Once they were inside, Ric felt immensely better.

The maître d' showed them to the private dining room where Mrs. Carlisle was hosting her luncheon. The hostess smiled widely when she saw Piper. Mrs. Carlisle dropped a dainty kiss on Piper's cheek.

"My dear, you look lovely." The older woman's assessing gaze moved to Ric. "My, my, and who is this?" She glanced long enough in Piper's direction to wink. "I'd heard there was a new man in your life."

Though she blushed, Piper didn't falter. "This is Ric Martinez, Mrs. Carlisle." Piper's gaze connected briefly with Ric's but she didn't say anything else.

Mrs. Carlisle made a sound of approval. "A pleasure, Mr. Martinez." She offered her hand.

His gaze never leaving the woman's, Ric accepted the beringed hand, leaned forward and brushed his lips across her knuckles. "The pleasure is mine, I assure you, *señora.*"

Mrs. Carlisle was properly impressed. Piper, however, was not. She glared at Ric. Confusion marred his brow. Didn't she want him to be charming?

"Please excuse us, Mr. Martinez," Mrs. Carlisle cooed. She turned to Piper. "Come with me, dear. We have a great deal to discuss." She looped her arm in Piper's and led her away.

Ric watched them go. Piper glanced back at Ric once but quickly turned away. A yearning so deep and so strong struck him that he felt weak-kneed with it. He knew better than to allow himself to feel this way. Ric cursed himself silently. What a fool he was falling for a woman who could never be his. No matter how she felt in his arms or how fiercely she kissed him. They were worlds apart. He scanned the elegant dining room. This was her world, always had been. There had never been anything but the best for Lucas Camp's lovely niece.

Ric accepted a glass of white wine from a passing waiter. He downed the liquid in one swallow, then licked the incredibly smooth taste from his lips. Expensive, very expensive, he decided. He thought about his little apartment back in Chicago, and the car he babied like it was a child. That was all he needed. He didn't need any of this. He was just a regular guy. His gaze instantly settled on Piper. He wasn't the right man for a woman like her. Their differences would only tear them apart even if they somehow managed to come together.

He had no desire to travel that path again.

Well, he amended ruefully, the desire was there, but he knew better.

PIPER WAS RELIEVED when the stuffy luncheon was finally over. She'd felt restless from the moment she sat down at the long, lavishly laden table. Martinez had been too quiet. He hadn't said a word to her after they'd taken their seats. In fact, he hadn't spoken to anyone. He'd simply eaten in silence. He'd acted nothing at all like the charming man she'd seen at the charity art auction only a few nights ago.

She hadn't missed the card Mrs. Carlisle had slipped to him. A card that, no doubt, contained her private telephone number. It infuriated Piper that women so openly threw themselves at Martinez, especially when he was supposed to be with her. One look at the man's handsome profile as he shook hands with the mayor on their way out the door served as a stunning reminder of precisely why this very attraction with which she struggled had happened. The man was gorgeous. Sinfully, decadently, drop-dead gorgeous. Women simply couldn't help themselves.

Piper hastened her stride. She might as well stop by the station and leave the desk assistant a blurb about today's luncheon. Couldn't let an opportunity like this pass without making the news. She would have Martinez take a few shots outside before they left. They could use that shot as a visual lead, then follow with any number of shots taken of Mrs. Carlisle at one society function or another. She'd have to do a voice-over at the station. Townsend would never agree to allowing Piper to stand around outside long enough to do the piece, but Martinez could at least pan the area.

The valet offered her keys as she passed him. Piper smiled and left the usual tip in his outstretched palm. She knew Martinez followed. She could feel him, but she refused to look back. She had no clue why he was brooding. She didn't even want to know why. She just wanted to get her job done. And somehow stop thinking about him as anything other than her cameraman.

Townsend and Green moved around her and toward their own vehicle. Piper resisted the impulse to shake her head at the whole situation. God, Jones, where are you? She wanted her old cameraman back. She wanted her life back.

"We'll need to get a little video before we go." Just as she reached her open car door, Martinez slammed into her with the full force of his weight. His arms went around her and they went down on the hard sidewalk. They hit the concrete, Martinez taking the brunt of the fall. He rolled her onto her back, covering her with his big body. The valet and the doorman plastered to the ground a few feet away, both wide-eyed and belly-crawling quickly toward the restaurant entrance.

What was happening?

Piper heard it then, the whizzing pop of a bullet as it flew by and then hit the sidewalk only a few feet away. Someone was shooting at them. Her heart pounded so hard, she could hear the blood rushing through her veins. Martinez's heart was pounding, too; she could feel it. His heavy body pressed into hers, making her pulse even more erratic in spite of current circumstances. She felt him reaching for something and then he had a gun in his hand. This one was smaller than the one he'd had before, but every bit as lethal-looking.

The next sound she heard was shattering glass very nearby.

Her car. A blast of fury had her pushing against Martinez's chest. "My car!"

"Take it easy, *querida*." Ric held her firmly against the ground with his weight. "The car can be fixed. You might not fare so well."

He didn't want her to be hurt. He was protecting her.

His gaze locked with hers, his breath ragged against her mouth. Piper couldn't help herself. She had to touch him. She wanted to feel those tempting lips...to trace the strength of that jaw. And when she touched him, the barest caress of her fingertips on that smooth jaw, those dark eyes filled with a yearning as savage as her own. The fingers of her left hand tightened on his jacket sleeve and the muscular bicep beneath. He winced. Piper jerked her hand away and stared at the warm, wet substance covering her palm.

*Blood.*

She blinked, her eyes trying to deny what her brain told her. Martinez was bleeding....

# Chapter Nine

Piper shook her head resolutely. "I don't want to hear it, Martinez. They shot you." She gestured to the thick gauze bandage encircling his bicep. "What if they'd killed you?" Her voice quivered slightly on those last couple of words.

"They didn't," he insisted calmly. "It's nothing but a flesh wound." It hurt, but he'd live.

Furious, she pivoted and started her neurotic pacing all over again. "Nothing but a flesh wound," she muttered hotly. "That's just like a man, gotta be a tough guy. I need to revise my out-of-date diary entry," she added, speaking more to herself than to him, Ric decided.

He massaged at the ache in his forehead. What did she want him to say? She'd gotten hysterical when she'd realized he was bleeding. It was all he could do to hold her down until the threat had passed. By the time the paramedics arrived, Ric wasn't sure which of them needed help more, him or her. She had refused a sedative, but had calmed considerably when the treating medic pronounced Ric as good as new. It was nothing but a nasty flesh wound. More a nuisance than a real problem.

Ric hadn't expected that kind of reaction from her. He'd tried to rationalize the extreme response by assuming that uncontrollable fear had played into the problem. After all, someone had been trying to kill her. But now, a full hour after they'd arrived safely back at her apartment, Piper was still more upset than she should be. Maybe she'd simply reached the end of her emotional rope. A lot had happened to her in the past few weeks. He wouldn't even pretend it could be anything else.

"I agree with Dave," Ric said quietly, in hopes of defusing the situation. She stopped and glared at him. "I think you should stay out of sight until after Tuesday's interview." Fishing for a way to make her see it his way for once, he went on, "That interview with the senator is too important to risk anything happening between now and then to put you out of commission."

A new kind of emotion, something between outrage and anger, sprang to life in those startlingly blue eyes. "You think this is all about me," she said in disbelief. Then she trembled right before his eyes.

He ached to hold her. Before he could stop himself, he had covered the distance between them, but refrained from touching her the way he wanted to. "You're safe now. And I don't plan on letting you out of my sight until there's no one left to threaten you." Raine had taken out the shooter. The trademark tattoo marked him as hardcore SSU. One down, and no telling how many more to go. Unless they somehow managed to track down and take out the leader, Piper could be dodging danger for the rest of her life. Ric hoped like hell that the FBI's undercover guy came up with something soon.

Piper looked directly into Ric's eyes, her own suspiciously bright. "You don't understand," she said wearily. "I made a conscious decision to go to that secret press conference last month." She pointed to her chest. "I knew the risk I was taking when I went. I know the added risk I take each time I walk out that door with SSU stalking my every move. I—'' She pressed her fingers to her lips to hold back the emotions shaking her.

Ric reached for her then. He couldn't bear to see her cry. "Don't do this—''

She batted his hand away. "You," she began, clearly grappling for composure, "didn't do anything to antagonize SSU. They shouldn't be shooting at you." She turned away from him. "This was all my fault. I shouldn't have let you go with me. It's not safe to be with me."

Instinctively his arms went around her. She resisted at first, then she sagged against his chest. He nuzzled her neck, reveling in the smell of her skin. "You shouldn't worry about me, *querida*. I can take care of myself."

She let out a big, halting breath. "I keep thinking that it could have been so much worse."

It definitely could have, Ric didn't say. She could have been hurt. He closed his eyes against the pain the mere thought sent hurtling through him. Townsend and Green had been standing by a few feet away, but neither of them had seen the shooter. It was pure luck that Ric had. He'd gotten just a glimpse of something in the second-story window across the street. If he'd been a mere second slower…

Ric frowned. It was almost as if the guy had wanted to be seen at that particular instant. The way he'd moved in the sunlight, causing that blinding glint. Whatever the case, he was dead now. Jack Raine was an expert shot.

Piper turned in his arms and looked up into his eyes. Ric felt his body harden at the feel of her against him, at the sweet concern in her eyes.

"You should stay away from me," she said firmly, but the little hitch in her breathing after her statement ruined the effort at determination. Her soft hands flattened against his chest. "I mean it, Martinez. I want you to go."

"I can't do that, *querida*." The rush of desire that shot straight to his groin made him tremble.

Her fingers fisted in his shirt. She was staring at his mouth and it was almost more than he could take. When she went on tiptoe and pressed her soft lips to his, he lost any control he'd hoped to maintain. She opened in invitation and Ric thrust into her. His hands found their way to her hair and he cupped her head, delving more deeply into her sweet mouth. The yearning that had been building inside him all week exploded into hot, searing need.

She tugged his shirt upward and Ric let go of her just long enough to pull it over his head and toss it aside. Her cool hands slid over his skin, making him crazy with want. Then she stopped and drew back from him.

For one long moment she simply looked into his eyes, drawing out the ache building inside him. He wanted so desperately to pull her back into his arms, but this had to be her decision. He knew the price he would pay, but he would not exact her cost, as well. If she wanted to cross that line and face the consequences that would come later, she had to do so of her own choosing.

Without a word she took his hand and led him across the room, down the hall and into her dimly lit bedroom. The late-afternoon sun couldn't quite penetrate the heavy, laced drapes, resulting in a room in deep shadow. When she turned back to him, he saw the sudden hesitancy in her eyes. She sat down on the side of her bed, looking anywhere but at him, her hands cradled in her lap.

Ric sat down on the end of the bed, allowing her to keep her back to him until she decided to face him again, but close enough to reach out to her. While he waited he studied the gentle curve of her shoulder, her tiny waist that flared into slender hips. Her skin where the dress scooped low off her shoulders looked as smooth and creamy as porcelain. He could imagine how she would taste there.

She looked at him over her shoulder. ''I'd like you to touch me. I know you want to.''

He trailed his fingers over that delicate, bare flesh that he'd imagined tasting only moments before. Her eyes closed and she moaned her approval. Taking that as license, he leaned forward and kissed her shoulder. She gasped. He eased the wide straps of her dress off her shoulders as he worked his mouth across that bare expanse of skin. The sound of her labored breathing sent another wave of urgency through him. He slipped the top button from its closure and pressed his lips there. He wanted to taste all of her. One by one he loosened button after button, kissing each vertebra as he bared it. He took special care when he unfastened her bra, lingering there.

When he'd freed the buttons all the way to her hips, she stood, allowing the dress to fall around her feet. She shrugged off the satin bra. Fire raced through his veins as he took in the beauty before him. Her skin was perfect, flawless. Her bottom was bared by a pair of thong panties, the sight of which made it very difficult for him to breathe. She stepped out of the puddle of lavender and moved around to stand directly in front of him.

Long, toned legs, made even longer by her spike heels, and then the barely veiled place at the center of her thighs made him weak with desire. The tiny Band-Aid at her belly button tugged his lips into a frown; he'd have to be careful not to hurt her. That worry dissolved as the need to see her naked breasts drew his gaze upward. Unable to help himself, he moistened his lips as he resisted the almost overwhelming urge to reach out and touch those small, firm breasts. They jutted upward, the tips rosy and pebbled into tight buds.

His gaze collided with hers then, and he saw the longing he felt mirrored there. Ric stood, needing to be closer to her. Her fingers went instantly to his fly. She dodged his mouth when he tried to kiss her and focused all her attention on unfastening his slacks. He groaned at the feel of her fingers along that highly aroused place. He felt ready to explode any second. She knelt before him, dragging his slacks and briefs down his legs. Looking at her kneeling before him like that sent a shock wave of heat hurdling through him. She tossed aside his shoes, then his socks. She stood as he stepped out of his discarded clothing, then leaned down and kissed his arm near the white bandage. When she looked up at him, the desire in her eyes had taken a back seat to the worry and regret that he'd been hurt. The idea that she cared enough to be concerned made him weak with tender feelings.

Unable to hold back any longer, he covered her breasts with his hands and squeezed gently. She threw her head back and cried out with pleasure. He kissed that delicate place at the base of her throat, all the while kneading those taut little breasts. She cupped his buttocks and pulled his hips against her. Her mouth found his and the kiss was filled with feverish urgency, making his heart pound harder, making him feel as if he were going to come before he got inside her. He couldn't wait. He broke free long enough to scoop her up into his arms, grimacing only slightly at the sting of his fresh injury.

Her fingers clenched into the flesh of his shoulders as she held on tightly. Ric lowered her to the bed and knelt beside her. He leaned down and quickly kissed her hungry mouth before moving down the length of her. He kissed his way along those shapely legs, until he was kneeling at her feet. He raised her foot to his chest and removed the high-heeled shoe. He tossed it behind him, then reached for the other foot and did the same. He traced her tender arch with his tongue and then on to her ankle. By the time he had kissed and licked his way back to the top of her thigh, she writhed with need. She reached for him, tried to pull him close, but he resisted.

He placed a gentle kiss next to her belly button, remembering the fear he'd felt in that hospital. A kind of fear he'd never experienced before. Using the fingers of both hands, he lowered her strappy panties. Careful not to hurry, he dragged the satiny material slowly down and off. When those lacy panties dropped to the pile of clothing already heaped on the floor, Ric turned back to her, ready to devour her completely. She was so beautiful. His full and ready erection urged him to take her now, but he held back, trying to slow his plunge toward release. He wanted to make this last, to make it special for both of them.

Piper watched intently as Martinez disposed of her panties, and then as he sat back, simply looking at her. She could hardly breathe, her anticipation was so great. His powerful body was completely, beautifully aroused. Her body responded so totally to him that it was frightening. She was wet and throbbing, aching with the need to be filled by him. His kisses and his wicked tongue had brought her to the brink of climax already. Merely looking at him now further aroused her, adding to the frenzy mounting inside her.

She had seen practically all of him that afternoon when she'd interrupted his shower, however, certain strategic areas had been covered by his towel. But not now. There was nothing left to conjecture now. He was gloriously naked. Martinez was not only drop-dead gorgeous, he was incredibly well endowed. He aligned his body with hers, staring down so very deeply into her eyes. Looming over her like that, he looked like a naked Latin god, his smooth skin an alluring contrast to the white bandage on his left bicep.

He lowered that magnificent body onto hers, and what little breath she managed stalled in her lungs. He kneed her legs apart and lowered himself expertly between them.

"Don't let me hurt you, *querida*," he murmured.

"Don't talk, Martinez." She breathed the words.

He took her hands in his and held them on either side of her head just as that dark gaze held her in a sort of trance. She longed to feel his mouth on hers once more, but he denied her that pleasure, though she knew he could read the want in her eyes. Never taking his gaze from hers, he nudged her intimately, prodding her entrance with his hard, smooth tip. Instantly she opened wider for him. His next thrust sent him deep inside her, stretching her, filling her.

She climaxed.

He held absolutely still as she shuddered around his thick arousal. When she could open her eyes again he was still watching her, but the fire in his eyes gave away his own proximity to the edge. His mouth came down on hers in a tender, yet all consuming kiss. It went on and on while her inner muscles continued to spasm around him.

Then he moved.

Piper whimpered, the sound lost in his intense kisses. He thrust his tongue deeply into her mouth, mimicking the move with his hips, finding full, deep penetration. Slowly he drew his hips away, allowing his heavy arousal to drag along her tingling feminine flesh. She wanted to touch him, to pull him back inside her but he held her hands firmly in his. Her body aching for his next move, she wrapped her legs around his and pushed her hips upward, taking him to the hilt. He growled a savage sound and kissed her harder, drawing on her senses so completely that she felt powerless to do anything but feel.

He pushed her back down with his full body weight, then withdrew to the tip, taunting her unbearably. Piper wanted to rant at him, she wanted him inside her. She wanted him moving. A new climax was already building with a pounding crescendo. He went deep again. She moaned her approval. He pulled back and thrust once more, harder. His fingers tightened around hers, his expression was intent, fierce, as he started a rhythm that left her powerless to do anything but stare into those dark eyes. Harder, faster, their mingled respiration matched the frenzied pace.

The world around her flowered into color and her eyes closed of their own accord as pleasure cascaded over her. This time her whole body rocked with release, and it just kept building. When she thought the tide would recede, a whole new wave crashed down on her. Then he crashed, too, his release so violent, he cried out with it as it shuddered through him. He slowed his pace but didn't stop, making it go on until the last ripple of pleasure subsided.

When he was spent, he collapsed beside her and tucked her body close to his. A sheen of perspiration slickened their skin. The cool air from the central air-conditioning made her shiver as awareness of her environment eventually came back into focus. Martinez pulled her closer, shielding her body with his own, just as he'd done on that sidewalk today. Protecting her, taking a bullet for her. Unbidden, tears welled in her eyes and she wanted to protect him more than she'd ever wanted to do anything in her life. Just when she would have asked him the question suddenly burning in the back of her mind, he spoke.

"I hope I didn't hurt you, *querida*," he murmured against her temple, a decidedly breathless quality to his tone. She smiled; she was breathless herself. "I tried to hold back." He pressed a kiss there. "But I wanted you so much...." He sighed, clearly unhappy with himself.

She turned in his arms, studying his concerned face for a time, her question momentarily forgotten. "Well, if you're not entirely satisfied with your performance, we could always do it again." She grinned as realization dawned in his eyes.

"Is that a challenge?" He kneed her thighs apart. "Because if it is, I never, ever back down from a challenge."

"Wait!" She pressed both hands against his chest, holding him at bay when her whole body yearned for his nearness. "There's something I have to know. Just one question." She had to ask while she still had the presence of mind. "Where did you learn to handle yourself so well under fire?" She had to know if what she suspected was right.

He frowned, just a little. "I told you already," he whispered, then nipped her lips. "Where I come from you never take chances."

Dodging his wicked mouth, she asked, "So you grew up in a neighborhood like Hope Place?"

He trailed a finger along her jawline, then down her throat. "Much, much worse, *querida.* Dodging bullets and bad guys was a way of life." His finger circled her nipple slowly, so very slowly, his gaze trekking the journey with fierce intensity.

Piper shivered, anything else she would have said or even thought gone. His hand slipped lower between them; she caught her breath. Surely she wouldn't come again even before he got inside her. But just watching him look at her, touch her, made her so hot she could barely stand it. Then that dark, sexy gaze locked on to hers and she was lost.

His mouth descended slowly toward hers.

She wanted him so desperately. She reached for him just as their lips touched.

The telephone rang.

Martinez jerked back as if someone had walked into the room and caught them red-handed. "I'm not answering it," she warned.

It rang again. "It might be important," he suggested, worry creasing his brow.

She shook her head. The damned phone rang again.

He grabbed the phone and punched the talk button. "Martinez."

Ignoring propriety, Piper trailed her fingers down his chest and encircled his already fully aroused shaft, still damp with their lovemaking. She just couldn't help herself; she needed to touch him. She stroked his length. He made a sound, not quite a groan, and placed his hand over hers to still her erotic movements.

"I understand." He paused. "No, we didn't go back to the station."

Whether it was from her wicked touch or the person on the other end of the line, he looked immensely distressed.

"Yes sir, she's right here." He held the phone out to her. "It's your uncle Lucas," he said tightly.

Lucas's timing was criminal, she decided as she accepted the receiver. Martinez got up and walked to the end of the bed to gather his clothes. The man had an amazing backside, too, she noted for future reference. "Hello, Uncle Lucas," she said, sated and contented beyond belief. She'd never enjoyed sex that much before. That, she realized, was the way it was supposed to be. Mind-blowing. The final item on her long-ago proposed future mate profile flitted through her mind, but she instantly banished it and forced her attention to her uncle's voice.

"Martinez?" she asked, surprised at her uncle's question. "Oh, he's unbelievable," she said dreamily. Martinez shot her a quelling look as he fastened his slacks.

"What?" Piper sat up. Weaver was dead. "When?" Less than two hours ago. Near the same time someone had tried to kill her. Piper listened as her uncle explained that Weaver had been shot while meeting his fiancée in what had been considered a safe location. The Feds hadn't wanted to allow the meeting, but Weaver had insisted. Now he was dead.

This was it. She was the only one left. She rested her head in her free hand and fought the urge to cry.

Her uncle's next statement grabbed her attention. "Senator Rominski is canceling his trip to Atlanta?" She repeated her uncle's words, certain she had to have heard wrong. Lucas refused to go into the details on the telephone. He informed her that Townsend and Green were being briefed on a secure line at that very moment and they would provide her with the rest of the details.

"I don't understand," she argued as the last lingering remnants of pleasure she'd found in Martinez's arms drained away, leaving her filled by this ugly reality. Lucas urged her not to worry, that everything would be fine. "I love you, too," she whispered before hanging up.

She pushed the off button and looked up. Martinez had left the room and she hadn't even noticed. She quickly dressed in a T-shirt and sweats and headed to the living room to find him. How could the senator back out on her like this?

*Weaver's dead.* Her uncle's words echoed inside her head.

And she was next in line on the hit list.

If it hadn't been for Martinez they would have ended it today. She and Weaver would both be dead. She paused in her journey and closed her eyes for a moment to gather her composure. She thought of the way he had protected her, and then of the way he'd made love to her with the same fierce determination, but with utter sweetness.

Battling back her emotions, Piper walked into the living room. Townsend was already there talking in a low voice to Martinez. They both looked up when she cleared her throat.

"So, I'm the last one standing, huh?"

At the look of devastation on Martinez's face, she instantly regretted her words.

"Miss Ryan, I'm going to brief both you and Martinez as to Mr. Camp's plan."

Piper dropped on the sofa and looked directly into the man's eyes. "I'm pretty sure that I'm a goner, so let's be frank here, shall we?"

Swearing a string of hot Spanish curses, Martinez looked away from her.

"You can't fight an enemy when you don't know who it is," she said, voicing what neither of them would. She fixed her growing anger on Townsend since Martinez wouldn't look at her. "The fact of the matter is that anyone could step out of the shadows and do me in at any time." Townsend stared at the floor and let her have her say. "So, if we don't know what the bad guys look like, then we're screwed, right?"

Martinez leveled a savage glare on her. "All we have to do is the unexpected. When the enemy is unknown and unpredictable, you make the target unknown and unpredictable, as well."

"And just how do you propose we do that?" She refused to acknowledge the hope his words engendered. She wanted so to believe him, but how could he possibly know? He was a cameraman, not a secret agent. No matter how tough the neighborhood he'd grown up in or how street savvy he was at saving his hide, these men were die-hard terrorists.

"Martinez is right," Townsend put in. "So we've come up with a plan. To date, you've been carrying on with your life as usual. If we go the route your uncle proposes, that's over."

Piper focused her attention on the G-man; she didn't need to keep looking at Martinez anyway. Looking at him only made her want to reach out to him. To somehow promise him that everything would be all right, when she knew she couldn't.

"In one hour we're flying to D.C. on a private jet secured by Mr. Camp. In D.C. we'll be staying in a hotel not far from one of the local television stations. Senator Rominski is taking a weekend trip to New York with his wife just to throw SSU off track. They won't expect you to be in D.C. if the senator's not there. Monday morning the interview will be done live from that station and aired right after *The Morning Show* and before SSU even knows you're in the city. We're keeping those who know your plans to a minimum. Only your news director and the senator himself will know you're in the city."

Piper was stunned. The interview was happening, and it was going to be televised nationwide for sure? Her uncle's plan sounded like it might just work to keep her safe and facilitate her career. Of course, he had been in the undercover business most of his life. If anyone could devise a plan to beat SSU and keep Piper happy, Lucas could. And the interview—national. This was good. Really good... wasn't it?

She looked at Martinez then. "Do you think it'll work?"

He held her gaze for a long moment before he answered.

So much feeling glowed there that it made her tremble inside. What was happening between them? This was about more than just sex, she decided hesitantly. It had been building since the first day she laid eyes on him.

"I think it can work," he told her without reservation.

Piper let go a long, shaky breath. Well, that settled it. If Martinez and Lucas thought it would work, it surely would. She met Townsend's expectant gaze. "Let's do it, then."

"There's just one more thing you need to know," Martinez said, drawing her attention back to him again.

It wasn't good. She could tell by his closed expression. "And what would that be?"

"The Bureau has a man undercover inside SSU." Martinez looked away for a moment before he continued. He had wiped all emotion from his face when he turned back to her. "They have some sort of grand finale planned for you. He doesn't know what it is yet, but whatever it is that's the reason they've kept you alive until now. He's pretty sure the attempts so far are just for show. Even the one today."

Piper's stomach roiled. So this is what he and Townsend had been whispering about. She tried to separate rational thought from emotion, but it wasn't working too well. *We could kill you…at any moment.* The memory of that threat echoed in her mind. What Martinez said was right. They were playing some sort of demented game with her. "So, they have something special planned for me," she ventured hesitantly.

"Apparently," Townsend answered her. Martinez had fallen silent. "We can only assume it has something to do with the interview of the senator. Since that wasn't scheduled with your station until a few days ago, we could be entirely wrong, but that's the thinking at the moment."

"Or—" Martinez cut in "—they could have someone in the right place and that someone could have known the senator was planning this interview days before the station knew it."

"That's possible," Townsend offered. "But the people working around the senator have all undergone rigorous security clearances and have worked with him for some time."

"All that means is that whoever it is, has a price," Martinez countered, his mushrooming agitation more than evident. "And SSU figured out what it is."

Piper didn't care what Townsend thought. She had to go to Martinez. She put her arms around his waist and leaned against his chest. When his arms closed around her she felt safe. With him holding her like this she could almost believe that this whole thing was somehow going to work out.

"Can you be ready in one hour, Miss Ryan?" Townsend asked.

She nodded, still clinging to the man who'd made love to her so thoroughly. "But I'm not going without Martinez. He's my cameraman. He goes where I go."

"Don't worry, *querida*," Martinez assured her, his deep voice rumbling from his chest. "You're not going anywhere without me."

## Chapter Ten

The hotel room was dark save for the glow cast by the lamplight from the sitting room. Piper stood near the window, staring into the night. She'd said little since they boarded the Learjet and left Atlanta behind. She'd shown no interest in dinner and had retired to her room soon afterward. Ric watched from the doorway, wishing he could say something—anything—to make her smile again.

He supposed he should just let her be. But he wasn't at all sure he could do that. She felt like a part of him now. He'd known from the beginning that something special clicked between them, and he'd wanted her more than he'd ever wanted any woman. But their lovemaking this afternoon had sealed his fate. He would never be the same again. He didn't know how she did what she did to him, but he only wanted to be with her. And that was going to end all too soon.

Ric closed his eyes and pushed away the pain that accompanied that last thought. Their whole relationship was based on a lie. He wasn't who she thought he was. And he had a bad feeling that she wasn't going to understand his reasons for keeping his real identity a secret...especially after what they'd shared this afternoon. He swallowed that hard reality and opened his eyes. He'd made a mistake. He should never have taken her to bed with that deception between them. He'd had the perfect opportunity to come clean when she'd asked him how he'd learned to handle himself under fire. But he'd been a coward, taken the easy way out.

He rubbed the back of his neck and considered the next forty-eight hours. The suite they shared had two bedrooms. Would she want him to share her bed tonight? And, if she did, should he with this lie still standing between them? Townsend and Green were right across the hall in a suite of their own. Lucas had hand picked the hotel. Raine would be somewhere nearby. Though Ric was certain he wanted to, Lucas wouldn't come near the place. He wouldn't risk being seen on the premises and compromising Piper's location.

Lucas and his people were working overtime in an effort to stop SSU. Ric hadn't prayed since he was a kid and had gone to Mass with his mother, but he'd prayed today. He didn't want Piper to be hurt in all this insanity. He wanted to protect her. Damn him, he wanted to make love to her again. His body stirred at the thought. More than anything, he wanted the chance for her to know him—the real Ric Martinez—and to forgive him for making love to her while this lie hung over their heads. He released a heavy breath, too mentally exhausted to think.

''You know,'' Piper said quietly, aware of his presence now, ''I still hate this city.''

''Why is that?'' Martinez crossed the barely lit room and leaned against the wall next to the window so that he could look at her. ''I mean, it's not like the greatest place on the planet, but it's not that bad.'' He'd had his share of good times in the nation's capital. None, however, that he cared to talk about at the moment. They either involved work or recreation: a Colby case; or a woman with whom he'd spent a weekend and would never see again. He was glad he'd finally outgrown that foolish need to prove he could have any woman he desired at any time he felt the urge. He settled his gaze on the only one who'd ever made him think past the moment—made him want a future with her in it.

Piper didn't answer his question for a while, nor did she look at him. She continued to stare into the dark night. The glittering lights from the windows in the high-rises across the street shone brightly, but not brightly enough to reach this far.

"I was eight years old when my father died," she finally said. "We lived not far from here. In one of those fancy town houses like all the rest of the people who worked in D.C., but thought they were too good to live in the city."

"What kind of work did your father do?" Ric already knew part of that answer, but he wanted to know more. And she seemed in the mood to talk now.

She folded her arms over her chest, but still didn't look at him. "He and my uncle Lucas were CIA field operatives." She glanced at Ric then. "You know, the black ops guys that aren't supposed to exist."

Ric nodded. He'd figured Lucas for the type.

"That's how my mother met my father," she went on, her gaze going back to the window. "Lucas brought him home after a mission and it was love at first sight."

She shifted, and set her chin defiantly as if she had no faith in the concept of that kind of love. "But, as it turned out, my mother was only a mistress. He was married to his career. He loved his job more than he did either of us."

Ric heard the disappointed little girl in her voice and his heart ached at the sound. "I'm sure the CIA required

exclusive devotion,'' he suggested in an attempt to throw
a different light on the subject.

She jutted that determined chin out again. ''It was more
than that. I can't explain it. I was too young to understand
fully at the time. But he didn't have anything at all left for
us. On the rare occasions when he was home, he was simply there. He didn't try to interact with me at all.''

''So you resented him for leaving you when he died.''

Piper laughed, but the sound held no humor. ''I resented
him a long time before that. I think I resented him even
before I was born for making my mother so unhappy.''
Piper shook her head. ''Despite her perpetual state of sadness, she was completely fooled, you know. Still is. She
thought he was this handsome, caring man who loved her
more than anything. But the reality was that he loved his
career more.''

Ric moved closer to her then. She needed to be touched;
he could feel it. He tugged one hand free of her firm
stance, and held it tightly. ''Is that why you're afraid of
falling in love?''

''I won't ever trust anyone that way,'' she affirmed.

Ric pulled her toward him, forcing her to meet his gaze.
''Are you sure it's not you that you're afraid to trust,
*querida?*'' She looked startled at the suggestion. ''Maybe
you're afraid you'll put your career before the man you
love, just like your father did to your mother.''

The man's perceptiveness astounded her. He was right.
The notion had crossed her mind, but she had refused to
consider it for long. She didn't want to be like her father,
not in that way. Though her mother had stopped grieving
for her father, she still loved him. Fear and that haunting
love kept her from having a relationship to this day. Piper
never wanted to find herself in that perpetual state of un-

happiness, whether caused by the man in her life or by her own single-mindedness toward her work.

"I guess it's a little of both," she reluctantly admitted. The new set of feelings his revelation invoked made her frown. No matter what else she felt, the bottom line was self-preservation. She would not end up like her mother. "I don't ever want to fall for a guy like my father. A regular guy who has no aspirations about saving the world will be fine with me."

Martinez trailed a fingertip along the line of her jaw, sending desire racing through her. She wanted him again. And then again after that. A smile chased her frown away. His tender touch vanquished the sadness that lingered in her soul.

"But you risk your life for what you believe in," the man who held entirely too much power over her countered. "Why would you not allow the man you fall in love with the same leeway?"

Piper clasped his hand in both of hers. "I know it sounds selfish. But I just can't let that happen. It hurts too much to lose that kind of man. I don't want to fall in love with a hero, Martinez. It's too hard to let him go when it ends." She lapsed into silence, remembering. She finally went on when she'd gathered her courage. "One night, a long time after he'd died—" she shrugged "—I don't know, maybe I was eleven or twelve, I woke up in the middle of the night with this feeling that he'd just been in my room." She peered up at Martinez. "You know, like he used to do. On the rare occasions when he'd be home, he'd come into my room and watch me sleep. My mother told me it showed how much he loved me and missed me." Piper shook her head. "But I didn't believe her."

"You woke up and he wasn't there," Martinez prodded, "and then what?"

Piper allowed the memories to come, something she rarely did. "I was so certain he'd been there. I could feel him." She held Martinez's hand to her chest. "So I rushed down the stairs looking for him. And I fell. Knocked myself out cold." She touched the tiny scar on her chin. "Mother had to carry me to the emergency room. She said it was the strangest thing. There was no blood on the floor and hardly any on my clothes. But the next day she found a bloody handkerchief in the washing machine. One just like my father used to carry in his back pocket. Mother swears his ghost came to my aid while I lay there unconscious." Piper made another of those strained laughs that lacked amusement. "But, knowing how hysterical my mother always got in a crisis, she probably used the handkerchief on me herself, then forgot about it."

Martinez wrapped his arms around her and held her against his chest. "We all have our ghosts."

"Still," she began again after a long pause, "so many times I could feel him." She frowned, remembering. "Like at my high school and college graduations. It was like someone was watching me." She shook her head. "No, not someone—him." She sighed, disgusted with herself for even remotely believing in such a silly notion. "What about you, Martinez?" She tilted her head to look up at him again. "Tell me more about your childhood."

He smiled and her heart did a little tattoo. "It was very different from yours, I'm afraid, *querida*," he said solemnly.

"Tell me," she urged, wanting to know more about this man who made her feel such alien emotions.

"We were very poor. My mother and father worked in what you would call a sweatshop. The work was hard and barely paid enough for survival."

He sighed, the sound making Piper feel sad. She asked, "Do you have any brothers and sisters?"

"One younger brother. We took care of each other while our parents worked their long hours. It was a rough neighborhood. It's a miracle either one of us survived it."

Piper turned in his arms and looked at him with new respect. "But you did." She touched that handsome face, relishing in the feel of his skin. "And your brother, I suppose he was named after your mother's other two brothers?" she teased.

Martinez grinned. "Carlos Jorge."

"Where is your family now?"

"Carlos lives in Chicago and our parents died a long time ago."

"I'm sorry," she murmured. He still missed them; she could see it in his eyes. She traced his full bottom lip, thinking that one or both of his parents must have been beautiful like him. "The relationship between me and my mother has always been so awkward, I forget sometimes that it isn't that way for everyone. She's always abroad lounging around some resort, and I'm always glad. She doesn't even know about this SSU thing."

He kissed her forehead so sweetly that Piper thought she might cry. "Love is not always like that, *querida*."

"Sleep with me tonight, Martinez." She pressed her cheek to his chest, needing to feel his heart beat. "I don't want to be alone."

He pressed another of those gentle kisses to her hair. "Don't worry, *querida*. I promise you won't be lonely tonight."

THE NEXT DAY dragged by like each hour was half a lifetime. Lucas called several times to check on his niece, but he had no news. The tension got the better of Piper by that evening and she started to pace. The old hurt she had revealed to Ric last night seemed to open up and fester with every passing moment. It was as if being in this city made her ill. He wanted desperately to make her feel better. At this rate she wasn't going to be in any shape to conduct the biggest interview of her career on Monday morning.

Ric finally understood why her career meant so very much to her. He'd thought at first that it was because she wanted to get to the top as quickly as possible, but he knew differently now. It was all she had. All she could trust, because she was in control there. Despite the poverty of his youth, he had never wanted for affection. His family had been close in spite of their circumstances. He and his brother were still extremely close. Just last year Carlos had lent Ric his brand-new SUV, and hadn't stroked out when Ric returned it a little damaged. Okay, a lot damaged. But Ian Michaels, Ric's mentor at the Colby Agency, had paid for the damages.

Ric had to find a way to get Piper focused on something besides her current situation. Unfortunately, sex wasn't the answer. No matter how good it had been last night.

Townsend had come in and out all day, checking on Piper. Green loitered in the hall acting like some sort of social deviant looking for an opportunity to pounce on someone. The guy was about as claustrophobic as Piper. It was a miracle the other guests hadn't complained. Finally, around nine, the two agents had called it a night. Ric glanced at the digital clock—9:30 p.m. He wondered if he could entice Piper into calling it an early night.

His attention came back to rest on the subject of his musings and her incessant pacing. She was working herself up into a real frenzy. He supposed it was a combination of cabin fever, fear and her own unhappy history. But there was little he could do about it. He wasn't at all sure his heart could take another night like last night, though his body was more than willing. They'd made love twice; each time she'd burrowed a little more deeply under his skin. She'd touched him so profoundly that last time that he'd been shaken to the core. Ric closed his eyes. He knew better. He'd promised himself that he'd never do this again. And here he was, head over heels in love with a woman who would never love him in the same way because of external reasons.

Oh, there was no doubt in his mind that Piper felt something for him. It just wasn't what it should be. It would never be enough to hold. Besides the major differences between them, she wasn't going to overlook his little secret when she discovered who he really was.

"I can't deal with this," Piper announced, jerking him back to the here and now. She stopped in the middle of the room and stared at him. "I have to get out of here. I'm losing it," she added, desperation in her voice.

He'd known this was coming. "You know it's not safe to leave the room."

She threaded her fingers through her hair and closed her eyes. "God, I hate this." She opened her eyes then and stared directly into Ric's. "Do you suppose this is what Sorrel and Weaver went through?"

He knew what she was thinking. They'd been so careful, hiding out like this and then they'd died anyway. "I don't know," he told her in all honesty.

"I have to get out of here." She grabbed her purse from the coffee table and started for the door. "If I'm going to die, it's going to be on my own terms. I'm not going to be murdered in this room like some sort of caged animal."

"Whoa, *querida*." Ric quickly moved between her and the door. "You can't do that. It's not safe. We have to stay right here."

"Why?" she demanded. "SSU doesn't know I'm here, remember? If they did they'd have made a move on this place already. Wouldn't they? That was the whole purpose of this little field trip, wasn't it? I'm safe because no one knows I'm here."

"Maybe." Ric molded his palms around her cheeks. "But I can't let you take that risk."

She closed her eyes and nuzzled her cheek in his hand. "I'm so tired of this, Martinez."

He wanted to make it go away for her. "I know, *querida.*"

She opened those amazing eyes and stared up at him, pleading her case even before she spoke. "Please get me out of here just for a little while. You can take care of me. I know it's not your job. But I trust you. You have a gun. You can keep me safe just as well as Townsend—better probably."

"Don't ask me to do that," he murmured thickly. She was playing havoc with his reasoning.

She clutched at his shirt, leaning into him. "Please, just for a little while. Besides, SSU doesn't even know I'm here. What's to worry about?" she argued.

He knew this city well, he rationalized. According to the latest intel, SSU hadn't suspected Piper had left Atlanta. That was true enough. The station had even run a couple of her old research segments, which had never aired for one reason or another, to make it look as if she were still in Atlanta and working.

"All right," he acquiesced. "But I make the rules. You do exactly what I tell you, when I tell you."

She nodded, her expression brightening already.

"I know a place where we can get lost in the crowd."

"What kind of place?" she asked, anticipation flashing in her eyes.

"A place where we can—" he jerked her close and did a little two-step "—dance our cares away."

"Give me five minutes to change."

Ric watched her mad dash to her room. He fished the cell phone from his jacket pocket and punched in Raine's number. He didn't have any idea how he was going to explain this, but he'd figure something out. Raine wouldn't have any choice but to go along with him. Ric wasn't about to let Piper down. He would just have to face the consequences later.

THE SUBWAY DOORS closed right behind them as Piper and Martinez bounded onto the train. She felt invigorated. Alive. Sneaking out of the hotel, and then the two blocks to the Metro station had her blood racing through her veins. She looked at the man standing next to her and couldn't resist the urge to touch him. He kissed her, lingering as if they weren't in a public place, as if nothing else mattered.

The ride to Columbia Square took only a few short minutes. Martinez held her hand as he led the way to the escalator. Two minutes later they were emerging onto the busy sidewalk.

"Two blocks this way," he told her, putting his arm around her shoulders as she walked beside him.

"Where are we going?" He still hadn't told her the name of the place.

He shot her a wink and heat instantly spread through her. "Just a place I used to hang out whenever I was in town."

"With a girlfriend?" she inquired innocently.

He grinned. "I'll take the fifth on that one."

"Oh, you are wicked, Martinez," she scolded teasingly.

"How dare you bring me to a place where you brought another woman!"

"I've been called worse." He grabbed her hand. "Come on, we're almost there."

Piper had to practically run to keep up with his long legs. The place he led her to occupied the corner of a block. The Millennium was emblazoned over the double doors in huge, glittering silver letters. When he opened the door, music rushed out to envelop them. The thunderous rhythm seemed to propel them forward, into the flashing lights and palpable energy of the inner sanctum.

Martinez passed a bill to the woman who greeted them. The woman stamped their right hands, then smiled an extraspecial smile for Martinez. Piper seethed, instantly wanting to scratch the woman's eyes out. Of course, it wasn't the woman's fault he looked like a Latin god. The tight black jeans and black form-fitting shirt left absolutely nothing to the imagination. He was muscular and gorgeous. The cell phone clipped to his waist added to the whole effect. And Piper had discovered where he kept his handgun when he was dressed like this—strapped to his ankle. He'd grown up tough and knew how to handle himself in a tight spot. Usually she was very uncomfortable with guns, but Martinez somehow made it okay. Made her feel safe.

The dance floor was enormous and round, not an angle in the joint. Even the bar was a half-moon. Crowded with gyrating bodies, a balcony circled the entire club. Spiral staircases were strategically located for easy access. The main dance floor was packed. Piper wasn't sure how one more body would manage to squeeze onto it.

Martinez leaned down to her. "Want something to drink now or later?"

She shrugged. "Later," she shouted back.

He nodded and led her onto the dance floor. Surprisingly, the throng automatically made room for them. Anticipation pounded with every beat of Piper's heart. She hadn't been dancing in a while, but that wasn't what had the blood coursing through her veins. The mere thought of seeing Martinez move was driving her mad.

He was right at home with the loud music, the swaying crowd and the fast hip-hop beat. That awesome body fell right into perfect step with the music. Piper could hardly keep her rhythm for watching him undulate those amazing hips. The memory of how those hips felt pressed firmly against hers made her mouth go dry. She had never seen a man who could move quite like that—not in real life anyway. Maybe on MTV. Every part of him was involved. There wasn't a muscle or a limb he couldn't wiggle or sway in a kind of motion that sent little shivers across her skin.

And he never once took his eyes off her.

By the end of the second song, Piper was matching him step for step, move for move. When the music slowed, he stopped and looked deeply into her eyes. Time stood still as the love song trembled from the speakers. The mass of dancers around them faded into the background and he moved toward her, his eyes only for her.

Martinez pulled her into an intimate position, one muscular leg planted firmly between hers, his arms around her waist. Her arms went instinctively around his neck. She tilted her head up so that she could maintain that soul-deep eye contact. His breath on her lips made her yearn for the taste of his delicious mouth. One hand slid down to her thigh and beneath the hem of her very short dress. Piper gasped at the feel of his palm as it ran across her skin. He tugged her closer, forcing the heat at her core fully against his hard thigh.

He watched her intently as he rocked her over and over against him. The intimate motion had her burning. One hand held her firmly by the waist, the other moved magically over her body, touching, tantalizing. The flames of lust dancing in his eyes told her that he was every bit as affected as she was. He squeezed her thigh, almost sending her over the edge. The music stopped and Piper thought she would die when he eased out of the intimate contact.

He leaned close, tempting her further with that subtle yet exotic scent he wore. "We need to cool down. Let's get a drink," he offered.

The music started again, loud and fast, before she could answer, so she simply nodded. Holding her hand, Martinez led her to the bar.

He held up two fingers and said something to the bartender she didn't hear. The man behind the bar nodded and went to work. Piper eased onto a vacant stool and Martinez took the one next to her just as the two tall glasses were set before them.

She raised an eyebrow in skepticism as she studied the exotic-looking drink. Martinez leaned down and whispered in her ear, "Don't worry, *querida*. You'll like it."

Piper took a long sip from the straw and almost moaned with pleasure. The fruity drink was marvelous. Martinez smiled knowingly. She was so glad he brought her here. Drink in hand, she spun around on her stool so that she could survey the ocean of shimmying bodies. She hadn't realized until just this moment how much she had missed a nightlife.

Something in his peripheral vision drew Ric's gaze to the left, beyond the bar. He snapped to attention. The man watching them so intently turned away. But something about the man struck a chord of recognition, making Ric's heart beat faster with anticipation. He'd seen that face somewhere before. He concentrated hard on the man's movements. Could he have simply seen him here before? It hadn't been that long since he'd been to this club. Maybe the guy was a regular.

Then a blond woman walked up to him. Recognition hit Ric. The blond woman who'd entered the ladies' room after Piper that night at the charity art auction. Her gaze connected with Ric's. She knew she'd been made, but quickly turned away as if nothing had happened.

Ric stood, dropped a twenty on the bar and snagged Piper's hand. She turned to him, a look of protest on her face. Her eyes went wide as she read his. She plunked her half-empty glass down on the bar and jumped off the stool.

He weaved through the crowd without slowing down. He held tightly to Piper's hand, not allowing her to slow down, either. It was two blocks to the subway, six minutes on the train, then another two blocks on foot to the hotel unless they took a cab. If this guy or his partner followed them, they would have to lose him or her before getting on the subway. Once they were on that train there was nowhere to hide. Ric burst through the doors into the unseasonably brisk night air and strode in the opposition direction than the way they'd come before.

"Wait, what's going on?" Piper dug in her heels in an attempt to slow him down.

He glanced back at her, but didn't slow his pace. "I'm not sure yet," he lied, not wanting to upset her. He hurried around a strolling foursome, then glanced back once more. The guy was definitely following them. No sign of the blonde. Ric swore.

He pulled Piper close, maintaining his hurried stride, then leaned his head down as if to kiss her. "We've got an unfriendly tail."

Her startled gasp was audible. "What're we going to do?"

Ric smiled, a good deal more confidently than he felt. "We're going to give him the slip." He hoped like hell the blonde hadn't taken another route to try and head them off.

Piper narrowed her gaze in determination, refusing to show her fear. "Sounds like fun."

They started to run. Just around the next corner Ric led Piper through a gap in the twelve-foot-high chain-link fence surrounding a construction site. If the blonde came around the corner at the end of the block, she'd run into her partner instead of Ric and Piper. Dodging piles of discarded materials from the old building's renovations, they rushed into the covering of darkness within it.

Piper flattened against one of the few remaining inner walls and Ric shielded her body. He struggled to control his ragged breathing, hoping Piper would do the same. She did. He removed his .32 from his ankle holster, then listened for the telltale sounds that would indicate their tail had followed them onto the site. The sound of rustling metal and a hissed curse served as a warning. He didn't intend to give up so easily.

They needed to move to higher ground. Careful not to make a sound, Ric eased along the wall that served as a shield between their position and the enemy. Piper did the same. When they were close enough to the stairwell to reduce the risk of being noticed, he led her across the open floor and through the open stairwell door. Once inside, Ric listened again. Their tail was headed in the opposite direction for the moment. Another lucky break. But where was the blonde?

Slowly, holding his breath with every step, they headed up. On the third floor they slipped out of the stairwell and

into the maze of precariously standing walls. Ric didn't
take the time to consider that he should never have allowed
Piper to talk him into this, or to wonder where Raine was
at the moment. They had to find a good hiding place until
their apparently somewhat inept tail gave up, or Raine
showed up—whichever came first.

The grill hanging haphazardly over a return ventilation
duct snagged Ric's attention. It was about six feet off the
floor. Perfect. He pointed to it, then made a stirrup with
his hands. Piper nodded her understanding. She took off
her shoes, and holding them in one hand, allowed Ric to
boost her up. It took a couple seconds longer than he
would have preferred, but she finally slipped inside.

Ric paused to listen again. He could hear the guy on the
floor below them. Apparently the guy's night vision wasn't
as good as Ric's. He seemed to stumble over everything
in his path. Satisfied that he had time, Ric gripped the edge
of the ventilation opening and pulled himself up and inside
it. Once inside, he pulled the grill back up into place. He
had to hunker down, since sitting up straight was impossible in the close quarters.

Piper was right behind him, breathing hard in the consuming darkness. He turned to her and pressed his fingers
to her lips, then pulled her close. "I'm going to take off
my shoes and move in front of you to lead the way." He
felt her nod. He kissed her cheek, allowing her to feel his
smile against her skin.

Ric slipped off his loafers and left them next to Piper's
shoes. He tucked his .32 back into its holster. Piper quickly
lay down and flattened against the sheet metal to allow
him enough room to pass. If they were going to run into
any rats or spiders, he'd just as soon be the one to greet
them. Adopting a low crawl, Ric started forward, careful
not to allow his belt buckle to scrape the metal.

The duct ran about thirty feet before it did a ninety-degree angle to the right. Twenty feet later another ninety-degree angle, straight up this time, halted their forward movement. There was no place to go now, but up. Ric eased into a standing position then flattened against the wall of the duct and allowed Piper to stand up in front of him.

She tiptoed, putting her mouth next to his ear. "What now?"

"We wait," he whispered against the shell of her ear.

She nodded.

It was a good thing it was an unusually cool night. Otherwise the heat would build fast in their dark, cramped hiding place. He couldn't see Piper's eyes in this deep darkness, but he could hear her breathing, could smell her sweet scent. The pull between them was thick and pleasant. It felt good just being near her. The silence that settled around them and beyond their hiding place slowly abated his uneasiness.

Piper touched him, her fingers splayed on his chest, then smoothed over him in a slow, seductive manner. He swallowed to contain the groan that rose in his throat. She brushed her thumb over one nipple, then repeated the action. Even through the thin fabric of his shirt, the action drove him crazy. He pulled her hand away. She was playing with fire here and this definitely was not the time. Not to be denied, she covered that same nipple with her mouth and sucked it hard through the thin material. His hands fisted at his sides, Ric clenched his jaw to restrain any response.

She moved to his other nipple and gave it equal time. Then tiptoed and captured his mouth. She kissed him hard, frantically. He kissed her back, harder, deeper. His fingers trailed up her arms and to the straps of her dress, he pulled them off and down, exposing her breasts to his searching hands. She gasped in his mouth when he squeezed the two small globes. Her hands went straight to his waist, greedily wrenching his jeans open.

This was crazy. They couldn't do this. He groaned into her mouth as her hands pushed his clothes away. He felt her reach for him. Oh, yes...

His body pulsing with need, Ric pushed her dress up over her hips and then lifted her against his chest. There wasn't enough room for her to wrap her legs around his waist, so he lifted her higher until he felt the heat of her center against his straining tip. He held her against his chest with one hand and guided himself into position with the other, pushing her scant panties aside with impatient fingers. Slowly, one searing inch at a time, she slid down onto his throbbing arousal. Mind-blowing sensations. Hot and tight. He kissed her, a deliberately slow, languid kiss that spoke of his desperation...of his need for her.

She rocked her hips against him, urging him to move. Slowly, carefully so as not to make a sound, he pressed her against the metal wall behind her and moved. Slowly. Silently. In. Out. And in again. She was so hot. Adrenaline was pumping through his veins at the danger...the risk they were taking, but he couldn't stop. Not now. He went in again, so, so slowly. And then almost all the way out. Her fingers fisted in his shirt. His own tightened around her slim waist. In again. Man, she was unbelievably hot and tight.

The sound of metal scraping across concrete jerked Ric from the haze of lust. He stilled, listening over the sound of their frantic breathing. His erection pulsed inside her slick walls. Another indistinguishable sound reached him. He strained to listen, to determine whether the sound was closer. Piper moved. Ric almost groaned out loud. He tried to hold her still, but she kept on moving. Slow. Little. Moves. His fingers tightened around her waist. He needed to listen…but she just kept on moving.

She moaned softly and started to come around him. He could feel her body clenching, squeezing him to the point of pain. The explosion hit them both at the same time. Light and sensation behind his tightly closed lids and the roar of blood in his ears. He covered her mouth with his and took her urgent cry as she took his.

They sagged together, holding each other tight, both struggling to slow their ragged breath. Ric listened for any sound beyond their savage gasping. Nothing. He would wait a while longer to be sure the guy wasn't coming back. Then he would go down and check things out. When Ric was satisfied it was safe for Piper to come out, he would get her back to the hotel.

But for now, all he could do was hold her and pray he could walk away from her when this was over.

## Chapter Eleven

Ric didn't breathe easily until he and Piper had reached the hotel lobby. And then it hit him like a sledgehammer in the gut. Tonight's little outing had been a huge risk. He should never have allowed Piper to talk him into it...but he would have done most anything to make her happy.

He punched the call button for the elevator and ushered her inside the moment the doors opened. If Townsend had knocked on their door for anything, he was going to be furious for being left out of the loop like this. And Raine was probably madder than hell that Ric had lost him. Just before the elevator doors closed, an arm poked inside, sending the doors gliding apart again.

Tension raced up Ric's spine. He had the weapon out of its holster and held carefully out of sight before the doors opened fully. He braced himself squarely in front of Piper. A tall, sandy-haired man, his mouth set in a grim line, stepped onto the elevator and leveled a hard, unyielding gaze on Ric.

Jack Raine.

*Damn.*

His eyes never deviating from Ric, Raine stabbed the button for their floor and leaned against the wall in a relaxed stance as the car jerked into motion.

From the clenched jaw to the lethal stare it was quite clear that Raine was pissed. Ric was too emotionally drained to work up any real anxiety over what the man thought of the fool thing Ric had done. He hadn't been thinking. He'd been feeling, which was a dangerous thing in this business. And he knew it. He tucked the weapon into his waistband at the small of his back and attempted to relax.

"Martinez," Piper murmured quietly.

He turned to her, seeing the question in her eyes. "Don't worry, *querida*. He's on our side." He vaguely wondered if she would remember Raine as their limo driver that first night.

She nodded, then peeked around Ric to get a better look at Raine. Ric was pretty sure the man had a few choice words to say to him. The bad part was, Ric didn't blame him. He'd screwed up big-time. Taken an unnecessary risk with the principal he was supposed to protect.

The elevator stopped on the top floor and Raine exited first. Ric and Piper followed. When they reached the door to their suite, Raine turned to Ric.

"The room's clear, so Miss Ryan can go on in, but *we* need to talk, Martinez."

It wasn't a request.

"All right."

Piper looked uncertain, but she obeyed when Ric angled his head toward the door to their suite. Once she was inside, he turned back to Raine. "Where are Townsend and Green?"

Raine nodded to the door across the hall. "You're in it deep, buddy," he said flatly. "In fact, I can truthfully say that I definitely wouldn't want to be in your shoes."

Ric met his lead-filled glare evenly. "You called Lucas."

Raine scoffed. "You're damned right I did. You call me and inform me that you and Miss Ryan are taking a little outing when you know she's been confined to quarters. Then you disappear from the club with not one but two hostiles hot on your heels."

"I lost them," Ric said, grinding out the words.

"I can see that. Otherwise you wouldn't be here." Raine's gaze changed a little; maybe just the tiniest bit of respect flickered there. "You know how to handle yourself, Martinez. That's not the problem."

Anger erupted inside Ric. "You're damned right I do. I've been the one who's gotten her out of harm's way every time. So don't give me any grief, Raine."

"Oh, you misunderstand, *compadre.*" Raine chuckled softly. "I don't have a problem with your job performance. Hell, I'd team up with you anytime." He leaned forward, putting himself nose-to-nose with Martinez. "But I ain't sleeping with Lucas's one and only niece. He's going to be supremely pissed, my friend. You have my sincerest sympathy. I'll be sure and come to your funeral."

A red mist swam before Ric's eyes. "What's between Piper and me is none of your business, man," he said tightly.

Raine shook his head. "You're right, it's not. But when Lucas gets through with you, you'll wish it wasn't yours, either." Raine hitched a thumb toward the door. "By the way, he's waiting for you."

Ric's anger dissolved instantly. Lucas Camp was here. Inside. No doubt waiting to take Ric's head off.

"Oh, yeah," Raine said, obviously noting the sudden pallor that slid over Ric's face. "For future reference, Martinez, when Lucas Camp gives an order, follow it. Don't deviate, don't even hesitate." Raine leaned forward again and sniffed. "And I think the first thing I'd do is wash off the scent of his niece. He's killed for a lot less."

Ric ignored that last remark. "The blonde from the art auction was with the guy."

Raine nodded. "Yeah, tailing her is how I lost the two of you."

"Did you nail her?"

"Of course." Raine glanced at his watch. "But she didn't want to talk."

Ric frowned. "You killed her?"

Raine shook his head slowly from side to side. "Didn't have to. When she realized I had her, she ate a bullet from her own weapon."

Ric swore.

Raine inclined his head toward the suite door. "Lucas is waiting." He flashed Ric one last look of sympathy then walked away.

Ric was a dead man.

If Lucas Camp didn't kill him, Victoria Colby would.

"UNCLE LUCAS, YOU DO NOT rule my life," Piper insisted impatiently. The nerve of the man showing up here in the middle of the night to chastise her for going out. She wasn't a teenager anymore. She was twenty-seven years old. She was way past being put on curfew.

His steady stare told her that she was wasting her time trying to get that concept through his thick skull. "You're in protective custody, young lady. You don't give the federal agents assigned to guard you the slip when you're in protective custody," he said calmly.

But Piper knew he wasn't calm. In fact, she couldn't ever recall seeing him this angry. His face was beet red and a vein throbbed in his forehead. She swallowed with difficulty, then sagged with defeat, dropping into the closest chair. She sure didn't want to be the cause of her uncle having an aneurysm or stroke.

"Now they know for sure that you're here," he added too evenly. "The whole point of bringing you here was to keep them from finding you."

Piper shook her head. "They had to know I was here. They had to be watching," she suggested meekly, not wanting to antagonize him further.

"Maybe so," he said tightly. "But you didn't have to give them such an open target."

"All right, I know I shouldn't have gone out. I guess it was a mistake," she admitted wearily. "But you know how I hate this town." She closed her eyes and pushed away the unbidden and painful images that tried to form in her head. "It brings back too many bad memories for me."

Lucas took the three steps necessary to stand directly in front of her. He lowered himself onto the table facing her. "I know you don't like being here, Piper, but it was the only way I could ensure your safety and at the same time facilitate this interview you seem so determined to do, come hell or high water." He patted her hand. "You know I've always tried to take care of you, to make up for your father's absence."

Piper rubbed her hands over her face. She didn't want to talk about this again. Rehashing the past would change nothing about how she felt. "I know, Uncle Lucas, and I'm grateful for all you've done." She reached out and cupped his very dear, and very worried, face. "I love you. But I'm not a child anymore." She dropped her hands to her lap and sighed tiredly. She really was extremely tired. A secret smile warmed her heart when she considered just how Martinez had worn her out. "I know what I did tonight wasn't so bright, and I'm sorry if I made you worry, but I had Martinez with me.''

The expression on her uncle's face changed instantly. Fury darkened his gray eyes. "So I've heard."

Piper frowned, uncertain what all that uncharacteristic animosity was about. "Anyway, I know he's just a cameraman, but he saved my life. Jumped between a bullet and me," she added emphatically just in case Lucas hadn't heard, which was highly unlikely. "I knew I'd be safe with him. He carries a gun and knows how to handle himself. I just couldn't stand it, cooped up here another minute." She took her uncle's hands in hers. "I hope you'll forgive me."

"You know I don't blame you, Piper." He studied her for a moment, before he continued, his voice tight. "Raine says that you and Martinez are…involved."

Piper blushed to the roots of her hair. She and Lucas had never talked about sex. For that matter, neither had she and her mother.

"Is that true?" her uncle prodded.

She adopted an indignant expression. "I can't believe you would ask me a question as private as that. I'm an adult. My sex life, and with whom I choose to conduct it, are most certainly none of your business."

Lucas looked away. "I'm going to kill him."

Appalled at her uncle's words, Piper's mouth dropped open, but the outrage she intended to display died a sure and swift death when she saw the lethal look in his eyes. He was serious. Martinez chose that precise moment to walk into the room. Piper could tell by the look on his face that Raine had already warned him that her uncle was not happy. She frowned. How was it that Ric knew all about Raine and she didn't?

Ric felt the muscle in his jaw begin to tic the moment

Lucas stood and faced him. Ric clenched it in an effort to stop the rhythmic jerk, but his attempt failed. Ignoring the fierce glare directed at him, he shifted his gaze to Piper, smiled and winked. She looked somewhat rumpled but so beautiful that his heart instantly melted. He didn't care what Camp had to say to him; what he'd shared with Piper was worth any price.

"It's time we told Piper the truth about who you really are," Lucas said bluntly.

Ric winced inwardly at the look of confusion that captured Piper's expression. *Any price,* he amended, *but this one.* "Can we talk privately first?"

Lucas shook his head. "I should have told her from the beginning and spared her the hurt she's going to suffer now because of your lack of professionalism."

"But you don't understand—" Ric argued, his blood going from boiling to freezing instantly.

"I understand perfectly," Lucas returned angrily. "You allowed my niece to become intimately involved with you while you were on duty."

"On duty?" Piper was standing now, looking from her uncle to Ric for an explanation.

"This is not what you think," Ric said quickly, in an effort to head off the hurt he knew would follow Lucas's bombshell. But there was no way to explain away the facts.

"This isn't entirely his fault," Lucas said tautly. "It was my idea for him to work undercover as your cameraman. Hell, I even set it up for him to stay in your neighbor's apartment, so he'd be close to you. But I never expected him to let it get personal." Lucas glared at Ric then. "He was supposed to protect you—nothing else."

Ric watched the color drain from Piper's face and his heart sank all the way to the floor. He'd wanted to tell her himself, to try and make her understand somehow. "I wanted you to hear it from me first," he managed to get past the lump at the back of his throat, but he barely recognized his own voice. The look of devastation on Piper's face trampled his heart already lying at his feet. No matter what was said, he couldn't take back the hurt he saw in her eyes at that moment. And he knew that hurt would grow. He could imagine no reason she would ever forgive him. He should have told her already. He'd had the perfect opportunity, but he'd been selfish. He didn't want to give up whatever time they had together. And now they were both going to pay for his selfishness.

Piper felt weak, as if she might faint. This couldn't be right. She shook her head in denial of her uncle's charges. But Martinez's words confirmed her worst fears. *I wanted you to hear it from me first.* He was working in one capacity or another for her uncle. He wasn't a cameraman. He wasn't the man she thought she knew at all. He had lied. He was a total stranger. And she'd trusted him, made love with him....

"Let me explain," Martinez said, starting toward her. "I didn't mean for things to happen this way."

Fury crashed down around her. She didn't want to hear his excuses or his explanations. She held up her hand to halt his coming nearer. "Don't." She shuddered inwardly at the look of hurt on his handsome face. But she refused to care if she hurt him or not. She was dying inside and it was his fault. He'd lied to her.

"I thought I was doing the right thing," Lucas said quietly. "I hired Martinez as your personal protector. I wanted someone right by your side every minute of every day to keep you safe. Someone outside all the political crap. It was my decision to keep his identity a secret. Not his."

She cut her uncle a scathing gaze. Was he trying to get

her to go easy on his hired help now? "Is that supposed to make me feel better?"

Lucas shook his head. "No, I guess not. But it is the truth."

She looked from her uncle to Martinez. "Oh, this is a fine time to decide to tell me the truth." She braced her hands on her hips. "Both of you lied to me." She glared at Martinez with all the disgust she could muster. "You could have told me while you were making love to me." Her voice trembled. Dammit, she didn't want to cry. "Or were you having too much fun to do the right thing?"

How could he look so sincerely remorseful?

He opened his mouth to speak, but couldn't seem to form the words for a few seconds. "I'll leave if that's what you want." He dragged his gaze from her to Lucas. "But I would prefer to stay on and finish the job I was hired to do."

Hurt and anger bubbled over inside Piper. "I want you to leave," she said shakily, very near tears. How could he even think of staying now?

Martinez only looked at her, his expression so distressed she could hardly bear to look at him. And she hated herself for caring.

"He stays," Lucas announced in a commanding tone that left no room for protest.

Piper protested anyway. "No way. I don't want to be near him." She hugged herself and tried to push away the images of Martinez making slow, sweet love to her.

"I'll keep my distance," Martinez offered quietly. "But, please, don't shut me out. You know I won't allow anything to happen to you. I'll do whatever it takes to keep you safe. You know that."

Piper rubbed her eyes with the heels of her hands. He was right about protecting her. He'd proven that to her more than once. Apparently encouraged by her silence, he turned to Lucas for confirmation, and something clicked in Piper's memory.

"It was you," she blurted, her gaze landing on a startled Martinez. The way he turned. She had noticed that before, but eventually dismissed it when nothing came to mind. "You were the one who took down the guy who tried to shoot me that day in the traffic jam." She blinked in disbelief. How could she have been this close to him and not known him at all? "It was you." She shook her head, still dumbfounded that she could have been so blind.

She'd lost it. There could be no other explanation. She'd never let anyone blindside her like this. Why didn't she question anything? Why didn't she see the odd coincidences? His showing up at the station, then right next door to her apartment. The tux. Who keeps a tux on hand? She'd swallowed that story about the rough neighborhood in which he'd grown up—hook, line and sinker. He was a professionally trained bodyguard, not some guy who'd turned his life around like he'd led her to believe.

"Martinez is good at what he does," Lucas said finally. "We need him on our team. We should put this...other issue aside for the moment. The only important thing right now is keeping you safe."

Piper sank back into her chair, her legs no longer able to hold her. If everything she knew about him was a lie...then the truth of the matter was that Martinez didn't really care about her. He'd only been doing his job. He was one of them. One of those guys who just do the job. Like Lucas. Like her father. Her heart fractured, making her want to cry out with the pain of it. She'd done the one thing she never wanted to do—she'd fallen in love with a man just like her father. One who would do anything to accomplish his mission. Even take her to bed...or out dancing even when instinct warned him against it.

"Are you listening to me, Piper?" Lucas sat down on the table in front of her again. "We have to do whatever it takes to make sure these maniacs don't get to you. That's all that matters right now."

She met his worried gaze and knew he was right. No matter what else Martinez was, he was very good at his job. He'd kept her from harm. And since she definitely didn't want to die, what else could she say?

"All right," she told her uncle. She turned to Martinez. "But don't even talk to me unless it's necessary for safety's sake." She looked away then. Despite the way he'd lied to her, she couldn't bear to see the pain in those dark eyes.

It was over.

She'd been a fool.

But it wouldn't happen again.

She needed to be alone. To wash the scent of Martinez from her body and to grieve for what would never be.

RIC SAT IN THE DARKNESS for hours after Piper had gone to bed. He should have told her the first time they made love. If he'd told her then... But he hadn't. He scrubbed a hand over his face and cursed himself for playing the "what if" game yet again. It was too late for that now. Whatever he'd thought she felt for him, his betrayal had squashed it.

She wouldn't forgive him for that sin.

Not that there'd been any real hope for them anyway. He pretty much fit the description of what she didn't want in a man. She would find his dedication to his job and his willingness to die for a client too risky. And he supposed he couldn't blame her. She had grown up with that kind of loss. Why would she knowingly seek it out in her adult relationships?

Relationship? Yeah, right. They hadn't had a relationship. They'd had an affair. And he was the bad guy. Ric blew out a heavy breath and pushed to his feet. He had to have some sleep. Though he didn't require a lot, he couldn't function without at least some. He paused when he passed Piper's door. He wanted so badly to turn that knob and look in on her, but she was off-limits to him now.

He headed for the shower, stripping off his clothes as he went. He didn't want to think anymore. It hurt too much. But Lucas's parting remarks kept replaying in his head. The man could definitely come up with some interesting torture techniques. He'd named off more than a few he fully intended to ensure Ric participated in if anything happened to his niece.

Ric closed his eyes and stepped beneath the hot spray of water. The feel of it sluicing over his skin quickly began to relax his tired muscles. He leaned his forehead against the cool tile wall and let the hot water do its magic as it flowed over and down his back. Before he could stop it, vivid images of his and Piper's lovemaking tumbled one over the other inside his head. He clenched his fists and struggled to suppress the emotions rising inside him like a tidal wave.

He wanted to hold her and make her believe that he hadn't meant to hurt her. He wanted to promise her the world if only she would trust him again.

But she wouldn't.

He'd had his chance and he'd blown it.

And now it was over.

## Chapter Twelve

Piper surveyed her reflection one last time. This was the moment she had waited for. Four long years of hard work and she finally stood on the precipice of that first giant leap into national recognition. After today she would no longer be known as simply Atlanta's sweetheart. In just two hours she would debut on national television in one of the most important interviews of the decade.

This was what she'd wanted more than anything else. The sole reason she'd given up a private life of any kind this past year so that she could focus completely on her career. The ultimate goal of everything she said and did, of every move she made was to reach this pinnacle.

Piper closed her eyes. Then why did it feel so hollow? Where was the anticipation, the pulse-pounding thrill of knowing her dream was about to come true?

God, she had made a mess of things the past few days. Piper forced her attention back to the mirror and took inventory of the pathetic person staring back at her. How could one week have changed her so much? She shook her head in confusion and defeat. It wasn't the passage of seven days' time that had done this to her. It was Martinez. He'd strutted into her life with that quick smile and devilish charm and stolen something she'd never given anyone before.

Her heart.

A thousand images bombarded her at the same time. Martinez wearing nothing but that towel when she'd interrupted his shower. Handsome as sin in a tux, charming every female who laid eyes on him. Dropping his camera and coming between her and those gang members. The blood on her hand that had come from him when he'd stepped between her and an assassin's bullet. The way he'd made love to her that first time. The feel of him inside her when yet another would-be killer searched for them just outside their hiding place. The fear of discovery, yet the irresistible, savage need to connect physically…to touch each other as intimately as possible.

How could she have fallen in love with a man so totally opposite to her? One she refused to call by his first name for fear of admitting that they were more than co-workers. For fear of acknowledging on a conscious level that he meant more to her than he should.

Piper smoothed a hand over her new, red power suit. A local boutique owner, who was also a friend of her uncle's, had dropped by yesterday with more than a dozen chic garments for her to choose from. When she hadn't liked any of those, another dozen had been sent for, all a precise fit. The hip-hugger silk slacks and matching double-breasted straight-line jacket were both figure flattering and a good contrast to her complexion and hair color. She stepped back and studied the end result yet again. Her uncle's friend had even provided the matching shoes and a pair of exquisite gold hoop earrings.

Everything was just perfect.

Except for her. Of course, the television audience wouldn't be able to see the sad emptiness she felt. They wouldn't be able to feel the hurt that speared through her each time she looked at Martinez or even thought about him. The pain in those dark eyes and the lack of a smile on that handsome face tore at her already-battered heart. Made her want to cry for the wrong they'd both suffered. He'd been doing his job, the job her uncle had hired him to do, and she'd simply been a fool.

And now they were both paying for the risk they'd taken by crossing that line. They had nothing in common; their future expectations were polar opposites. No power on earth could change that. She'd seen this same scenario too many times. People who meshed on every level had a hard enough time keeping a relationship going these days; how could she expect one to stick where the odds were against them from the outset?

Piper sighed, a weary, terribly unsteady sound. Twenty-four hours of walking on eggshells around each other had her nerves frayed. Twenty-four endless hours of avoiding eye contact, of ignoring the pull of his presence. She summoned her crippled resolve and squared her shoulders. It wouldn't hurt this badly forever. Time was all she needed.

Eventually Ric Martinez would be nothing but a bitter-sweet memory. Piper grabbed her purse and ignored the instant denial that surged inside her. She would return to Atlanta when this was over and never look back. It was the only way.

The best thing for both of them.

She opened her door and stepped into the small hall that led into the suite's large parlor. She would get over this hopeless feeling. Sex, she decided. It was mainly about sex anyway. Nothing else. You couldn't fall that deeply in love with anyone in just a few days. Especially someone you really didn't even know. *Could you?*

"I'll get back to you as soon as this is over," Martinez

said into his cell phone, his back turned to her as she entered the room. He closed the phone and deposited it into the pocket of his jacket.

Piper braced herself against the effect the sound of his voice always had on her. "I'm ready," she announced in what she hoped was a cool, professional tone. "Was that Townsend?"

Martinez turned toward her, his gaze locking instantly with hers. She was totally unprepared for the rush of feelings…for the breath-stealing, heart-stopping emotions that gathered in her chest.

"No, that was Alex Preston from the Colby Agency," he explained.

The Colby Agency was where Martinez worked. She didn't want to hear about that; it hurt too much. She summoned her waning resolve. "Can we leave now?"

"The car's ready." Those too-serious dark eyes held hers steadily as if he wanted desperately to relate something that he couldn't bring himself to say. Like hers, his tone sounded just a little too cool and even. There was no mistaking the un-Martinez-like quality of it.

Piper looked away first. "Good." Seeing no point in continuing the awkward conversation, she started toward the door. "I don't want to be late."

Strong fingers wrapped around her upper arm and stopped her. Piper shivered at the feel of his gentle, yet commanding touch. He held her like that for one long beat, but didn't offer to pull her around to face him.

"I don't want it to end this way, *querida*," he murmured in that silky, accented voice that was all Martinez.

She blinked back the hot sting of tears. "Don't," she said tightly. "This is the only way it can end."

He moved in close behind her, his body telling hers what she refused to allow him to say out loud. Piper squeezed her eyes shut and forced the image of Martinez in that elegant black suit he was wearing from her mind. She didn't want to think about him and she definitely didn't want to feel what he was making her feel.

"You can pretend that you don't feel this...." His free hand slid over her hip and to her waist, pressing her closer against him. "But I can't."

Need ached through her, nearly overwhelming in its intensity. She drew in a deep, bolstering breath and fought to steel herself against his touch. "You lied to me... betrayed my trust." She pulled loose from his hold, difficult as that proved. "Don't expect me to pretend to be grateful you did it to protect me." She reached for the door in front of her, knowing if she didn't make her exit soon, she wouldn't be able to hold it together. "Sex wasn't part of the deal you made with my uncle." Anger kindled inside her; she trembled with the effort to keep it inside. "I certainly hope your fee is adequate to cover the extra effort."

Martinez reached past her and flattened his hand against the door when she would have opened it. "Don't sweat it, *querida*," he said harshly, his tone deadly and his lips only inches from her cheek. "I wouldn't dream of charging you extra. You were worth the trouble."

Piper forced a calm she didn't feel and deliberately opened the door when he at last moved. Fury whipped through her, testing the limits of her self-control and making her want to turn around and slap his smug face. But she wouldn't give him the satisfaction of a reaction. His words only helped her to see the added foolishness of her lingering feelings for him.

She'd had him pegged right from the beginning. He was nothing but a smart-mouth charmer, not unlike a gigolo. He was bought and paid for...had a job to do. He didn't care about her. The opportunity to play hero was likely just an ego trip for him. He was most likely an adrenaline junkie at heart, like every other guy she knew in law enforcement or private investigations.

A little voice that she wanted desperately to ignore nagged at her. The horrible thoughts she was having about Martinez weren't entirely true, she admitted as she stepped onto the elevator Townsend had waiting for them. Martinez was damn good at his job. Like her, his job came first; anything else was just a perk. No matter what else he was, he was an excellent bodyguard. And he did care, at least on some level.

Once on the elevator, she and Martinez claimed opposite corners as Townsend stepped aboard and pressed the button that would take them to the lobby.

"We'll be leaving by the service entrance," Townsend said to Piper. "Lucas has a car waiting at the back."

"Fine," she acknowledged.

Townsend turned to Martinez then. "Raine is riding shotgun."

"Excellent."

Piper cursed herself when the sound of that one word coming from Martinez curled around her and warmed her from the inside out. One way or another she was going to get the man out of her system. If it took her the rest of her life.

She swallowed back the lump that rose in her throat when she considered that if the SSU had its way, her life would end very, very soon. Like today. Piper glanced at Martinez's grim profile. He'd promised to keep her safe. She prayed his determination to do the job he'd been hired to do wouldn't cost him his own life.

That was the one thing Piper was certain she couldn't live with.

RIC STOOD OUTSIDE Piper's dressing room and watched as the makeup lady scrutinized Piper's lovely face. The woman was complaining that she'd be out of work if everyone required as little in the way of on-screen preparation as Piper did.

"Wipe that besotted look off your face, Martinez."

Ric jerked to attention at the sound of Lucas's voice. His glare toxic, Lucas paused on the opposite side of the open doorway. Ric cleared his thoughts of the woman who had his gut twisted into knots. He leveled an annoyed look at the older man. He didn't need Lucas looking over his shoulder on the job.

"I assume you have something to say that relates to the mission," Ric suggested with clear irritation.

"Wear this." Lucas handed him a tiny earpiece. "You'll be able to hear whatever communications take place between me and my men. My whole team's here. I decided the Feds needed a little backup. No one else will be on this frequency." He pressed a miniscule black disc beneath the edge of Ric's lapel. "With this," Lucas explained, "we'll be able to hear you if you have anything of interest to say." He glared at Ric. "But don't open your mouth unless it's necessary. We want to keep the line clear for emergency transmissions only."

Ric glanced at Piper, then turned his attention back to Lucas. "Do we have any new intel?"

The grim line of the older man's mouth and the hard look in his eyes spoke volumes. "Whatever's going to happen, it's going to be today. And, unfortunately, it looks like it's going to be real time. No warning." Lucas looked away. "According to the man inside the SSU, the finale, whatever the hell it is, is already in motion." Lucas swore hotly. "We've got the whole damned place locked down tighter than a drum. We've scoured every square inch of this studio." He shook his head. "The place is clean. There has to be someone on the inside here."

A sense of helplessness flooded Ric. "There's nothing else we can do but wait for them to move." It wasn't a question, and Lucas knew it.

"Nothing. Everyone on the premises has been cleared to be here. Whoever the mole is, he or she is in deep."

A production assistant paused in the corridor. "Excuse me," he said, then leaned between Lucas and Ric and through the open door. "We need you on the set, Miss Ryan."

Lucas's solemn gaze settled once more onto Ric's. "My men and I will be watching every move anyone on the premises makes. No matter what happens, don't take your eyes off her, Martinez. Not even for a second. I don't want your attention on anything else."

Piper hesitated long enough as she passed between them for her uncle to kiss her cheek and offer a heartfelt good luck. She didn't look at Ric. She just walked away. He followed.

No matter how bad it hurt to have her ignore him like this, it wasn't important. The only thing that mattered was protecting her from whatever the SSU *bastardos* had planned. Today, Lucas had said. Whatever they had planned was going to happen today.

PIPER WALKED ACROSS the set, her heart pounding so hard she could barely hear herself think. She plastered a professional smile into place and forced her respiration to slow. She had to forget Martinez. She had to forget the SSU and all those dead reporters with whom she'd taken that fateful journey just five weeks ago.

Right now, she had to be Piper Ryan, the cool, objective journalist. A pivotal part of her career depended upon what happened in the next minutes. She and the senator would be introduced during the last five minutes of the morning broadcast. Once the show ended, the interview would begin after a commercial break. She had a full half hour.

Piper held the three-by-five-inch index cards containing the agreed-upon questions in her left hand. Yesterday she and the senator had run through the interview by telephone. Piper had placed the least important questions at the back of the stack in case the senator got a little long-winded on live television. She'd taken considerable time last night and studied the questions, her research and the senator's bio. She was ready.

"Miss Ryan." The senator extended his hand and smiled that charismatic smile that had gotten him elected four times already.

Piper accepted his hand and shook it firmly. "Senator, looks like we're a go. I hope you know how much this opportunity means to me."

"This is an excellent opportunity for both of us," he agreed. "Getting the full half hour this morning was the President's doing. I'm sure neither of us will let him down."

No pressure there, Piper mused at the same time she felt her pulse go into double time.

The senator released her hand and turned to the younger man standing at his side. "I wish I could take the credit for working out the necessary details to make this day happen, but I can't. Miss Ryan, this is Jacob Watts, my personal assistant. He's the man responsible for setting this whole thing up with the network."

Piper shook the other man's hand. "Thank you, Mr. Watts. I'm forever in your debt."

Jacob Watts flashed a smile as equally charming as that of his mentor. "You were the only logical choice, Miss

Ryan. We want you to make history with us today. This is your moment. Enjoy it.''

His sincerity seemed almost too genuine. Piper resisted the urge to frown. Before she could respond to, or consider, his comment any further, a commanding male voice interrupted their conversation.

"Miss Ryan, Senator, we'll need you to take your seats now so that we can adjust the lighting and get a level on your mikes,'' the set director announced.

Watts withdrew what looked like a slim pocket watch and glanced at it. "I guess that's my cue to go.''

Allowing him one last smile, Piper turned toward the homey arrangement that served as their set, with its overstuffed chairs, intricately carved oak table and Tiffany lamp. She started in that direction at the same moment Jacob Watts headed stage right. Their paths collided. She tripped over his long leg, but he caught her. One steadying hand connected with her waist, flattening against her stomach, the other closed around her arm. The palm covering her belly button caught the brunt of her weight, pressing firmly to upright her. A twinge of pain shot through her from the nearly forgotten incision. She winced before she could repress the gesture.

"I'm so sorry, Miss Ryan,'' he offered contritely when he'd steadied her fully. "I guess this is why I don't spend any time in front of the camera.'' He laughed at his own ungainly blunder, then looked at his pocket watch again as if he feared he'd damaged it somehow.

"It's all right. I'm fine,'' she assured him. She smoothed a hand over her suit and offered him a patient smile. No wonder she'd experienced that twinge of pain. The guy still had his watch in his hand.

His cheeks a bit flushed, Jacob Watts backed up a couple of steps. "I'll just get out of the way before I cause any more damage.'' He hurried away, suddenly quite adept at dodging the numerous obstacles in his path.

Maybe she made him nervous. Though Piper couldn't fathom why, she didn't have time to dwell on that mystery at the moment. Thankfully she hadn't dropped her cards and gotten them out of order, and she quickly took her seat next to the senator. In only a few short minutes the whole country was going to be looking at her. Her heart thundered back into a deafening staccato.

While the set director and floor manager ensured that all was as it should be, Piper took long, slow deep breaths to calm herself and to prepare for the moment when the cameras went hot. She focused inward to the years of discipline and hard work that had made her the excellent interviewer she was. An award-winning interviewer, she reminded that little worrisome voice that chipped away at her self-confidence.

The next few minutes were going to be the most important of her life. And she intended to give a stellar performance.

RIC WATCHED from stage left. It had taken him a full two minutes to calm after that clumsy Watts guy had all but bowled Piper over. The jerk was standing on the opposite side of the stage now, mopping his sweating brow with a handkerchief. It was a miracle the man survived in the world of politics if he was half as nervous and graceless as he appeared this morning. But then, cutting the man some slack, tension was running high at the moment.

Especially Ric's. That instinct he'd honed as a kid in one of Chicago's toughest neighborhoods was nagging relentlessly at him. Something was going down and there wasn't a damned thing he could do to stop it. He had never, ever felt this helpless. He wanted more than anything to protect Piper, but every instinct warned him that whatever was going on was somehow out of his hands.

And he didn't like it at all. There had to be a way to keep the situation under control. Townsend and Green, a dozen members of the senator's own recently beefed-up security team and four of Lucas's own specialists were on-site. They had the place thoroughly covered.

Ric listened carefully as Lucas's team called the all-clear on one area after the other. There were no hostiles in the vicinity. Not one.

But there had to be. SSU didn't make idle threats.

If the intel Lucas had was up-to-date, and Ric was certain it was as current as could be obtained, then something was going to go down today. Considering Ric's own instincts were humming with dread, he felt sure it was only a matter of time until trouble made itself known.

Ric frowned when his gaze shifted to the other side of the stage. Watts was no longer loitering there. Maybe the guy had had to walk off some of the tension.

"Logan here. We've got one on the move." A male voice, one of Lucas's team members, sounded in Ric's earpiece. "He's out the side door."

"I've got him in my sights," a decidedly female voice said next. "It's that guy Watts."

"Stand down, Callahan," Lucas ordered. "Don't fire unless necessary."

"He's heading east. I'm right behind him." Logan again, breathless from running.

"I can cut him off," another male voice added.

"Hold your position, Ferrelli," Lucas instructed. "He may be a decoy."

Thick silence lurked in the tense moments that followed. Ric's pulse rate tripled as he strained to hear any sound. What the hell could Watts be up to? Ric's gaze never left

Piper. She looked so beautiful that it made his chest ache. He had to focus hard on keeping his mind on business while keeping his eyes on her.

If he could just find the right words to say to make her trust him again. Would it matter? he wondered. Would she overlook his betrayal, set aside what he did for a living and let this thing between them go where it would?

No way. She'd made her standing clear. She had no intention of falling in love in the first place. And definitely not with a guy like him. His past aside, Ric represented the precise kind of man she did not want to be involved with. She didn't want a hero or a guy who put his career above all else. She would risk her life for the story, but she didn't want the man in her life to do the same. He thought about the story she'd told him about her father and he tried to understand her feelings on the issue.

But he wanted her. And he wanted her to want him. Nothing he could call to mind was reason enough to keep him from wanting her or to stay his desire for her to return the feeling.

"I've got him." It was Logan again, his voice strained as if he was struggling. The choice words that echoed next, followed by a couple of heavy thuds confirmed Ric's estimation.

"Hold him. Raine and I are on our way to your location," Lucas cut in.

Ric breathed a little easier now that the guy had been caught. He wondered briefly how the hell Jacob Watts had slipped under the security net and gotten that close to the senator. Or maybe he'd already been in place and simply got an offer he couldn't refuse. Fury twisted inside Ric at that thought. What kind of lowlife put a price on life? He wanted his turn at using Watts for a punching bag. And it had to be Watts. Why else would he run at this pivotal moment?

"Lucas, we have a situation red," Logan said, his voice eerily calm. "The guy's carrying a palm-size, very high-tech device that could be some kind of activator, considering it has a timer that's counting down as we speak."

Lucas swore.

Ric tensed.

"Should we evacuate the studio?" Ferrelli suggested.

"Hold on, sir, we have incoming intel from a land line. It's an FBI field supervisor." Another new voice. Male, and apparently, the communications coordinator.

"Nobody moves," Lucas ordered. He was breathing hard. "If we've got intel coming in on a land line we've got intel that can't wait. Hold on to that son of a bitch, Logan, I'm almost there."

Ric released the breath he'd been holding. The FBI agent undercover at the SSU headquarters must have something hot. Maybe he'd obtained the lowdown on what SSU was up to this morning.

The interview had begun. Ric directed his full attention back on Piper. Logan apparently had Watts under control. Lucas was in charge of the situation. If the studio needed to be evacuated, he would give the order. Ric's job was to keep Piper safe. He smiled as he watched her in action. She was smooth. The senator was charmed. The viewing audience would be, as well. Ric felt something shift in his chest. Piper was on her way up. There would be no stopping her.

She definitely wouldn't have time for a guy like him.

As much as it hurt, he was happy for her. She wanted this so much. He wanted her to have it.

"Martinez."

It was Lucas. He sounded strange. "I'm here, man."

"I want you to get Piper out of that studio any way you have to. A car will be waiting out front. The engine will be running. I'll feed you instructions on where to go. *Do it now.*"

Ric frowned. "Piper isn't going to like it. The interview—"

"Screw the interview," Lucas snapped. "That bomb is going to go off in twenty minutes. There's no time to waste. We're notifying the bomb squad right now. So move!"

Ric was already walking toward Piper before Lucas finished his last statement. "What about the rest of the people?" Surely Lucas didn't intend to leave everyone else in the building.

"Hurry, Martinez. I'm too far away to do it myself. You have to hurry. There's no time for me to get back there." Urgency tightened the voice echoing in Martinez's earpiece. "I don't know how the bastards did it, but the explosive is implanted subcutaneously in Piper's abdomen. You have to get her to a hospital. *Now.*"

Ric stalled halfway to his destination. "What did you say?"

"You have nineteen minutes, Martinez. In nineteen minutes Piper and anyone close to her is going to die."

# Chapter Thirteen

"How do you see the role of this new organization as different from the other agencies who have worked to stop terrorism, Senator?"

Piper listened attentively as the senator offered his practiced answer to her question. They were only a few minutes into the interview and things were off to a great start. She was nervous, her palms a little damper than usual, but otherwise she was in control. She told herself again that this interview was no different than the dozens of interviews she had done back home in Atlanta. Of course, having a news legend introduce her had been a little unnerving. But the moment Piper had asked her first question, she'd settled right into the role.

*This* was what she'd wanted to do for as long as she could remember.

"I believe this kind of narrowed focus will make all the difference," the senator was saying. "Fighting terrorism will be our only goal. Our attention will not be splintered in any other direction. And we have a strong message for groups like the SSU," he went on. "Their time is very short. Acts of terrorism will not be tolerated. We will stop them."

Piper nodded her solemn agreement. She hoped SSU

was watching right now. "To the extent you can share with our viewers, how do you plan to deter terrorism?"

"Well, Piper," he began with that charismatic smile, "it's our belief that—"

The senator stopped abruptly, his gaze moving to someplace beyond Piper's right shoulder. She resisted the near-overwhelming urge to look behind her, but years of on-camera training kept her looking directly at her guest.

"You were saying, Senator," she prompted. Whatever was taking place behind her, she had to get the senator back on track. Now was not the time for anyone's attention to wander, most certainly not his.

A strong hand clamped around Piper's right arm. Startled, she whipped her head around to see who had grabbed her. *Martinez.*

"We have to go. *Now.*"

"What?" Why was he on the stage? Go where?

Piper glanced at the camera, then back at the man effectively pulling her out of her chair. "Martinez, what are you doing?" she demanded beneath her breath. Had he lost his mind?

He jerked her microphone from her jacket and tossed it onto the table next to the artificial flower arrangement. "There's no time to explain."

She dug in her heels. "Are you insane?" A peculiar mixture of fear and anger erupted inside her. This could not be happening. She had to be hallucinating.

Martinez's hold on her tightened. This was no hallucination. "Don't argue," he growled from between clenched teeth.

The senator was on his feet then. "What's the meaning of this?" He started toward Martinez.

Piper glanced at the control booth and hoped like hell that they'd gone to another commercial break, but one look at a nearby monitor told her they hadn't. Surely the director would do something fast.

Townsend suddenly appeared behind the senator and ushered him back into his chair. Green was arguing with the station's security guard a few feet away.

What on earth was happening? Piper stared in disbelief at the sheer number of people, Feds as well as the Senator's security personnel, who suddenly flooded the set. What was going on? She turned to glare at the man now dragging her off the stage. Had there been a bomb threat? She frowned. Surely they would evacuate everyone if that were the case. Why wouldn't Martinez simply tell her if that were the problem.

"Three minutes until we're live again," a male voice announced from the control booth. "Someone had better get the situation straightened out. I can't stretch it."

Thank God. They had finally gone to a commercial break. Piper seized the opportunity to jerk hard against Martinez's ironclad grip. "What are you doing? If there's no immediate threat, I have to finish this interview."

He didn't answer. He just kept tugging her along. Cold, hard reality slapped Piper in the face then. He'd ruined her interview. She was done for. She could see the headlines now. Jilted Lover Drags Television Journalist From The Most Important Interview Of Her Life. Journalist Will Never Work Again! Her career was over. And why? No one was shooting at them. There didn't appear to be any bad guys nearby.

Martinez pushed through the studio exit and out into the bright morning sun. Piper twisted, pulling with all her might to stop him. "Dammit, Martinez, where are you taking me?" Where was her uncle when she needed him? Why hadn't Townsend helped her instead of letting Martinez drag her out like this?

She jerked hard again. "I said, let me go!"

Ric stopped abruptly and glared at her. Without a word he swept her off her feet and into his arms and started striding away from the studio again.

Furious, she pounded his chest with her fists. "Get your hands off me!"

He ignored her.

The dark sedan they had arrived in over an hour ago was sitting at the curb, the engine running. Piper frowned. They'd parked in back. Why was the car up front now? Why was the engine running?

Martinez jerked the driver's side door open, dropped her to her feet and pushed her toward the open door. "Get in."

Piper placed one foot against the vehicle and used it for leverage against him. "No way," she snapped. "Not until you tell me what's going on."

"Get in the car, Piper," he demanded. "I don't have time to explain."

"Take the time," she bit off. "You just ruined the biggest interview of my career, bucko. So you'd better have one amazing excuse!" She pushed back when he again attempted to force her inside the car. He would tell her what was going on or she wasn't going anywhere. She whirled to face him, but the words she intended to hurl at him died on her tongue when she met his dark gaze.

Something changed in his eyes. The irritation was gone, instantly replaced by utter desperation. Before she could figure out what that meant and react, he'd reached beneath his jacket and snagged his big mean-looking gun. One of the two he'd used to protect her all this time when she'd thought he was just a cameraman.

He leveled it on her now. "Get in the damn car."

Piper blinked, stunned. *He had lost his mind.*

"Okay," she said quickly. She definitely didn't want to argue with a man who had a gun aimed at her, even if it was Martinez. Her heart pounding with the adrenaline now flooding her body, she all but hurled herself into the car. She scrambled across the bench seat to the passenger side. Before she could grab the door handle and escape as she'd planned, she heard the click of the power locks. He shoved the car into gear when she would have tried hitting the unlock button.

"Buckle up," Martinez instructed.

The car lunged onto the street, propelling her back against the seat. After a couple of false starts, her fingers numb and clumsy with the fear pounding through her veins, Piper finally snapped the seat belt into place.

"Where are we going?" she demanded hoarsely, her voice shaking in spite of her best efforts to keep it steady.

"Just be quiet," he snapped. "I have to concentrate."

Ric listened intently to the voice coming through crystal clear on his earpiece. Lucas confirmed that the bomb squad was en route to the hospital, as well. Ric studied the street ahead as Lucas rattled off the directions that would take him and Piper to that same hospital. Lucas's next words shook Ric to the bone. The private hospital he'd taken Piper to last week had been closed for two months. It had been a setup.

He'd known it. Dammit, he had known that something wasn't right with that Dr. Petersen. The lack of personnel…the missing vending machines…the interview charade with the mother of one of the SSU members…Piper getting sick. It was all one big elaborate plan to ensure the opportunity to implant the explosives. With the tiny explosive in place, they could kill Piper and the senator in one fatal blow, live—on national—television, allowing

SSU to make a huge statement. But how had they managed such a flawless setup?

An idea filtered through the worry and fear inside him. "Did you eat or drink anything that morning before the interview with the Olsen woman? Before you got sick?" he asked, glancing at Piper as he maneuvered swiftly down the crowded street, darting in and out of the lanes of traffic to avoid slowing down.

Piper glared at him as if he'd lost his mind. "You need help, Martinez. This is kidnapping!"

"Answer the question," he roared, then clenched his jaw in an effort to regain control. Fear was vibrating inside him. He refused to consider that in a few short minutes she could die. He didn't care if he died, but he couldn't let anything happen to Piper.

She shrank farther against the passenger side door. Then, as if suddenly remembering his question, she shook her head in response. She stopped suddenly. "Wait. I had coffee. Keith brought me a cup before we left the station."

"Who took the call from Mrs. Olsen?"

"Keith—"

"The desk assistant back in Atlanta," Ric said for Lucas's benefit. "He's in this." Martinez hit the brakes and made a hard right at Lucas's barked instruction. Tires squealed. Martinez fought the inertia pulling them into a tailspin, then stomped the accelerator to launch the car forward into the middle of the slowly moving traffic.

*Fifteen minutes,* sounded in his earpiece. *Faster, Martinez. Right on Twenty-First.*

He had to hurry.

He swerved to miss a pedestrian who stepped off the curb when the traffic signal turned red and the crossing light said Walk. Piper screamed. Horns blared as cars on the cross street screeched to stops.

"Slow down, Martinez. You're going to get us both killed!"

*Left on K Street.*

"Now you tell me," Ric muttered as he slammed on the brakes and turned in front of the oncoming traffic. His heart rushed into his throat when a moving van bore down on them before it came to a rubber-burning halt. More horns. Shouts. But he ignored them all. He had to concentrate.

"Let me out of this car!" Piper demanded suddenly. "You're going to kill us both." She depressed the unlock button and reached for the door handle. "Stop the damn car!"

"Shut up before you make me do something we'll both regret!" Ric sent her a look that stopped her cold. He couldn't risk telling her the truth right now. She might be angry, but he could deal with her anger. Hysteria was another story.

*Right on Twenty-Third.*

*The emergency room entrance is on the left.*

"Listen to me, Martinez. There's no way to stop it," Lucas said quietly, uncharacteristic fear in his commanding voice. "Once it's activated, there's no turning back. No way to disarm it. Watts must have gotten close enough to trip the timer right before the interview began. He had to have touched her with the device we found on him. It was the only way to start the countdown."

The memory of Piper tripping and Watts steadying her flashed in Ric's mind. "Did Watts touch you in any way that seemed odd at the time?" Ric demanded of his now-sullen passenger.

"I don't know what you mean," she snapped. "The only thing odd around here is your bizarre behavior. I swear, Martinez, I'm not going to forgive you for doing this.''

''When you ran into him and tripped,'' Ric barked impatiently. ''Think, Piper!''

Her hand went to her abdomen, right over her belly button. ''He caught me.'' She frowned. ''I remember it kind of hurt. But I didn't think anything of it. Too nervous about the interview, I guess.'' She met Ric's gaze when he glanced at her ''Why?''

*Son of a bitch.* Ric was going to kill Watts when he got his hands on him. And any of the other SSU *bastardos* Lucas rounded up.

''We're here,'' he told Lucas. Ric slammed on the brakes directly in front of the emergency room doors and shoved the gearshift into park. He was dragging Piper out of the car before it stopped rocking.

Ric shoved his gun back into his waistband beneath his jacket as he tugged a still-reluctant Piper through the automatic doors.

''What are we doing at a hospital?'' she demanded, again trying to slow his forward movement. ''Is my uncle here? Is he hurt?''

Ric ignored her questions as he listened to Lucas explain that Raine was still trying to get the seriousness of the situation across to the 9-1-1 operator. Clearance to direct assistance was still pending. No one was waiting to help them. There'd been an automobile accident on Pennsylvania Avenue and the bomb squad was still three minutes away.

Ric swore.

*Twelve minutes.*

A dozen people were crowded around the admissions desk. He didn't have time for that. He glanced around the crowded waiting room. Piper tried to twist free.

"Be still," he hissed in her direction, pinning her with a deadly glare.

She glowered right back at him. "Not until you tell me what the hell is going on!" She stepped closer. "Dammit, that was national television, Martinez, and you dragged me off the set like...like..." She flung her free arm heavenward. "Like a maniac. Do you have any idea what you've done?"

A nurse called the name of one of the waiting patients. The woman, holding a crying child in her arms, hurried to follow the nurse through the double doors. Ric jerked Piper close and slipped through the doors marked Authorized Personnel Only behind the mother and child.

He scanned the frenzy of white uniforms rushing in and out of exam rooms. Personnel preoccupied with the business of saving lives and helping the sick buzzed around the nurse's station. Ric needed a doctor. He stuck his head in each exam room he passed, until he found one empty. He paused then and surveyed the starched white coats for the name tags.

*Eleven minutes* sounded in his earpiece.

Time was running out.

"You do know that they're going to arrest you for your actions, don't you, Martinez?" she snapped. "They're going to take you away in one of those straitjackets and lock you in a little room."

*Dr. Devers.* The name tag grabbed Ric's attention at the same instant that he'd decided his only choice was to draw his weapon and demand that a doctor step forward.

"Dr. Devers," Ric said before the man could rush past, "we have an extreme situation here."

Devers frowned and glanced at the file in his hand. "Are you Lester Phelps?"

Ric nodded. "We have to hurry."

The doctor motioned to the empty exam room behind Ric. "Right in here, Mr. Phelps."

Ric ushered a fuming Piper into the room. "On the table," he ordered. "Now," he demanded when she folded her arms over her chest and simply stood there in defiance.

She rolled her eyes and hopped onto the examination table.

Dr. Devers frowned again at Ric's ordering Piper onto the table. "It says here, Mr. Phelps, that you're suffering from severe gastric upset." He glanced at Piper. "Or is it your wife who has the problem?" The doctor shook his head in confusion. "They seem to have the age wrong here, as well."

Ric snatched the folder out of the man's hand and tossed it onto the counter across the room. "Forget about Phelps for now. We've got bigger problems."

"See here," the doctor said sharply. "What's the meaning of—?"

"Lie down," Ric ordered Piper.

"Get real, Martinez," she retorted. "I've had just about enough of this madness. Tell me what the—"

*Ten minutes.*

Fear seared through Ric's veins. "I said lie down," he commanded.

Startled, Piper complied.

Ric turned back to the doctor. "Listen to me. I don't have time to repeat myself. There's something implanted subcutaneously near her belly button." He gestured to Piper who looked appalled at his suggestion. "I need you to get it out. *Now.*"

"You must be joking," the doctor scoffed.

"No joke." Ric leveled a lethal glare on him. "You have ten minutes to do it."

"This has gone too far," Piper muttered heatedly. She started to get up but Ric stopped her with a look.

"We don't have time to waste, Doc." Ric turned his attention back to Devers.

The doctor laughed a choked sound. "I can't cut into this young woman without an ultrasound or X rays. You must know that what you're suggesting is impossible, not to mention unethical."

"I'm out of here." Piper sat up. "There's no way anyone's cutting into me without my permission."

"That's right," the doctor chimed in. "There's paperwork that has to be done. Tests." He shook his head in confirmation of his words. "I simply can't begin a surgical procedure without the proper preop tests and authorization."

In one fluid motion, Ric slipped the weapon from beneath his jacket and leveled a bead directly between the good doctor's eyes. "This is your authorization, Doc." Ric flicked a look at Piper. "I said lie down," he growled.

Though she trusted him on some level, real fear of his intent flickered in her wide eyes. "You'll never see the light of day again after this, Martinez," she told him, her anger still simmering despite her mounting anxiety. "They'll throw away the key."

"Now." Ric turned his attention back to the doctor who'd gone a sickly shade of white staring down the barrel of Ric's weapon. "The previous incision is where you need to begin. It's probably very close to that spot. But I can't be certain. You'll have to do a little exploring. It's small enough you can't feel it through her skin. It might be in more than one part." He swallowed tightly. "You'll need to be careful, very careful."

The doctor shook his head again. "I—I can't just cut into her like that."

Sweat dampened Ric's forehead. He snugged his grip on his weapon. "Nine minutes," he said, echoing the voice in his ear. When the doctor still hesitated, Ric added, "What you're looking for is a very tiny, very deadly high-tech explosive. If you can't find it and get it out in the next nine minutes then she's going to die." Ric stared directly into the doctor's eyes then. "And if she dies, you'll die." Ric cocked his weapon. "One way or another."

"Explosive?" Piper echoed. She reached for her abdomen, her gaze colliding with Ric's. He watched realization dawn there. "Do it!" she screamed at the doctor. "What're you waiting for? Get it out of me!"

Ric glanced from Piper back to the doctor staring, stunned, at him. "Now that I think of it, maybe you'd better clear the E.R., too," Ric added as calmly as he could.

The doctor jerked the door open and shouted at the top of his lungs. "Get me a local and a surgical pack in here, stat! And get this area cleared. Now!" His movements jerky, Devers grabbed a pair of latex gloves from the dispenser on the wall and tugged them on.

Finally, Ric thought with a twinge of relief. Now they were getting somewhere.

A frazzled nurse rushed into the room within seconds. She squeaked in surprise when she saw Ric's drawn weapon. "The local you ordered...D-Doctor," she stuttered as she handed the prepared syringe to him. "They're clearing the E.R. but...I...don't..." She looked back at Ric's gun and fell silent.

Piper winced when the doctor injected the local anesthetic. Ric focused on the doctor's movements instead of her frightened expression. His own fear was bordering out of control.

"Scalpel," the doctor ordered brusquely.

Her movements clumsy, the nurse struggled to break open the seal on the surgical pack and uncover the implements.

"Eight minutes," Ric announced, his whole body going numb with fear.

"Scalpel," the doctor shouted.

"But, Doctor, I'm not sterile," the nurse protested. "I need—"

"Give me the damned scalpel!"

The nurse slapped the instrument in his gloved palm. He poised the scalpel above Piper's belly button. "Can you give me an idea of what I'm going after here?" he asked. His gaze locked with Ric's. Sweat had beaded on the man's forehead.

"All I know is that it's implanted subcutaneously and that it's set to go off in eight minutes."

The doctor swiped his forehead with the sleeve of his coat. "What if I hit it…cut into it or something?"

Ric clenched his jaw against the muscle throbbing there. "I can't answer that question. Just get it out. Okay, man?"

The door burst open and two police officers wearing protective gear and wheeling a detonation control container between them stormed into the room.

"Do we have it yet?" the older man, the one in charge Ric surmised, demanded. "For safety's sake I need to get it out to the parking lot."

Ric shook his head. "We're working on it." He nodded to the doctor. "Let's do it, Doc."

Ric's gaze fixed on Piper and he tried to calm the fear in her eyes with the promise in his own. "Everything's going to be fine, *querida*," he said softly. She reached for him, and Ric wrapped his fingers around her hand. ''Hurry, Doc,'' he urged.

The doctor pressed the scalpel to Piper's flesh and bright red blood pooled in its wake.

*Seven minutes…*

## Chapter Fourteen

Ric adjusted the covers around Piper once more. With a weary sigh he sat down on the edge of the bed next to her. Lucas had wanted her to stay at the hospital, but she'd refused. So he'd sent them to his Georgetown apartment along with Townsend and Green to stand guard.

The sedative Dr. Devers had prescribed had finally kicked in. Ric glanced at the two bottles sitting on the bedside table. Sedatives and antibiotics—just the trick for surviving a foiled assassination attempt.

He closed his eyes and thanked God one more time that the intel had arrived in the nick of time. A few minutes later and…

Ric shook the horrifying thought away. The guys from the bomb squad had only managed to get to the parking lot with twenty seconds to spare. The blast hadn't been earthshaking, but it had been more than enough to do the job. SSU only intended to kill Piper and the senator. The senator's assistant, Watts, had been the one to suggest Piper for the interview. Allowing SSU to kill two birds with one stone. He'd set everything up to make a very public, very blunt statement. Between the desk assistant back at WYBN and Watts in D.C., SSU had known Piper's and the senator's every move.

Keith, the desk assistant, was young. He'd joined SSU because of his older brother. The woman who'd called herself Mrs. Olsen turned out to be their mother. Ric shook his head. But Watts was a different story; he'd done it solely for the money. Ric swore silently.

Lucas thought it was probably too late to determine what kind of poison they'd used to give Piper the abdominal cramps, but a sample of her blood had been sent to a special lab to see if they could find any lingering traces of whatever substance had been used. Petersen had lied about the laparoscopy. They'd merely put Piper under so that they could implant the explosives. While he'd patched her up today, Dr. Devers had explained that the tiny three-part unit had been implanted much like a Norplant contraceptive. Ingenious, Devers had said once the danger was passed.

Ric didn't think it was ingenious at all. He wanted to kill the *bastardos* with his bare hands. Between Raine and the FBI, the SSU was being dismantled from the inside at this very moment. They might never know the names of everyone involved, but the headquarters in West Virginia had been brought down. Watts had spilled his guts, giving the FBI plenty of evidence to take down the upper echelon of the organization that had hired him.

A relieved sigh hissed past Ric's lips. Piper would be safe now. He doubted there would be any renegade members looking to make such a high-profile hit with no backup from their former commanders. What would be the point now? Ric would know more when Lucas returned from his teleconference with Raine and the federal agent in charge on site. Lucas had wanted Raine on site as an advisor. Ric's assignment wouldn't be over until he'd turned Piper safely over to her uncle's care.

Ric was to keep Piper comfortable until Lucas returned

home. When he arrived, the two of them would have a little talk, Lucas had informed Ric. Right now he was too tired and too thankful that Piper was safe to care what Lucas had to say to him. Nothing he could threaten Ric with would compare to what it was going to cost him to have to face the rest of his life without Piper.

"Martinez," she murmured.

"Rest, *querida*, you're fine now," he assured her. She looked tired and vulnerable, but more beautiful than any woman he had ever laid eyes on. He couldn't help himself; he had to touch her. He caressed that soft cheek and wished for the umpteenth time that things could somehow be different between them.

She sighed and licked those full, pink lips. He resisted the urge to lean down and kiss her. Just when he was certain he would have to kiss her or cease living altogether, her gaze locked on his and she smiled dreamily.

"I love you, Martinez." She touched his face, her soft fingers cupping his jaw. "I'm sorry I got so mad at you for not telling me the truth." She blinked twice, clearly having difficulty keeping her eyes open.

If only she meant those words. "Shhh, *querida*, it's only the drugs talking. You'll be much better tomorrow and wondering why you said such foolish things."

And it was foolish. He knew better than to even hope that Piper could feel that way about him.

Her sweet features scrunched into a frown. "No, Martinez, I mean it," she insisted. "I really do love you."

"Piper—"

"Don't say anything," she insisted. "Just think about it and give me your answer later."

Answer? Ric frowned. What answer? Piper smiled another of those sweet, most likely drug-induced smiles. His frown deepened when he realized she wasn't actually looking at him any longer. She was looking somewhere past his shoulder. The drugs, he decided.

"Daddy," she murmured.

Ric stilled. The hair on the back of his neck stood on end. Someone else was in the room. And he'd been too tired and too worried about Piper to notice. "Rest now, *querida*," he suggested, as if unaware of the presence behind him. "I'll check on you again a little later." Ric stood and slowly turned around, his hand going instantly to the weapon in his waistband.

"I wouldn't do that if I were you," the man said, a 9 mm in his hand and pointed at Ric's chest.

Ric noted the resemblance immediately. Same dark hair, only the man's was peppered with gray. Same startlingly blue eyes. *Daddy.* This man was Piper's father.

The same man who'd been dead for nearly twenty years.

"Daddy, you're here," Piper said unevenly, surprise, disbelief in her tone. "But I don't understand." She sat up. "Where have you been?"

Fear slammed into Ric. Any man who'd faked his own death couldn't be back for anything good. "Don't move, *querida*," he said softly, praying she would have the presence of mind to listen. He didn't even want to consider what had happened to Townsend and Green.

"You betrayed me, Piper."

She stared at the man standing at the foot of her bed. She looked confused and wounded by something she didn't understand. The drugs kept her from fully comprehending the seriousness of the situation.

"This can't be," she mumbled.

"Look, man, I don't know what this is about—"

"Of course you don't," the man said, cutting Ric off. "You couldn't possibly understand what it feels like to watch your country—the one you've risked your life for—

sell itself out.'' He laughed, a bitter sound. "So I decided to take charge of my own destiny.''

Ric glanced at Piper, who was still staring at the man before her. "She thinks you're dead.''

Cold blue eyes stared straight through Ric as if he weren't there or didn't matter in the final scheme of things. "I am dead to her.'' He shifted that emotionless gaze to his daughter. "You betrayed me just like all the rest. Cast doubt on what we stand for. I've watched you from a distance, all these years. Hoping you would be what I knew you were capable of. After all, my blood runs through your veins. But you failed me. Betrayed me.''

He shifted the barrel of his weapon toward Piper. Ric's breath stalled in his lungs. "She didn't betray you, man,'' he urged. "She doesn't even know you.''

"Daddy, what are you doing? I don't understand this.''

"You should have listened,'' the man snapped. "I gave you every opportunity—much more leeway than the others, but still you spoke out against me. My followers—my sons—are all that matter to me now. You are as dead to me as I have been to you all these years.'' His lips curled into an evil sneer. "You could have given your life for me and killed that gutless senator who dares to believe that he can stop us. Instead you've ruined what should have been one of our finest moments.''

Piper shook her head, clearly struggling with her confusion. "But you're my father.''

He laughed, a dry, ugly sound. "You think that makes a difference?''

Ric's tension escalated. This man, Piper's father, had come here to kill her, to finish what he'd started. He was the SSU. "Look, man, if you're PO'd about what went down today—'' Ric shrugged nonchalantly "—it isn't Piper you should be angry at, it was me who messed up

your little surprise party. I dragged her out of that interview against her will.'' Ric tapped his own chest. ''And,
you know, I'm glad I did, because I really hate you sick
*bastardos.*''

Fury danced in those blue eyes so very much like
Piper's, but the man quickly schooled his expression as if
not wanting to give too much of himself away. Thankfully
his expert aim moved back to Ric. ''Well, then, perhaps
you should be the first to die, Mr. Martinez.''

''No!'' Piper struggled to free herself from the covers.

''Don't move!'' Ric commanded as he braced himself
for the hit, his right hand already itching to reach for his
own weapon in hopes of putting this guy down before he
went down himself.

''Then again, maybe not.'' The son of a bitch shifted
his aim back to Piper. ''Why not let the lady go first since
she seems willing enough?''

Ric snatched his weapon from his waistband at the same
time he hurled himself between Piper and her father. As
if in slow motion, Ric saw the fire fly from the barrel
aimed at him, felt the round when it hit him in the left
shoulder, too low for his liking. He returned fire, hitting
the guy somewhere in the chest. ''After you,'' Ric suggested, hoping the hit was deadly as he struggled to push
himself up.

Piper's father stared for a moment at the neat, round
hole in his chest made by the bullet that had obviously
missed anything vital. The wound was seeping blood onto
his tan shirt. Ric felt the warm sticky stuff spilling from
his own injury. He swore. He had to kill this guy before—

Ric struggled to his feet, forcing his right arm into a
firing position. Frowning, he gasped for air. Couldn't catch
his breath. Something was wrong. He stared down at the
wound in his chest. It was frothy with bloody bubbles.

*Mierda.*

He was screwed.

He tried to breathe. The sound was strange. The air wouldn't fill his lungs.

The undeniable click of a weapon engaging echoed in the room. Blackness threatening, Ric tightened his grip on his weapon and aimed it at the man now aiming his own weapon at Ric yet again. Why didn't the bastard die?

"Stop!" Piper stumbled from the bed, trying to get between the two men.

Ric shoved her away and fired. The other man fired simultaneously. Ric staggered back from the hit that nailed him high on the shoulder. Piper's father dropped to his knees from the second round he'd taken, but he didn't go down. Ric tried to suck in another breath. The hole in his chest whistled. *Mierda.* Piper was scrambling to her feet again. Ric lifted his now-heavy arm and took another bead on the man struggling back to his feet.

A gunshot exploded. Piper's father fell facedown on the floor. Where had the shot come from? Ric shifted his gaze to his left. Lucas stood in the doorway, his weapon still aimed on Piper's father.

*About time.*

Ric closed his eyes; the weapon in his hand slipped from his useless fingers as he slumped facedown across the bed. He could hear Piper screaming his name but he couldn't respond. He needed air.

"Don't you even think about dying on me, dammit!" Lucas ordered as he rolled Ric onto his back and ripped his shirt open, sending buttons flying. Ric gasped for breath, the sound oddly strained and futile, the whistle from his wound high-pitched. He needed more air.

Piper was crying and begging her uncle to do something. There was a sudden pressure against Ric's chest. He could hear Lucas talking on his cell phone. Something about an ambulance. And then there was nothing at all.

PIPER SAT in the intensive care waiting room, feeling utterly numb. She had cried—which she rarely did. She had prayed. Now she simply existed, waiting on some kind of word on Martinez. If she lived a dozen lifetimes she would never be able to put the images she had seen out of her mind. Martinez's lifeless body had been sprawled across the bed. Blood was everywhere. Her stomach roiled at the memory. Lucas was doing something…trying to stop the bleeding or help Martinez breathe. The sound. She would never forget the sound of him gasping for breath, of the wound sucking in air.

Even through the haze of her sedative she had known it was bad. But she couldn't help. She'd huddled nearby, useless and sobbing. Piper closed her eyes and fought back the tears. She simply didn't have the strength to cry anymore.

The idea that her own father—who, unbelievably, had been alive all these years—had tried to kill her, and that he had built the SSU from the ground up, still boggled her mind. How was this possible? How could the man her mother had loved so dearly, the man she herself had loved like any child will love her father, have done all these horrible, horrible things?

"I can't believe he was still alive." Piper lifted her gaze to her uncle who sat directly across from her. "You knew it all along, didn't you?" She wasn't really accusing, just stating a fact.

Lucas studied her for one long, silent moment. "On some level I think I did."

"Why didn't you tell me?" Piper shook her head at the

whole far-fetched idea. "How could you have allowed us to go on believing he was dead?"

Lucas sighed. Both hands were propped on his cane before him. "I knew he had turned. I just didn't know to what extent until it was too late. When that South American village burned to the ground, I guess it was just easier to believe that he'd died there. Why ruin the memories you and your mother had by telling you that he had become one of the bad guys before biting the dust?"

"Didn't anyone suspect that he was still alive?" she demanded. She just didn't see how all this was possible.

"I had known your father, worked side by side with him, for almost a decade. He was my brother-in-law for chrissakes. And even I couldn't be sure. I knew if he didn't want to be found, we'd never find him. He knew all the tricks, Piper. If he was alive, as long as he didn't try to interfere with yours or your mother's lives, what difference did it make? He was dead to all of us long ago. What I had to do today had nothing to do with the man we once knew. Would it have been easier on you if you had believed him to be a criminal rather than dead?"

Piper couldn't answer that one.

"Maybe I made a mistake by not telling the two of you about my suspicions years ago, but think how it would have affected your mother. How could any of us suspect that he would turn out this evil? And then come after his own flesh and blood?"

She couldn't blame Lucas. He'd done what he thought was right. Piper shivered to think that all those times she'd had that eerie feeling of being watched, or that she'd awakened and believed her father had been in her room, she was probably right on the money.

Piper rubbed her temples with her fingertips to relieve the insistent throb there. She still felt like a zombie. The drugs, she supposed, and complete exhaustion. She leveled her gaze back on Lucas. "You know Mother isn't going to take this well."

"I'll take care of your mother," he assured her. "Right now you need to concentrate on taking care of yourself. You've been through the wringer, young lady."

He was definitely right about that. Pain speared through her at the memory of the hurtful things she had said to Martinez when she learned the truth about his identity. She had ignored him as if he didn't exist, and now he was in surgery fighting for his life.

And it was all her fault. He'd been protecting her.

"You're in love with him, aren't you?"

Piper's head came up at her uncle's question.

He scoffed. "Don't look at me that way. I'm not blind. You're in love with that cocky—"

"Lucas," she warned.

"Young man," he finished smoothly.

"Yes, I am." The admission was liberating. She loved Martinez and she wanted the whole world to know it.

"As far as I can tell, you don't have a thing in common," Lucas ventured.

Piper grinned. "Except great sex."

Lucas swore under his breath. "I don't need to hear about that, young lady."

Her expression grew solemn. "He's funny and sweet." Her heart fluttered at the thought of his kiss, of the way he looked at her. "He's thoughtful, and so good-looking—"

"And too damned cocky," her uncle interjected.

Piper felt her lips drawn downward. This was the part that worried her. "He's a hero." She gave her head a slight shake. "I didn't want to fall in love with a hero. He takes too many chances. Just like you, and my father...before."

Lucas lifted an eyebrow in clear skepticism. "And you don't? Give me a break. Look at the risks you take in your job. Who are you calling a hero?" He chuckled. "I would just imagine that Martinez has the same worries where you're concerned."

Piper considered her uncle's words for a moment. He was right, she knew. She met his wise, caring gaze. "So, what do I do?"

Lucas grinned, one of those mesmerizing expressions that affected every breathing female that wasn't related by blood to him. "That's simple. You marry the guy."

Piper twisted her fingers together. She'd hurt Martinez deeply. Hadn't believed anything he said. Lucas had told her sometime during the endless hours since they'd arrived at the hospital that Martinez had told her the truth about his past. He was exactly the man he said he was. And she had treated him terribly.

"But what if he doesn't want to marry me?" The thought tore at her heart.

"Then I'll have to kill him."

Fighting a new wave of tears, Piper pushed carefully out of her chair. She had five abdominal stitches this time and she was definitely sore from the doctor's probing. She moved to sit beside her uncle and then wrapped her arms around him. "I love you, Uncle Lucas."

He held her tight for a long moment. "Ditto," he murmured.

"Excuse me, are you Lucas Camp?"

Piper drew back and stared up at the brunette who'd ask for her uncle. She looked to be in her late twenties, and she was very pretty. Tall and slender, with an air of confidence.

Lucas stood. "The one and only," he returned, all charm.

The woman smiled widely, the gesture only making her more attractive. She extended her hand. "I'm Alex Preston, from the Colby Agency. I've come to check on Martinez. We weren't briefed on the extent of his injuries, only that he was here."

This woman worked with Martinez, Piper realized, still a little slow on the uptake. As Lucas explained what they knew of Martinez's current condition, Piper rose from her seat, some emotion she couldn't quite label propelling her. Was this Alex anything to Martinez other than a co-worker? The thought turned Piper inside out. She remembered him mentioning the name, now that she thought about it. But Piper had thought Alex was a man. That couldn't be further from the truth.

"The last report we received from Martinez," the woman—Alex—continued, "SSU had fallen."

"That's right," Lucas told her. "There may be a few stragglers we didn't round up in the bust, but they won't amount to much without their leader."

"I hope you're holding up all right, Miss Ryan," Alex said, turning her attention to Piper.

Piper manufactured a smile. "I'm fine. It's Martinez that I'm worried about at the moment."

Alex inclined her head, searching Piper's face, reading between the lines of what she'd said. "Martinez is a tough guy. He won't go down easy."

"Mr. Camp."

All three turned at the sound of the doctor's voice. "Mr. Martinez came through surgery with flying colors. He's out of recovery, but we'll keep him in ICU for a day or two. One bullet passed through without doing any real damage. But the other one, the one that worried us, penetrated the left upper lobe of his lung, then lodged in a rib." The doctor released a heavy breath. "He's one lucky young man. It could have done a lot more damage in there. The chest tube has reinflated his lung. He's young and strong. There's no reason not to expect a full recovery. He'll be out of commission for a while, though.''

"When can I see him?'' Piper wasn't sure if she could live one more minute without seeing for herself that he was indeed going to be okay.

"He can have visitors one at a time, but make it brief.'' He glanced at this watch. "We don't normally allow visitors at this time, but we'll make an exception this once.''

Lucas shook the man's hand. "Thank you, Doctor.''

Piper appreciated that her uncle had the presence of mind to thank the man. All she could think about was getting to Martinez. Relief surged through her at the thought that she could finally see him. Piper flicked a glance at Alex Preston and dared the woman to suggest that she be allowed to see him first.

As if reading the challenge in her eyes, Alex offered, "I can see him later. The two of you go ahead.''

"Let me go in first,'' Lucas said, dousing Piper's hopes.

"Lucas,'' she protested.

He held up his hands stop-sign fashion. "I'll only be a minute. Hold your horses. You heard the doctor say he was fine.''

Piper glowered after her uncle. If he threatened Martinez in any way...

"So,'' Alex said, drawing Piper's attention back to her, "how long have you been in love with Martinez?''

RIC OPENED HIS EYES and then blinked to focus. Where was he? The hospital. Oh, yeah. *Piper*. Fear surged through his veins. Then he remembered. Her father was dead. Lucas had finished him off. And saved Ric's life.

He frowned, trying to remember the details of what happened next, but nothing came. He'd passed out, only regaining consciousness for a few seconds in the emergency room.

Another, much more pleasant memory, made him smile. Piper had told him that she loved him. He wasn't foolish enough to believe that she really meant it. She had, after all, been under the influence of a sedative. But it warmed his heart even now to remember her words.

"I hope you know that I don't intend to make this easy on you."

Ric looked up to find Lucas standing in the opening of his cubicle. Ric smiled in spite of the pain he was in. He felt like hell but this man had saved his life. Ric owed him a smile at the very least.

"Don't give me any flak, old man. I ain't in the mood." Ric's smile fell. "What about Townsend and Green?" Piper's father couldn't have simply walked past them.

"They're fine. Both were wearing their vests."

Ric was immensely grateful neither of the men had been killed. He'd gotten kind of attached to them.

Lucas crossed the room, his cane clicking on the tile floor, and paused next to the bed. He studied Martinez for a moment before he spoke. "You're not exactly the man I would have chosen for my niece, but I guess you'll do."

Ric stifled a laugh. "I don't think you have anything to worry about."

"I hired you to protect my niece, not make her fall in love with you."

The impact of his words hit Ric like another bullet. "Is that what you think?" He tamped down the hope that wanted to expand in his chest. He had to be certain.

"What I think obviously has nothing to do with it," Lucas countered. "She's in love with you. Hell, she's out there now shooting daggers with her eyes at Alex Preston.''

Ric frowned again. ''Alex?''

''Yep. Victoria sent her to check on you. I imagine I should get back out there and let Piper come in before she blows a fuse.'' He hesitated before he turned away. ''You did good, Martinez.'' He leveled that too-knowing gray gaze on Ric. ''There are no words or tangible rewards that would be enough to repay you for saving my niece's life.''

''There's just one thing I want,'' Ric told him, his gaze never wavering, despite the tension now filling him.

One corner of Lucas's mouth hitched up in a grin. ''You already have that.''

''And your blessing?''

''Without reservation.''

Ric relaxed. ''Thank you. That means a great deal more to me than you know.''

''In fact,'' Lucas added pointedly, ''it could prove rather unhealthy for you should you ever break my niece's heart.'' With that said, Lucas walked out of the room.

Ric closed his eyes and allowed the memories of holding Piper close, of kissing her, of making love to her, to fill his mind. Warmth spread through his body, easing the pain in his chest and shoulder.

''Martinez.''

He opened his eyes to find Piper hovering near the foot of his bed. He smiled, his fingers yearning to touch her already. *''Querida.''*

She moved to his side. ''I'm sorry you got shot again.'' Her eyes were misty, and red-rimmed.

He found her hand and covered it with his own. ''It's okay. It's over now.''

She moistened her lips and stared down at their joined hands. ''And I want to apologize for getting so angry with you when Lucas told me who you really were. I should have listened to you." She shrugged. "Given you a chance."

He squeezed her soft fingers. "I should have told you in the first place."

She looked at him then, tears trickling down her cheeks. "None of that mattered when I thought one or both of us was going to die. I realized what a fool I'd been to put anything before the feelings I had for you."

Ric let go a heavy breath. "It's not going to be easy, Piper. We live in different worlds."

"We're both flexible—we can adjust to the other's needs."

"You don't mind that I might have to take another case like yours and risk my life for someone else's?"

"Of course, I mind," she said softly. "But that's part of what makes you the man you are. And I wouldn't want you to change." She shrugged, the barest lifting of her shoulders. "I take plenty of risks myself. We'll work it out somehow."

He pinned her with a still-skeptical look. "You don't have a problem changing your last name to Martinez?"

"I was thinking Piper Ryan-Martinez," she offered with a watery smile.

"And children," Ric pressed. "How do you feel about children? I'm Catholic. We like big families."

Her smile grew wider. "I was thinking two, a few years down the road," she qualified.

"You're sure about all this?"

She leaned down and kissed his forehead gently, like the brushing of a butterfly's wings. "I'm more sure about this than I've ever been of anything in my entire life. I love you, Ric."

He grasped her chin in his hand and looked deeply into

her eyes. She'd called him Ric. "I love you, Piper," he whispered, then touched his lips to hers in the briefest of kisses.

"Should we take the big plunge right away or take things a bit more slowly?" she ventured hesitantly, drawing back to search his gaze once more.

She still didn't realize the depth of his commitment. "I plan to marry you, Piper Ryan, the day I get out of this hospital if not sooner. I don't need any more time."

"That could be arranged, I think," she mused.

Ric frowned. "There's just one thing."

Piper tensed. "What's that?"

"Where are we going to live?"

A mischievous grin slid across those pouty lips. "Oh, I'm certain we'll arrive at some sort of amicable agreement."

Ric pulled her mouth back down to his. "Good," he said against her lips. "Because I'm never going to let you out of my sight for long."

# *Epilogue*

Victoria Colby stared at the case folders fanned across her desktop. Now was not a good time to be lending out one of her finest investigators. Was there ever a good time? Still, the Colby Agency had a long-standing reputation of assisting the local police in their time of need. Chicago PD was always happy to reciprocate. In this business it paid to maintain the right connections. With Ian still on leave with his and Nicole's new baby girl, Victoria was left to make these decisions on her own. She lifted her gaze to the two members of her staff, Alex Preston and Zach Ashton, seated on the other side of her desk, waiting patiently for her to begin.

"Okay, Alex," Victoria said finally, "we'll give them three days. With Martinez taking an extended vacation with his new wife and Ian still on leave, we're bordering on overextending ourselves at the moment."

"I agree." Alex flipped through the notes in her pad. "I think three days will be sufficient to work up a profile on the crime scene."

Trained at Quantico as a special agent for the FBI, Alex was an expert at reading crime scenes. It was more than her training, however, that made her a highly sought after expert in her field; she had a kind of sixth sense. Alex formed amazingly accurate impressions not only about the crime scene itself, but also about the perpetrator. She was good. Very good. The Colby Agency was lucky to have her.

"All right, then," Victoria affirmed. "Three days it is. And you tell Detective Cusack that he owes me his first-born child."

Alex smiled. "I think we're up to his grandchildren now," she teased. "And since his wife has just found out that she's expecting, I'm sure he's glad that we don't really intend to collect."

Victoria felt a twinge of regret at her own childless state, but quickly suppressed it. She'd learned long ago not to dwell in the past. "Congratulate him for me. And as soon as you're back in the office I want you to look into this Jasna Bukovak case."

"The pro bono with the missing sister?" Alex shuffled back a few pages in her notes. "Down in Tennessee, right?"

"That's the one." A frown creased its way across Victoria's forehead. "Something about that whole scenario really concerns me. I have a feeling it's going to be more than a simple missing-persons case."

"I'll keep you posted on what I find," Alex assured her.

Victoria turned to Zach, the agency's most trusted legal adviser. He was one of the best attorneys in the country. "Did you get in touch with Judith at WWIN-TV?"

"I did." Zach inclined his head and zeroed in on Victoria with those killer baby blues and that lopsided smile. "She was thrilled at the prospect of stealing Piper Ryan away from WYBN. She wants both Piper and her cameraman, Jones. I told her they were a package deal."

A knowing smile curled Victoria's lips. "I'm quite sure that Judith is very pleased to have a rising star like Piper added to her news staff, but I'm more than certain that any thrill she may have experienced was from the possibility of dinner with you." Victoria arched an eyebrow in question. "Her place or yours?"

Zach's smile widened to one of his famous all-charm grins. "Hers."

"I'm sure," Victoria added, "Martinez will appreciate your efforts at seeing that his new bride is employed nearby."

"Since I've had the pleasure of meeting Piper—" Zach stood and shoved his hands into the pockets of his slacks "—he won't be the only one who'll appreciate it."

Smiling and shaking her head at Zach's exaggerated playboy rhetoric, Alex pushed to her feet. "If there's nothing else, then I'll see you in three days."

Victoria nodded, dismissing the two. She watched as Zach, ever the charming gentleman, opened the door for Alex. Instinct niggled at Victoria. The Bukovak girl's story disturbed her. It had been a long time since she'd been this troubled by an impending case. American families hosted foreign exchange students all the time without incident. But not this time. This time something had gone wrong and a young girl was missing. Vanished into thin air.

But, dead or alive, she had to be somewhere. Victoria could only pray that it was the latter.

"Mrs. Colby."

She looked up; Mildred stood in the door. Victoria shook herself from the unpleasant thoughts. "Yes, Mildred."

"Lucas Camp is here to see you."

Startled, Victoria straightened. Her hands went instinctively to her tightly coifed chignon. "Thank you, Mildred. Send him in."

Victoria rose from her chair, but waited behind her desk, using it as a shield. She'd known Lucas for more than twenty years. They were friends...family, actually. But in the last couple of years, she'd felt drawn to him on a different level. She sighed. Maybe it was simply because James had been gone so very long now. She was lonely. As true as that fact was, she would not risk the friendship she and Lucas shared. Not for anything.

Lucas strode into her office, leaning a bit more heavily than usual on his cane, but his smile was that of a fit, young man half his age. Neither the passage of time nor the sprinkling of gray at his temples had lessened his commanding presence. Lucas was as handsome and charming as ever.

"I hope you don't have plans for lunch today," he announced, clearly pleased with himself for some reason that only he knew.

She flared her hands and lifted her shoulders in the barest of shrugs. "You know I can always make room for you in my schedule, Lucas. What brings you to Chicago?"

He paused in front of her desk and eased one lean hip onto its edge, then braced his hands on his cane. "It's a twofold mission," he offered, a twinkle of amusement in his gray eyes. "I'm recruiting and celebrating."

Suspicion narrowed Victoria's gaze. "Don't you even think about trying to recruit any of my investigators," she warned.

He chuckled softly, the sound doing strange things to her ability to breathe. "Don't worry, Victoria. I know better." He shook his head slowly. "And I have to say, you certainly come up with the best. That Martinez is something."

Victoria smiled at the admission she knew hadn't come

easily for Lucas. "Apparently your niece thinks so, as well."

Lucas shrugged. "I've forgiven her for that."

Victoria suddenly remembered the second part of his mission. "What are you celebrating?"

He grinned. "By special order of the President, my little organization has just been given carte blanche for doing research and salvaging missions. We can now overrule anyone."

She raised a skeptical brow. "I'll bet your old buddies at the CIA love that."

"Don't you know it. My specialists are going to keep those other guys in line," Lucas bragged proudly.

Victoria skirted her desk and offered him her arm. "In that case, I say we start celebrating a little early."

He stood and gently tucked her arm in his. "There's no one else I'd rather share this with than you, Victoria."

Warmth spread through her at the sincerity of his words. "Thank you, Lucas. That means a great deal to me."

And it did.

*     *     *     *     *

*Don't miss the next*
**COLBY AGENCY** *case*
*PHYSICAL EVIDENCE*
*July 2002.*

# Prologue

Victoria Colby watched the early-morning commuters on the busy street beyond the parking lot four stories below. Deep inside, where she harbored her most secret thoughts and feelings, she knew something was very wrong. This September morning would bring bad news. She could feel it in her bones.

Drawing in a heavy breath, she considered that she had worked hard since her husband's death to make the Colby Agency the best in the business. She employed only the very finest in the fields of research, investigation and protection. She knew better than most that no amount of planning or strategy could ward off the unexpected twists and turns life took.

A soft knock on her office door drew Victoria's attention back to the present. She stiffened her spine and turned to greet the attorney she had summoned so early this morning.

Zach Ashton entered the office, his expression nothing short of grim. "Is Hayden here yet?"

"Not yet." Victoria gestured to one of the wingback chairs flanking her desk as she settled into her own chair. She braced herself for Zach's report. "Have you been able to reach Alex?"

He shook his head slowly from side to side. "I've called at least a dozen times in the past two hours with no luck." He looked away briefly, and Victoria knew that he was having difficulty considering the possibilities of why Alex had not called in. "I couldn't reach the Bukovak girl, either."

An uncharacteristic feeling of helplessness welled in Victoria's chest. The sensation was not completely foreign to her; she had known it well during the long months immediately following her husband's death. And she'd known it another time she refused to consider, even after all these years. Doggedly pushing it aside, she leveled a determined gaze on her trusted attorney. "We'll have some answers when Sheriff Hayden arrives."

Zach stared at the floor for a long moment. Victoria knew that he was assessing the situation and reaching the same conclusions she had. And the bottom line was not good. Neither of them was willing to admit that fact just yet.

Alexandra Preston had worked at the Colby Agency almost as long as Zach. She was very good at her job. Trained in Quantico as a special agent for the FBI, Alex was nobody's fool. She was attractive, smart and tough. But now she was missing in action. They'd had no contact with her in forty-eight hours. No one stayed out of touch that long unless they were stranded without communications, severely injured...or worse. Victoria wished she could have saved Zach this gut-wrenching wait, but he knew Alex better than anyone here. Victoria needed his input. Usually she carefully avoided teaming two people who were or had been involved on a personal level, but whatever had been between Zach and Alex was over long ago. Both appeared to have moved on, but remained close friends. And right now Alex needed Zach on her team, just as Victoria needed his expertise in the upcoming meeting.

Zach lifted a worried gaze to meet Victoria's. "We could be looking at a very bad situation here. Maybe there's someone else you'd rather have making assessments."

Victoria considered her words for a long moment before she spoke. "We can only hope for the best, but I doubt that the sheriff from Rutherford County, Tennessee, would drop everything and fly up without strong motivation. As to your involvement, I believe you're the best man for the job."

The intercom interrupted whatever Zach intended to say next. "Sheriff Hayden is here," Mildred announced.

"Show him in, please." Victoria stood to welcome the man who had gotten her up at the crack of dawn demanding a meeting.

Sheriff Mitchell Hayden strode across Victoria's office without hesitating until he stood directly in front of her desk. The first thing that grabbed her attention was his too-long hair, which was secured at the back of his neck. The next thing she noted was intense, cool blue eyes.

He extended his hand. "I'm Mitch Hayden, Mrs. Colby. Thank you for seeing me."

His deep, whiskey-smooth voice held a hint of an unmistakable Southern drawl. He was tall, six-one or two, she surmised. And solidly built. Victoria resisted the urge to frown when she considered his faded jeans and plain white cotton T-shirt. The running shoes didn't quite fit the bill, either. She couldn't recall having ever met a lawman who looked quite like this one.

"Sheriff Hayden," Victoria acknowledged as she gave his hand a brisk shake. "This is Zach Ashton, the agency's attorney."

Already standing, Zach clasped their visitor's hand next. "I hope your flight was pleasant, Sheriff."

"It was fine," he said curtly, then turned his attention back to Victoria. "I have several questions that need answers."

"Make yourself comfortable, Sheriff." She indicated the chair adjacent to Zach's as she resumed her own. "Why don't you tell me what brings you to Chicago this morning?"

The sheriff's posture didn't relax as he sank into the seat she'd offered. He was intent, poised for whatever came his way. "Why does your agency have an investigator nosing around in my county?" he asked bluntly.

"If this visit is in regards to Alex Preston, you're right, she is one of my investigators," Victoria acknowledged. "However, you must be aware that the information regarding the case she is investigating is private, Sheriff. Was there anything else you wanted to know?"

Only the slightest tightening of his jaw gave away Mitch Hayden's irritation. Victoria was impressed. The man had traveled a considerable distance to get stonewalled in the first two minutes.

"Don't jerk me around, Mrs. Colby," he warned. "I've been up all night and I've come a long way. All I need are some answers."

"Is Alex in some sort of trouble? Is that the reason for your visit?" Zach suggested pointedly, his courtroom demeanor going a long way to hide his anxiety.

An unbearable silence hung for two long beats.

"I think you already know the answer to that question," the sheriff replied quietly. Too quietly.

"If something has happened to Alex," Victoria said firmly, "I demand that you tell us now."

He leveled an unreadable gaze fully on Victoria's. "One

of my deputies is dead, and Alex Preston is in the hospital under protective custody. She's also my prime suspect.''

Mitch knew he'd gotten their full attention with that announcement. The attorney looked downright sick to his stomach, but the woman, Victoria Colby, seemed almost relieved, as if she'd feared worse. Maybe now Mitch would get some straight answers.

"What happened?" the attorney, Ashton, wanted to know.

"Is Alex all right?" Mrs. Colby demanded.

"She's fine other than having trouble remembering what happened," Mitch explained with as little detail as possible. "The two were found in Deputy Miller's car early yesterday morning. Miller was dead. It looks as if they shot each other. There was cocaine in the vehicle." Mitch paused, allowing them to absorb the ramifications of his words. "If you want to help clear her of a murder charge, I'd suggest that you start talking."

"I can assure you, Sheriff Hayden," Mrs. Colby said, more calmly than he would have expected, "that our investigation has nothing to do with drugs, nor is Alex a drug user."

"You're skirting the issue," Mitch snapped. His impatience was showing, he knew, but at this point he didn't really give a damn.

"And you aren't?" she returned.

This was pointless. "I can get a warrant."

Mrs. Colby smiled. "Just so you know, Zach is one of the finest attorneys in the country. You may be in for a long wait."

"Is that a threat?"

"Absolutely not," Zach said emphatically, offering the sheriff his best, practiced smile. "Just fair warning."

Mitch suppressed the curse that raced to the tip of his

tongue. "Look, I want to get to the bottom of this just as much as you do. And, like you, I know my men. Deputy Miller would never have shot anyone unless it was in self-defense, and *he* sure as hell wasn't involved in drugs."

"Sheriff Hayden, I can assure you that we will do whatever it takes to help you determine what happened," Mrs. Colby offered.

Mitch knew she meant it. He had the distinct impression that Victoria Colby was a woman of her word. But the last thing he needed was further involvement from their agency. All he wanted at the moment was answers.

"So—" Mitch relaxed fully for the first time in more than twenty-four hours "—does that mean you're ready to cooperate?"

"Only if you're ready to cooperate with us," she offered frankly.

Mitch inclined his head and considered the no-nonsense lady seated behind the big oak desk. "What will it take to get the information I need now? *Today.*"

"If your office cooperates completely with mine, then I'll return the favor," she explained. "Considering the geography, I would request that one of my people accompany you back to Tennessee. I want a full report on Alex's well-being. I would also require that he and Alex be allowed to participate in every aspect of the investigation to clear her name."

"Is that all?" Mitch asked sarcastically.

She dipped her head in a gesture of acknowledgement. "I believe that will be sufficient."

Mitch let go a heavy breath. It crossed his mind to simply say no, but he had the feeling that she would not give in quite so easily. She would hold back the information he desperately needed until some judge made her give it up. He didn't want to waste time. Miller was dead. He'd been not only a friend but one of Mitch's best deputies. Mitch had every intention of solving this case as quickly as possible. Nothing. Not Victoria Colby or her fancy agency was going to stop him.

"All right, Mrs. Colby. Tell your man to be ready in three hours. That's when my flight leaves. Now—" Mitch leaned forward in anticipation "—will you give me the details regarding Alex Preston's case?"

"Certainly," Mrs. Colby said in an accommodating tone. "Zach will fill you in on the way. There's no need for you to wait three hours. I'll have my pilot take the two of you back to Nashville in the agency jet."

*Agency jet?* Mitch tamped down his surprise, but couldn't suppress his renewed irritation. She was hedging again. "The case, Mrs. Colby," he insisted. "Tell me about the case."

She stood, effectively dismissing him. "Zach will answer your questions en route. I want him with Alex ASAP. She's entitled to legal representation."

Frowning, Mitch pushed hesitantly to his feet. Just what he needed—some hotshot, smart-mouth attorney dogging his every step. Especially one who looked ready to rip off Mitch's head and spit down his throat. "I'm not sure—"

"I'm sorry to interrupt," the secretary announced from the door. "But there's an urgent call for Sheriff Hayden."

Mrs. Colby ushered the telephone on her desk in his direction. "You can take it here, Sheriff."

Tired and annoyed and definitely not up for any more problems, Mitch snatched up the receiver and depressed the blinking button. "Hayden." It was Colburn, one of his deputies. "Slow down, Colburn, and tell me what the problem is." The deputy's next words stunned Mitch. A mixture of fury and anxiety clenched his gut. "I'm on my way," he said tersely, then hung up.

"Is there a problem, Sheriff?" Mrs. Colby studied him closely, as if reading the new worry even before he spoke.

"That was one of my deputies," he said, his voice oddly devoid of inflection. "Alex Preston is missing, and the deputy who was watching her is dead."

# A ROYAL MONARCH'S SEARCH FOR AN HEIR LEADS TO DANGER IN:

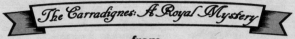
*The Carradignes: A Royal Mystery*

from

## HARLEQUIN®

# INTRIGUE®

Plain-Jane royal secretary Ellie Standish wanted one night to shine. But when she was mistaken for a princess and kidnapped by masked henchmen, this dressed-up Cinderella had only one man to turn to—one of her captors: a dispossessed duke who had his own agenda to protect her and who ignited a fire in her soul. Could Ellie trust this man with her life…and her heart?

**Don't miss:**
## THE DUKE'S COVERT MISSION
### JULIE MILLER   June 2002

**And check out these other titles in the series**

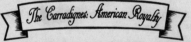
*The Carradignes: American Royalty*

**available from HARLEQUIN AMERICAN ROMANCE:**

## THE IMPROPERLY PREGNANT PRINCESS
### JACQUELINE DIAMOND   March 2002

## THE UNLAWFULLY WEDDED PRINCESS
### KARA LENNOX   April 2002

## THE SIMPLY SCANDALOUS PRINCESS
### MICHELE DUNAWAY   May 2002

**And coming in November 2002:**
## THE INCONVENIENTLY ENGAGED PRINCE
### MINDY NEFF

*Available at your favorite retail outlet.*

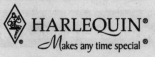
## HARLEQUIN®
*Makes any time special* ®

Visit us at www.eHarlequin.com                    HICR

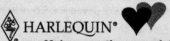

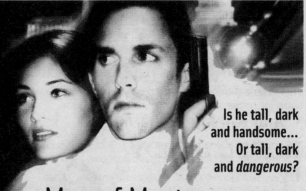

# TRUEBLOOD, TEXAS

Coming in May 2002…

# RODEO DADDY

by

# B.J. Daniels

**Lost:**

*Her first and only love.*
Chelsea Jensen discovers
ten years later that her father
had been to blame for
Jack Shane's disappearance
from her family's ranch.

**Found:**

*A canceled check.* Now Chelsea
knows why Jack left her. Had he ever loved her, or had she
been too young and too blind to see the truth?

**Chelsea is determined to track Jack down and find out.
And what a surprise she gets when she finds him!**

*Finders Keepers: bringing families together*

# HARLEQUIN®
# INTRIGUE®

## TWO MODERN-DAY COWBOYS—
## ONE ANCIENT FAMILY LEGACY

### BACK BY POPULAR DEMAND!

## THE MCKENNA LEGACY

### BY PATRICIA ROSEMOOR

The thrilling family saga lives on as two more McKenna
grandchildren face a legendary legacy. In the McKenna
family, true love comes with a heavy dose of heart-
stopping suspense and breathtaking romance.

## MYSTERIOUS STRANGER
**May 2002**

## COWBOY PROTECTOR
**June 2002**

*Look for these exciting new stories
wherever Harlequin books are sold!*

# HARLEQUIN®
*Makes any time special*®